THE WHITE FIELD

DOUGLAS COLE

Relax. Read. Repeat

THE WHITE FIELD
By Douglas Cole
Published by TouchPoint Press
Brookland, AR 72417
www.touchpointpress.com

Copyright © 2020 Douglas Cole
All rights reserved.

ISBN: 978-1-952816-07-9

Editor: Kimberly Coghlan
Cover Design: Colbie Myles
Cover Photo: James Scott Smith

First Edition

Printed in the United States of America.

Praise for *The White Field*

"There's a realism and a spiritualism here that summons John Updike's classic *Rabbit, Run*. Rarely will a reader find the grittiness and beauty intertwined so compellingly."
 —Mark Spencer, Winner of the Faulkner Award for the novel, The Omaha Prize for the novel, The Bradshaw Book Award, and author of several books including *Ghost Walking* and *Trespassers*

"If you enjoy Le Carre and Hemingway, Douglas Cole's novel, *The White Field*, will engage your mind and your heart. Here is writing that carries the awake reader into new terrain and taps on the soul for this journey into the self."
 —Jeff Kamen, Award winning journalist and documentary producer for NPR, NBC, CBS, ABC, and author of *Warrior Pups*

"The White Field is a rabid yet tender odyssey into the oscillating abyss of an ex-convict degenerating into redemption. Cole writes with haunting splendor, illuminating the dreams of the doomed."
 —Matthew Dexter, author of *The Ritalin Orgy*

"With his debut novel, *The White Field*, Douglas Cole delivers a taut, well-paced thrill ride rife with keenly observed lyricism, a startling and refreshing addition to the literary world of misfits: gripping, thoughtful, and unquestionably alive."
 —Sara Lippmann, Author of *Doll Palace*, Dock Street Press

"Author Douglas Cole's breakneck prose places us squarely in the hectic mind of a man influenced from all sides, seeking a life free from fear. The result is a stunning narrative that is simultaneously frightening and familiar."
 —Kerri Farrell Foley, Managing Editor *Crack The Spine*.

"Douglas Cole's writing is lyrical jazz, shifting effortlessly between smooth syncopation and frantic riffs with practiced perfection."
 —David LaBounty, Managing Editor, *Blue Cubicle Press*

"*The White Field* is a blend of classic archetype with breathtaking prose. Douglas Cole beautifully sculpts noir themes, gripping characters, and vivid imagery in a story that glues you to the pages.

—**Amy Kisner, Editor** *Lit Literature*

"With a poet's ear, Douglas Cole records the pulse of a work-a-day life's tedium and, cogently, that of his narrator who dares to escape it."

—**Dennis Must, author of** *Hush Now Don't Explain* **and** *The World's Smallest Bible* **plus three short story collections:** *Going Dark, Oh, Don't Ask Why,* **and** *Banjo Grease.*

"Here's a rarity. Few accomplished poets have crossed the Rubicon into major literary fiction with such confidence. This is a novel whose feet are in the Beats and its head in transcendence. It's a genre-stripper. Cole, like Joyce, is as much an innovator as Daedalus. *The White Field* - alternately bewitching and terrifying - is a clear coup: the ultimate existential thriller."

—**Michael Feeney Callan, author of novels such as** *The Woman and the Rabbit, Lovers and Dancers,* **poetry books,** *Fifty Fingers* **and** *An Argument for Sin,* **as well as critically acclaimed biographies on Robert Redford, Sean Connery, Anthony Hopkins, Richard Harris, and Julie Christie.**

For Jenn

Portions of this work appeared in the following publications: *Airgonaut, Alternating Current, Bitter Oleander, Bluestem Magazine, Best New Writing Anthology* (Hopewell Publications), *Clackamas Review, Contrary Magazine, Counterclock, Crack the Spine, Dimeshow Review, Edge, Eclectica, The Forge, Ginosko, Iconoclast, Lit Literature, Litbreak, Longshot Island, Owen Wister Review, Solstice Magazine, Sou'wester, Torrid Literature, Unreal, The Wayfarer, Wellington Street Review, Wilderness House, The Wisconsin Review*; and a Blue Cubicle Press limited edition novella called *Ghost*.

Suppose this prisoner could not turn back but was instead dragged forcibly up the steep and rough passage to the mouth of the cave and released only after he had been brought into the sunlight. The impact of the radiance of the sun upon his eyes would be so painful that he would be unable to see any of the things that he was now told were real. It would take some time before his eyes became accustomed to the world outside the cave.

—**Plato**

Where shall wisdom be found? And where is the place of understanding? Man knoweth not the price thereof; neither is it found in the land of the living.

—**Book of Job**

I
Awake

I walked into the sun. It seared the road and the rooftops, intense, blinding. I went up Eighty-Eighth Street through the homes and the old elms with their heavy summer growth and darkness along their limbs, light strobing through the shadows. I knew someone might recognize me. They might even call the police. But I couldn't resist. I was free, now. Nobody could touch me.

Only those who cared, and by now there were none, would have known my release date. My wife may have known. At one time, I imagined her writing it on a wall calendar, marking off each day leading up to it with a big, black X. But I knew I'd fallen far from her thoughts.

I couldn't be sure of my children, though. They were so young when I went in they could have forgotten all about me. My wife had remarried. Very likely, they called her new husband daddy. Very likely, they thought he was. Events had erased me. After all, I'd made no contact. And while I had no idea what my wife might have told them, unless she'd changed in ways I couldn't foresee, I knew she'd tell them the truth if they asked and say nothing if they didn't. At worst, they believed I was dead.

And that life seemed like something unreal. There were no traces of it around here. But my sense of time was way off. From counting, literally, minutes as they passed, I went into a vast timeless trance-zone where whole years vanished. In the midst of this, I reemerged from time to time to peer into my little cell of life with seconds hanging like drops of water on a window ledge and refusing to fall. But now, walking this street, I was the last person anyone around here was expecting to see.

So, as I went up Eighty-Eighth to the old house, I had this strange feeling that I was invisible. In the dusk light, I saw the windows of the houses blazing. Commuters on their way home shot by and curved around the meridians in the intersections, their faces steel traps that snapped and flashed mirror eyes and grim lips and frenzy, frenzy for home, motion so fast they blurred into tracer ribbons. And the sun only cloaked me that much more. Even my shadow was a rail.

And I heard it, that high tension ping, like my own past ringing from the driveway and those days when I was a kid, too, playing into evening as our faces disappeared in the darkness with only the square of the backboard above and the black sphere of the ball and the heat and breath of the other players around me. Then I saw them, three boys playing basketball in the driveway. One was a

2

tall gangly kid with long black hair and ripped jeans and a T-shirt with the word ENEMY printed on it. Another kid stood beside him, but the light made it hard to see his features. Then, the ball landed on the rim, bounced up, arced over to the other side of the rim, hung there suspended in the net for a moment and then dropped through. The third boy stood back from his shot with his hands on his hips, breathing hard, turning his head slowly as I saw, I swear, my own face there in front of me. With a brow of concentration like a hawk's predatory gaze, he looked at me as our eyes locked for an eternal moment that I thought carried some recognition, but the moment changed before I could read it. Then, I was passing on, and my son returned to his game.

I was on time for my first day of work. First job as a free man. Larry Paterson, the shop owner, was a bloated hungry ghost with a greasy brown beard and a puffed up, sweaty face. Even in this heat, he wore an enormous flannel shirt tarped over his frame and spotted with sweat. When I came in, he looked at me like I was another part of the machinery, another guy he had hired out of prison. I followed him back through the shop. "Timecards here," he said, pointing at an old timeclock on the wall with a rack of punch cards. When he spoke it was like he was out of breath. "Fill your name out on one. You get paid every Friday."

The little shop office he occupied looked like the spot where the whirlwind dumped the leftovers, moldering papers and brown boxes and one steel desk in the middle and a filing cabinet tilting with drawers half open, some of them empty. He had a calendar on one wall with a picture of a balloon-breasted woman in a yellow bikini lying back with sexual vibrato over the seat of a motorcycle. The trash can overflowed with twine and packaging and soda cans. The desk was covered with stained invoice sheets, pens, envelopes, a clipboard and a phone, a half cup of cold coffee, and old fast food burger wrappers with hard glistening corners of cheese. There was a strong smell of metal filings. Otherwise, the room had a bare, almost temporary look, though it also seemed like this was the place where Larry spent most of his time, a little prison of his own. I stood there as he scanned my information.

"You're on temporary for now," he said. "Trial basis. Three weeks in, if you make it that long, we'll talk. I'm going to start you off with paint prepping. You ever use a phosphorous gun?"

"Nope."

"Doesn't take a brain surgeon. Go out to the shop and ask Raphael to show you what to do. He's in the painting bay." He looked down and pushed around some papers. But something about his actions looked like an act. When was he going to say, just kidding? And I wondered if he was going to tell me something else or ask me any questions. I wanted to ask him if he had told any of the other workers that I'd been in prison, but I decided that wasn't such a good idea. They probably didn't know. And if they did, most likely they didn't care.

"Anything else?" I asked. I had this floating disbelief that anything, even this, could be so simple. I still felt unreal, and I wanted to avoid making any mistakes. I felt I should double check everything, just to make sure. I wanted to be certain there was nothing else I was supposed to do.

"No. Go to work."

I hesitated. "Which one is Raphael?"

"He's the big guy, painter, Mexican. You can't miss him."

The shop was a shabby little building, a double Quonset hut like a tin can cut in half lengthwise with the two halves laid side by side and a hole cut in the middle to pass through from one side to the other. At the ends of the tin cans were tall sliding wooden doors with slats so far apart you could put your arm through, and on the curved sides of the huts were darkly sooted windows so obscured by filth no light came through. On this side of the shop were two painting bays and two large kilns that looked like missile silos with wheel-lock doors and steam blurred temperature gauges. They swelled and radiated a ring of infernal heat. The painting bays were medieval, paint splattered, scrimmed-in structures with protruding hooks from which hung the various parts to be painted: what looked like fuselage plates and wing blades, but I had no idea what they were. Spray guns and metal tongs hung down from the ceiling on swivel arms, and two painters stood in their bays, paint mist swirling around them as they swept their spray guns over the hanging parts. They wore goggles

4

and overalls and were covered with a Jackson Pollack blast of colors. The taller one, who had to be Raphael, was about seven feet tall. I waited, watching as he swiped the gun back and forth, laying down white stripes of enamel onto a wedge of gray steel.

I raised my hand like a kid in school, and he stopped and shoved his paint gun into a rack on the wall and lifted his mask. I was surprised to see a wide, friendly smile as he nodded and said, "Yeah? Wha's up?"

"I'm starting here," I said. "Larry told me to ask you about the phosphorous gun."

"Clean-up, huh?"

"I guess."

"Raphael Ephastus," he said. And he extended a hand the size of a bear claw. I took hold of it. It felt like he could pulp-crush my hand if he wanted to. I'd seen guys like him in prison, so big nobody bothers them. But I detected a genuine kindness behind the large-handed grip. I still had cobweb thoughts to get rid of.

"Tom," I said.

"Tom? Good. Welcome to..." He looked around, smiled, then shrugged, and said, "Wanna smoke?"

"Sure," I said, even though I was a little anxious to get started. Trial basis. I still felt like eyes were watching me.

I followed him to the doorway and out into the gravel lot, and he handed me a cigarette, put one between his lips, lit his then mine.

"Thanks," I said.

"No problema," and he rolled his head from side to side, making it snap with a ripple that sounded like a string of wet firecrackers going off. "I can use a break. I didn't sleep last night."

"Yeah?" I asked. I'd lost the art of casual conversation, and it wasn't really my habit to ask questions. It's time now, I thought, so I said, "Why's that?"

"I've been working another job, too, you know? And sometimes when I get home, I just can't sleep."

"What's your other job?"

"Painting."

"Full-time?"

"Yeah."

"You have two full-time jobs?"

"I do. The other one is a nightshift at another shop."

"Jesus!"

"Wife and kids, you know? Life costs." And he took a deep breath, a smoke, gave his big head another roll and said, "Come on."

I followed him back in and through the opening to the other side of the shop. He stopped for a moment and took a drink from a water cooler. That side was filled mostly with racks of drying parts and wide metal tables. One other guy was working alone at one of the tables, hunched over and sitting on a high stool, doing something with boxes full of little metal plates. "Hey, Tony," Raphael said. "This a new guy name Tom."

I nodded to Tony. He lifted one hand without looking up and then went back to his work.

We went through the tables and out through another set of sliding wooden doors, and I followed him across the gravel lot over to the spot where I would be working. A huge rusted drum with a pump attached to it stood there in the corner of the lot. A hose came out of the pump, and on the end of the hose was a long-barreled spray gun with a trigger handle. Raphael flipped on the pump, and an engine thrummed, the hose went taut, and phosphorous steam leached, hissing snake-like from the coupling on the gun. Next to the gun was a mountain of large aluminum crates. Raphael threw down his cigarette, grabbed a crate, lifted it like it was nothing more than a cardboard box, set it on a wooden pallet, and began spraying it with the phosphorous gun. He sprayed it inside, sprayed it outside, flipped it over, hit every surface. When he had finished, he set it down, turned to me and said, "See that?"

"Yep."

"Tha's what you do."

"I think I got it."

"Do all these crates, okay, and stack them next to the side of the shop there to dry. You keep them off the ground, though, you know, on those pallets. They have to be clean, no dirt on them anywhere, so we can paint them. If you finish today, let me know. I'll set you on something else. You got it?"

"I got it."

"Tha's good."

He picked up his cigarette, looked up at the sun, shook his head, grinning. As he went past me, he slapped me on the shoulder and said with a little chuckle, "Good luck, amigo."

"Thanks."

He went back into the shop, and I stood there looking at my mountain of work and smiled. I was alone, completely alone out there, with no eyes on me at all. And it was a beautiful feeling, that no one was watching me. It was freedom. I still felt the pressure of phantom walls, even in the open yard outside the shop, but I also felt free. I was hyper-aware of space. When I breathed, I breathed the whole sky.

The sun was only three fingers high, but already it was blazing hot. I went over to the gun, grabbed the barrel, and the moment I picked it up I felt a sharp, hot stab of pain. I dropped it. I knew I'd made a bad mistake. I looked down and saw a white burn welt filling up over my palm. Then it began to hurt. This was not good, but I wasn't going to go in and say anything about it. It was my own fault. I would just have to power through.

I had to maneuver the crates using my forearm to lift them, which wasn't easy. I avoided any contact with my palm. When my palm did touch anything, it sent a bright pain shooting up my arm. The blister throbbed sickly. I had to spray left-handed. That wasn't easy, either. And little by little, the day got hotter as the sun rose higher and I sprayed box after box. Each one weighed about eighty-five pounds, and the more I sprayed, the more soaked I became in that hot, phosphorous steam. I could even taste it. My shirt hung so heavy with sweat I finally took it off. But after a while I felt my skin burning, so I put my shirt back on. I sprayed the crates and lined them up against the shop, and I nearly had a whole row done by the time the sun hit its zenith. But a tower of boxes remained.

It was noon, and it was hotter than hell. My eyes and mouth were burning. I stopped and looked around for a space of shade to sit and smoke a cigarette. But there was no shade, so I sat down on one of the crates, lit a cigarette, and stared out over the gravel lot. Across the street were dirty little white houses with bars on their windows. The street was lined with shrunken oaks. And off across the field to the south, the airport buzzed with the flicker of planes taking off and landing in the amber air.

I worked all afternoon on that tower of crates and was nowhere near done by the end of the day. I was soaked, burned, exhausted. I punched out with my new timecard, half dead, and shuffled out with the rest of the workers. Dust rose up in the parking lot and the alleyway as the cars pulled out. I got into my car and lit another cigarette. I looked down at my open palm and saw the popped blister of pulpy, burned flesh. So this is it then, I thought. Well, so be it. I started my car and drove one-handed into the whiteout of the road.

B ack at my studio apartment, I opened a cold beer and drank it down, the whole bottle, in one gulp. I opened another and sat by the kitchen window. My eyes ached and my hand pulsed with pain, wrapped now in a homemade bandage. I tried to ignore it, to let it be. But it kept up a nice, insistent throbbing, trying to keep my attention on it. The last of the sunlight was coming through the thin row of trees behind the apartment building. Sparrows hopped around on the branches, sending up quick puffs of dust as they shook the leaves. Sometimes they stopped and looked in at me.

My little furnished studio apartment was not much bigger than a prison cell. It felt like something out of centuries past, with a Murphy bed that folded down out of a wall closet and a tan couch with consumption-saturated cloth and a low back, a wooden chair with green cushions crushed in by years of flop house sitters, a coffee table with a surface full of cup rings and cigarette burns, a green Formica kitchen table and a small gas stove that looked like a miniature Cadillac. I even had a nice walk-in bathroom with a door that closed and a window that opened by turning a crank arm, though the window ledge was rotting out. But it was mine. I could do what I wanted with it. I could come and go as I pleased. And I had a television set, which I put on the end of the coffee table so that I could catch up on the news and see some shows. And though the walls were still bare, I thought, if I wanted, I could go down to the thrift shop and get some pictures, some art, or even make some of my own.

I had a little radio up on top of the refrigerator, and I turned it on as the sunlight went and the world filled up with darkness. I listened to a jazz station and smoked a cigarette and blew the smoke out the window. Chet Baker came on, playing a song called *Night Bird*, and I listened as he laid down the first few statements, repeated them, and then took flight. Right out of whatever that song was originally about, whatever you could have written down, he took off on his own. Free of the structure. Improvising but never wrong, every choice fluid and graceful. He flew, smooth and connected, tethered to the other players but far away, too, because he was flying up and out of it. And I went with him and closed my eyes and knew in the dark sky sound I am going and go and boundless go just like that night bird flying with no walls and no doors and no home at all—just going and going in all directions in the endless dream. Then whatever I was hearing sort of fell back, and I felt myself pulling away and going further and reaching higher and holding there in such beautiful stillness true and pure and perfectly poised—free for as long as I wanted. It was an old trick of the mind I'd mastered in prison. Then, a kind of lightning branched out, winds rolled again, and the whole world trembled into being again. Here I was back in the nerve and the blood and the body of sound, and like a friend speaking to me, that trumpet player's voice put me right back in my little kitchen space with all his trumpet variations concluded.

I was too tired to cook anything, so I drank another beer and smoked another cigarette and ate a piece of bread out of the Wonder bag.

I got up from the kitchen table and turned on the television. I flipped through channels, no permission necessary. It seemed like there were so many stations, now: stock car races, an exercise show (hmm), shopping channels, phony reality shows, game shows, music shows, politics, disaster, fix this, sell that, shows and shows. Then I stopped on an old Fred Astaire movie. I left the sound down, turned the television so it faced the kitchen, and sat down by the window again. The night air was warm and still. I opened the refrigerator door, and cold air rolled over me.

I smoked and pulled another slice of bread from the bag. Freedom. Everything was charged with it. It was in the shape of doorknobs and the color of white paper. I drank another beer. Night closed the book, saving its place with a finger, and headlights punched through the blinds of my front window and arced across the ceiling. Could I just be in this and love it and let it all go? I propped my feet up and leaned back in the chair. My kingdom.

I listened to the sounds outside: music, people talking, cars passing, my neighbors not in their cells but in their apartments. I watched Fred Astaire dancing, listening to the jazz on my radio, and it seemed like Fred was dancing to my jazz. His steps coincided with my music. I laughed. Go, Fred, go. And I watched him dance in a room all by himself, taking a hat rack as a partner, running up the walls as the room began to rotate around him, dancing on the walls, dancing on the ceiling.

I was back at those boxes, the sun coming up like a bleary eye in the white haze. I dragged the boxes onto the pallet and shot them with the phosphorous gun, mist blasting up hot around me. I had wrapped my hand in a cloth, but it was still a mess and sent angry messages when I touched anything. The bandage was soaked through and rubbing against the raw flesh of my palm, but I didn't take it off.

At about ten o'clock, I took a cigarette break and ate an apple and sat in the open yard by the side of the Quonset huts. The sunlight was warm and diffused, not too hot yet. Then I heard someone singing inside the shop, a beautiful song in Spanish. As I sat there smoking, I had a pleasant, drifting moment, and I watched with exhausted hungover calm the way the light rose and fell in the faint mixture of morning fog and city smoke sidling through the withered oak trees and the little white shacks along the street.

The shop was on an alleyway, and across the alleyway was a small, run-down house with a front yard pounded to nothing but dirt, and while I sat there, I saw cars drive up and park in front, guys going into the house and then coming out shortly after and driving off. It was a steady stream, constant coming and going, and I knew something was up. A criminal nerve tingled inside.

Next to the house was a fenced-in yard where a German Shepherd paced and plopped down panting in the shade and barked every time a new car drove up. It never ended, that barking, except for brief intervals when someone inside would shout through the screen door, "Shut the fuck up!" Then the dog would sulk for a while and nuzzle down next to the fence and restrain himself and paw at his ears and snuff the dirt, until another car came and he was up on his feet and barking again.

But I kept hearing that singing, someone inside with a beautiful tenor voice singing in Spanish. And so I went over to the painting side of the hut and looked in and saw Raphael there painting and singing. He saw me. I nodded and held up my cigarette. He pulled off his goggles and hung up his paint gun, but he kept on singing, looking back towards Larry's office. And he came outside with me, smiling and singing.

"Smoke?" I asked.

"Ah." He took a cigarette from a pack in his shirt pocket. He stretched out his long, paint-splattered arms and wrapped them around the sun. Then he put the cigarette between his teeth, and I lit it for him.

"Get any sleep?" I asked.

He shook his head slowly, smoking, humming the song he was singing, folding his arms across his chest. "No," he said. "You know, I never sleep, not much. I get home..." He shook his hand by the side of his head. "I just can't do it."

"How long you been working two jobs?"

"Maybe six months, now. It's killing me."

"Why two jobs?"

"I told you. I need the money, you know?"

"Yeah?"

"Yeah. I got my whole family, my kids and my wife's mother. We need the money."

"You got kids, huh?"

"I do."

"How many?"

"Five."

"Whoa! All right, Patron."

Raphael smiled. "Three boys and two girls."

"What are their ages?"

"Jorge is twelve; he's the oldest. He's kicking my ass, you know. Thinks he the man, now." He counted them off on his fingers. "Juan is ten. Sandra is seven. Isabel is five, and little Raphael is two." He nodded, count done, proud.

"Nice," I said. "A full house."

"What about you?" he asked.

I shrugged. "Yeah. Well, yeah. I've got a son, a daughter. They live with their mother, though. We're divorced."

"I see. You miss them? You see them?"

"Sure, I see them," I lied. Why did I lie? "Sometimes," I said. "But they're with their mother full time."

"Tha's rough," he said, looking out across the alleyway as a car plowed through the mist and into the dirt lot in front of the house. "I love my kids. Tha's the only reason why I do this."

"So where you from, Raphael?"

"Mexicali, Mexico. Jalisco, before. My parents and my brother are in Jalisco."

"Yeah? What'd you do down there?"

"I was a cop."

"A cop?"

"Yes I was," he said, drawing hard on his cigarette. "Ten years."

"Wow, a cop."

"I was a cop. I make a lot of money, too, doing that, you know? Down there is different. I had jewelry, you know? Gold. Lots of gold." He held out his hands, paint splattered and bare, and turned them over as though they were laden with rings and bracelets of gold. "People would just give it to us. Me, my partner. We go to the bars and clubs, you know, and everyone likes us and give us things because we are the protection. They give us respect. The girls like us, too." And he smiled. "They come up to you, and we never buy drinks, there. I had this ring, big ring. Someone try to mess with us, I'd hit them, and my ring," he tapped his right ring finger and then his cheek, eyes narrowing, "would leave a mark on them, you know. A reminder. They remember who they don't mess with."

"I bet they didn't forget."

"It was good. We made a lot of money. We never pay for nothing. Food. Bars give us free drinks. Everybody give us things. They wanted to, you know? Is respect for us and what we do."

"I get it," I said. "So why'd you leave? Why come up here?"

He smoked and rolled his huge head, snapping those vertebrae. Another car came down the alleyway. "My partner, he commit suicide. It look like he commit suicide."

"Really?"

"Yes. I come back to the car one night, you know, and find him there. And it look like he shoot himself." Raphael held his hand like a gun against his stomach and said, "Pfow. When I see him that way, tha's the way it looks. You know what I mean? It look like he kill himself, but there's no reason for that. He don't want to kill himself. It was a message for me, too. That could be me. I know that, and I know who send that. I know what that mean. It change things for me. Things change after that."

Larry came over then, and Raphael took a deep breath and shook his head. Larry looked like he was pissed off, saying, "Hey, you lazy fucker. What are you doing? Teaching the new guy bad habits?" Raphael didn't say a word, but his eyes got narrow as he smoked the last of his cigarette. "Come on you big wet-back, I don't pay you to stand around jerkin off." He was the small man with the power. I'd seen a lot of that. It was guard talk, guard power. "And you, too, new guy. Get back to work," he said to me. I don't think he remembered my name. I didn't really exist to him. Raphael, though, was twice his size. But Raphael stayed cool. He nodded, threw his cigarette down and twisted his foot on it, nodded again and grinned, but he never looked at Larry. "Come on you fuckers," Larry said. And he was smiling like he was being funny, like he was playing a game. "Ya big lazy fuckin bean eater, go on." And Raphael just kept nodding with a look I had seen before, like his mind had a trigger lock on for now.

After work, I took a drive by the house. I knew it was a risk, but I wanted to see it once more. I guess I was hoping to see my son, Stephen, again, and if I was lucky, I might even see my daughter, Melissa. The boy I had seen playing basketball had to be him. I was sure of it. The age was right. The kid I saw looked about sixteen, which fit the math. But as I approached the house this time, I didn't see anyone. It was dusk, and nobody was out on the street. As I passed the house, I tried to look in through the windows, but they were just deep maroon reflections of the sky.

I cruised around for a while, looking for places I knew. Some were still there. The grocery store was still there. So were the drugstore and the liquor store. There was a new kids' play area south of the reservoir, with kids spinning on the merry-go-round and mothers pushing their toddlers on the swings. I turned on the radio, jazz, the only thing I could listen to, now. Anything else just made me edgy. I smoked. Air flowed through the open windows. I felt good; moving felt good. The light was going, but it was one of those slow descents, streetlights fluttering off and on.

I headed west toward the water and rolled down the hill and parked by the marina. I turned the engine off and sat in the car. A smooth Miles Davis tune was playing on the radio, a song called *Blue in Green*. Why should I go anywhere? The music was soft rolling into the water itself, and Bill Evans was laying down the code as if constructing piece by piece the elements of the world from a dialogue inside his mind, from the upper register to the lower, from the waters sliding to the gulls gliding above, matching rhythm for rhythm with the light of Miles ascending through the Chamber bass waters and then rising through thin reeling high hat clouds and the wind beat of Cobb drums and the slow freighter cruising of Coltrane saxophone, smoke trail rising in the shape of geese flocks heading home. They played it all, and I watched the light fall back behind the horizon, a few thin clouds lingering as the song played out like liquid metal burning in the sky and the far stark jagged line of blue heartbeat mountain peaks on the tail end of the peninsula. Music. It was all music. And gulls swept overhead with glowing red wings curved to match the horizon, their trumpet calls drifting across the waters of The Sound.

I awoke from a deep sleep that night to the sound of someone screaming. Or was I dreaming? Some commotion. A fight. I got out of bed. I couldn't hear any specific words, but it was definitely a fight. Right outside my door I heard a thump, a banging, then more screaming. So I opened my door, and right there on the walkway, I saw a big, bald man dragging a woman by her feet—or at least he was trying to. She was holding onto the railing and had a good grip it looked like because he was lifting and pulling at her legs, trying to yank her loose, but she wasn't letting go. I stayed there in the doorway. Then I said, "Hey! What are you doing?"

They both froze in place. The man's eyes burned mad-dog fury at me. His face had that sweat-sheen of a high-octane fever mind. The woman gripped the railing, her head down. That was a righteous grip. A life-grip. There was nothing I could imagine that would break her loose. Oh man, I thought, this is someone else's problem. What am I doing? Why did I open my door? This can only lead to trouble. But I stood there. I just waited to see what would happen.

And then like a deflating ego, he dropped his shoulders and let go of her legs. Then he turned and looked straight at me for a moment. I braced myself. And without saying a word, he turned and went back down the walkway and down the stairs. That was it. He was gone. I couldn't see where he went after that, into which room down below, but I had a very real fear that he might come back.

I looked down at the woman lying there on the walkway. She didn't move. Her hands were vice grip tight on that railing, and she was breathing hard and trembling.

"Are you all right?" I asked.

It felt like I stood there a long time in that open door. She didn't say anything, and she didn't move. I could sure hear her breathing, though. I bet you could hear that breathing everywhere in the world.

"You okay?" I asked again.

And then she looked up. I could see the fight-haze clearing from her, could see her coming around. I knew something of that space. And I could see the energy of her fear like bolts of graffiti flaring up from her chest. She looked around, and then she stood up. She was tall and slender, with straight black hair that was messed up from the fight and wide, black-smeared eyes. She had on ripped blue jeans, no shoes, and a green sleeveless t-shirt.

"So—?" I said.

"Can I come in for a minute?" she asked.

That was the last thing I wanted, to have her come into my apartment, especially if that man, her man I guessed, came back looking for her. I didn't want anything calling attention to me or in any way messing up my parole, and this felt like something that could cause a lot of trouble. But what else could I do? I couldn't say no.

"Sure," I said, and I stood back and let her come in and closed the door.

She sat down on my couch, her leg jittering fast. "You mind if I smoke?" she asked.

"No, you go right ahead." I said. I stood as far away from her as I could in that little room.

She lit up a cigarette. She smoked it hard. I could see her mind working fast, calculating every escape route. Then she jumped up and looked out through the window. I almost asked, is he there? I wanted to know, too. Then she turned around and looked at me a moment. I thought she was going to head out the door, but instead, she went across the room to my little kitchenette and looked in there. I don't know what she was looking for. Then she came back. "Do you have a phone I could borrow?"

"Sure," I said, and I picked it up off the table next to the bed and handed it to her.

She went back to the kitchen, and I heard her trying to talk quietly to someone in those loud hiss-tones. "Can you get me?... yeah, Rob's back... same old shit... now... please... no, I can't stay here... please... yeah... just wait out front... I'll see you."

I looked out the window, but I didn't see him out there.

She came back into the room and gave me back my phone. "Thanks," she said. "I appreciate this, really. I know it's fucked up. Do you mind if I wait in here for a bit longer? I promise it won't be long. I've got someone coming to get me."

"That's fine," I said.

She finished her cigarette and started a new one. Then she sat down on the couch again, her leg going like a piston. I sat down on the edge of the bed. And we both waited.

"I'm sorry about this," she said. "And thank you. For all I know, you might have saved my life. I mean, I don't know. But this time, the way it was going, he might have killed me. He's capable of it. I know that. And no one else around here came out. Did you see that? Bunch of cowards. I'm sure they all heard it, though."

I didn't say anything. I was hoping that the person she called would come get her fast.

"He's fucking crazy. Fucking high. Fucking...criminal. Fucking asshole."

She was trembling, close to crying, hands shaking, cigarette shaking in her fingers.

"He's your boyfriend?" I don't know why I said that. It seemed obvious, and now I felt stupid for asking. And it didn't matter to me.

She snorted and laughed. "I wouldn't call him that," she said. She looked at me then, hard, eyes narrow. I don't know what she was looking for. Judgment? "Yeah, he's my boyfriend. Or *was*. That's the last time he ever touches me, though. I swear to god. I'll kill him. He moved in with me a little while ago, fucking stupidest thing I ever... He's supposed to be in prison right now. Seriously. He was arrested. And he should be in prison. I mean it. He's such a fucking loser. A thief. A dealer. He would've gone to jail, but the cops fucking fucked it all up and forgot to read him his rights or some stupid shit. So they had to let him go. He was arrested for assault, right? And possession? And they had to let him go. Can you believe that? And then I let him move in with me." She hung her head and then looked up like she was giving a confession. "I let him move in with me."

"You two live downstairs?"

"Yeah, I mean, I did. I've been here about a year. You just moved in, didn't you?"

"Yeah. I did."

"I've seen you. I'm Sharon. Sorry about this."

"Tom," I said. "And don't worry about it."

"That rat's asshole is Rob. And I'd avoid him if I were you."

"I'll try."

A silent, nodded, minimal but formal agreement passed between us then, strange and intimate in the middle of what was probably one of the worst moments, or what looked like one of the worst moments, of her life. But what could I know of her life? Or who wrote her twisted dreams? You open a door...

"My friend will be here any minute, I swear, okay? And then I'll be out of your way forever," she said.

"Seriously, it's okay," I said. But I knew I would feel better once she was gone. Both of us would feel better. Although, now that I had opened that door, I had no idea what would happen next, what I had let myself into, what this guy, Rob, would do about it. She seemed to know what I was thinking, and she gave me a look, something that said she didn't know either.

And so she smoked. And I smoked. And the room filled up with our smoke as we listened and waited.

"He's insane," she said. "And he's a speed freak, so watch out. That's what was going on tonight. He gets ugly when he's on speed." Her leg was jittering so hard I could feel the floor shaking. "He better not fucking come back up here. If he does, I'd call the cops." I couldn't let that happen.

We listened. And we waited.

Every sound jolted us both with the thought that he was coming back. She got up and looked out the window, then sat down, smoked, rubbed her upper arm, dropped ashes on my floor, rose, looked out the window again, sat back down, smoked and smoked. I sat there, trapped in my own apartment. Heavy dread.

The friend arrived at last and gave a little toot of the car horn. Sharon jumped up when she heard it. She looked out the window. "That's them," she said. "Hey, thanks, really. I appreciate it. And you know... Ah, I'm sorry about this."

I stood up. "Don't be," I said. "Don't worry about it."

Then I stood back, and she opened the door but hesitated. There was still the gauntlet to pass, going down the stairs, getting past the troll-cave below and the troll-man in it waiting down there. The red corona of her fear pulsed from her. She glanced at me, smiled, then went out and ran down the stairs fast. I watched. Her friend in the car below opened the passenger door for her. She jumped in, and the car took off with a sound like I'm outta here.

I waited a moment after she had left, looking down the stairs to see what was coming next, listening, feeling the empty street cool and radiating. I swear I could feel his energy like electric spider wires splayed out over the apartment building. Then I closed the door, turned off the lights and went to bed. I lay awake for a long time, nothing myself and listening to the nothing out there.

I finished the boxes on the third day. Then Larry moved me to the storage and prep room where he handed me off to Tony, who was supposed to show me what to do next. He was a little guy with one of those thin, scraggly beards that never fully comes in, like he didn't punch all the way through puberty. He was about my age, though, with long hair tied back in a ponytail. He wore a Doors shirt with Jim Morrison reaching out a warlock hand at me.

"Now what you do," he said, taking me over to a table covered by a beat-up sheet of tin and a couple of large boxes full of little metal plates, "is you take one of these..." He took out a plate that was about the size of a book cover. Then he produced a jar of what looked like red putty. "You get yourself a hunk of this..." He pulled out a gob of the putty and rolled it between his fingers. "And roll it into a ball…and you…" The plate had holes of various sizes in it, and he worked the putty into the holes. "You've gotta get it in there and make sure it fits all the way around the inside edge of the hole," he said, "so that no paint can get in. But you can't get any of it on the surface of the plate, here, you see? Ya got it?"

"I think so," I said.

"And you've got to fill every hole," he said.

He spoke softly, working the putty into the holes of the plate with a delicate, jeweler's care. Sometimes his tongue would appear between his lips. And as he worked, his thin fingers flipped the plate around like a spider wrapping up a fly.

"Get a plate," he said. "By the time you're done, you'll know how many holes it takes to fill the Albert's Hall."

"Nice," I said, and I laughed. "All right, *John.*"

I took a plate from the box, grabbed a hunk of putty out of the jar, and started working on my new assignment. It wasn't as easy as it looked, though, especially with my blistered hand still puffed up and raw and the flesh on my palm buckling when I gripped the metal plates. Sometimes the putty wouldn't stick to the edge, and sometimes, after I had gotten nearly all of the holes filled in, a putty disc would pop out, or I'd knock it out by accident when I set it down on the table, or my hands would sweat so bad from the dreamy swelter of heat in that room that the putty would smear on the surface of the plate.

"Ah! Tony," I said, laughing, "I don't think I'm doing too well, here."

"Don't worry about it," he said, rotating the plate in his hand so fast he hardly seemed to touch it. "You'll get the hang of it." He was done with about eight of those plates by the time I had finished two. But I kept at it. I felt determined to master this one task. And for a long time, we didn't say anything to each other. We worked while we listened to the radio that was sitting up on one of the metal shelves. It was set to a classic rock and roll station: Janis Joplin, The Beatles, The Stones, Led Zeppelin, Steely Dan, that sort of thing. And every once in a while, I heard Tony humming along with one of the songs.

Finally, I asked him, "So how long you been working here, Tony?"

"About four years," he said. "I've been here the longest."

"Really? And you've been doing this the whole time?"

"Yeah. Adam's curse. I do this, and I'm pretty much in charge of opening and closing, which just means opening the doors in the morning and closing them at night, though I like saying 'opening and closing' because it sounds more official. So if someone asks me what I do, I say 'I'm in charge of opening and closing the shop.' Doesn't that sound good?" and he smiled ironically, pointing back to the wide, sliding doors.

"So you're the one in control of letting us in and out," I said.

"That's right. You know, I've actually been here longer than Larry."

"Yeah? Who was here before him?"

"His father. Weird guy named Hurd. He's the one who owns the place. Or he *did* own it. I think he might be dead, now."

"Ah."

"But Larry doesn't know what the fuck he's doing."

I laughed.

"In fact, you watch. It's pretty funny. Larry does all the silk screening, right? You know, for instrument panels and that sort of thing. You have to use stencils, and it's pretty delicate work. I mean, it's not that hard, either. But Larry thinks he's the only one here who can do it right. He thinks we're all a bunch of idiots. I used to do it, when his father ran the place, but whatever. The problem is, and what Larry doesn't seem to understand after…I don't know, more than a year?…is that, when it gets hot like this and you try to silk screen the panels— well, you'll see. He's such a dumb fuck he doesn't know that the paint will just run in this heat. It's the paint that—he always fucks it up. And then he gets all pissed off and starts cussing and screaming and throwing a total tantrum."

"__"

"Oh, you'll love it. Poor guy. I do feel sorry for him, though, sometimes. And he didn't used to be this fat, but he's got diabetes or a heart condition or something, I'm not sure what, and they put him on some medication about six months ago, and he just bloated up overnight. It changed him. He was always a punk, but now he's a sick, fat punk. I can't imagine he's got much time left."

"That doesn't sound right."

"Yeah, but you watch. The next time he does a silk screen. You watch. You'll get a kick out of it."

"All right."

And for the rest of the afternoon we worked in the dream heat, fixing putty balls into metal plates, listening to the radio play songs like *Waitin' on a Friend* and *People are Strange*, Jim Morrison coming out of the radio and through Tony's chest with that hand reaching out and leveling on me a charge or a command or a final request to follow—I could never be sure what—while Tony hummed along with the music.

I drove down to the Blew Eagle Café, knowing it was risky, wanting it to be after the tedious machine shop work. Traffic howled on the bridge overhead as I cruised along the river road past the concrete plant. And through my open window, I heard freighter horns out in the Sound and train whistles running through the night. Yellow cones of security beams lit up the boxcars in the terminal yards and the transient camps tucked up under the viaduct. Rain fell lightly, a faint drift, cool, soft and gray. I parked in the gravel lot among the pick-up trucks and Peterbilts, got out and walked over to the café and pushed through the doors with their dark green porthole windows.

Inside, nothing had changed. It was the kind of place you go to when you want to disappear. Nets with green globe fishing floats hung from the ceiling overhead, and along one wall human backs curved into deep, dark grotto booths with red glass candleholders flickering under their eyes. The long amber mahogany bar glowed, and behind it gleamed a row of bottles in the evermirror casting back layers of phantom faces. Here, no time had passed. Jimmy was tending bar, and the time machine music played through a sad muffled jukebox speaker—Loretta Lynn, Waylon Jennings, Patty Page and Merle Haggard, blues and soulful drinker's tunes drifting down a padded tunnel from the mouths of the ghost singers themselves. And in a row, drinkers sat hunched in eternal crucifixion on bar stools.

I took my place. It happened to be open, as though an invisible hand had saved it for me all these years. But at first nobody noticed me, like I wasn't even there. I looked around for familiar faces, and pretty quickly I saw one. Eddie Ferris. Little con man, beggar, thief. He was a drifting, circling barfly, slipping through the veils into every bar I ever entered. Nobody trusted him, nobody liked him, but you could count on him to be there, tipping his empty glass your way. His presence was a strangely comforting thing. He was mildly schizophrenic. Often, I wasn't sure what he was saying as he fast-talked about some crazy deal you knew wasn't real or the agents with their eyes looking through the electronics and their ears listening through the plumbing. One time he told me a florist shop was a front for human trafficking, and his story turned out to be true. How he knew that I'll never know, but after that he became more deeply and religiously committed to various delusions, and everything he ever said concluded with "Gimme a little something to tide me over." Charity for poor old Eddie, charity I gave to on many occasions because Eddie hadn't always been this way. He was a sweet kid who wanted to teach, but somewhere in his early twenties, things started to slip. First, numbers began running through his head, and that was all he could say. Numbers. Then, Zeus was on his trail and punishing him with nightmares and lightning storms at every turn. He chained himself to his girlfriend's car to save her from the oblivion cloud. He was in and out of mental wards after that. That's when people started calling him Poor Eddie. He'd sell you out for a dime, and he always smelled of alleyways and dirt yards, always needed a shave, always seemed one step away from the grave. Poor Eddie. But he'd do anything for you. I once found him sleeping in my car. He was just this side of being homeless and probably was homeless much of the time. And like a ghost, he came and went, drifting in and out of our lives, but as far as I knew, for all his petty crimes, he had never gone to prison.

When I saw Craig, there too, I felt like a ghost at my own funeral. Now, I've heard it said we're born innocent, and the world turns some of us bad. I've also heard that some people are born without a soul. I've known Craig my whole life, but I still can't be sure what happened to him. His family had money, but for whatever reasons of fate or broken circuits in the brain, he drifted over the line. He could get you anything: guns, drugs, you name it. I went to his twelfth birthday party, and all I remember is that some kid went home crying. The party was over, and Craig stood there in his window watching us go with a look like he was going to burn the place to the ground. In that inarticulate adolescent way of understanding, it became clear that something was a little off in him. The most basic, simple human qualities of compassion never developed in him. And it showed most in the way he loved guns. We were in the same class at school, and one time when we went on a field trip to the Museum of History and Industry he ran straight to a display case full of old rifles and Lugers and Colts, shouting, "Outa my way—guns!" Early on, he always had them, could get you any kind you wanted. He was a gun historian and knew everything about the designs and designers of guns, the famous killers who had used them and every detail of their lives, who was killed by them and the different kinds of damage done by different kinds of bullets, which guns were used in every war and which guns were preferred by all the gangsters. And so he became Gunman Craig, or just Gunman. Yet, when I saw him there in the bar, he was still just a big kid who liked to play with guns. He never told me, but I heard from others that he had killed someone. I never asked him about that. Would you?

Some other people I didn't know were in the back playing pool. Every once in a while, I heard the crack of a shot. And when at last Jimmy caught sight of me with his peripheral sensor, he slid down the bar with his face lighting up into a satyr's grin, and he said, "Tom, you wily ghost, where the hell did you come from? What'd you do, break out? Hey! Slapper there," and he threw out his hand. Jimmy was a broad-chested, thick-armed son of a coroner, with eagle features and sharp, watchful eyes that saw everything. A charmer of devils with a little devil in him, too.

"I'm a free man," I said. "Free and clear."

"Well just look at you. And don't you just glow."

"I do believe I do," I said.

"When did you get out?"

"You could count the hours."

"Hey! You're just a newborn, aren't you!"

"I'm learning to crawl."

"Well, we'll get you up on your feet here in no time."

"I could use a lift."

"Hey, I think I saw Thane—"

"Ah let that wait, let it wait," I said. "What I'd really love to do is just sort of soak it all in for a moment, you know what I mean? I'll see those guys soon enough."

"Sure. Sure. Of course. I gotcha. They'll sniff you out here before too long anyway."

"I'm sure they will," I said. "In fact, it's inevitable."

"Life's not a rehearsal, but it might be a simulation."

"Let's call it reality for now."

"Let's call it a dream within a dream."

"Let's have a drink before I wake up."

"I think I'm trained for that. Say, there, what happened to your hand?"

"Ah, this?" And I held my hand up with its dirty bandage. "This is from a little on-the-job injury."

"Looks a bit raggedy, man, but, hey, you've got a job. That's good."

"Yep. I'm blessed with work, and I'm a contributing member of society."

"Well, I've got the antidotes for that! So, what can I get you? Hey!" He snapped his fingers. "I know, I know." He poured me a shot of whiskey and then a tall pint of beer and placed them before me and laid his towel over his arm like he was a priest administering the Eucharist. "And you're not paying for anything, either, buddy. You hear me? Your money's no good here tonight. Everything's on me."

"Ah, thanks, Jimmy. Thank you very much. I appreciate it."

"Really, I mean it," he said, patting his hands across the bar, fingers going like he was playing piano keys, flicking coasters into towers, tossing a stir stick between his teeth. "But you know," and he looked at me with squinting scrutiny, "you look pretty good. In fact, you look great. You look the same, man. So what's the deal? Time hasn't touched you?"

"Well... it has. I feel it."

"Naw, man. You escaped its claws, somehow. Somehow you did." He stood there staring at me and shaking his head. "It's good to see you. I missed you. You're the only person around here I ever thought of as having any kind of substance." He sneered. "Most of these guys are just a bunch of fuckin' bozos. But not you. You're real, man, and when I found out you were going to prison. Fuck. I knew something was wrong with the world!"

"It's nice of you to say that."

"I'm serious."

He was conning me, in some way, and I knew it, and he knew I knew, which was always the code of our connection. I wasn't sure of the angle, but I didn't care, and we got along fine. He and my brother were close friends at one time, and on my seventeenth birthday, he gave me a copy of Gabriel Garcia Marquez's book, *One Hundred Years of Solitude* with a fat joint taped to the inside cover. But whom the gods love... His mother was a jazz singer, his sister an Episcopal priest, and his brother became an actor in Hollywood. Jimmy had written a novel himself that was well received, and that was a big deal in our mostly under-achieving crew. But for some reason, he stayed here in this dive bar, bought from the previous owner and now his own underwater grotto dream. You could find a thousand poems in your destitute soul, here. I could say he was a bad influence, but who knows? People have said the same about me.

I took a drink of the whiskey and sipped the beer. "All right," I said. "This is the first real drink I've had in...ah...thanks."

"Just what the doctor ordered," he said.

"And you. You look hyper as ever. Charged up. What's going on with you?"

He did an exaggerated set of karate chops. "I'm the lord of Hades, man. What can I say? I've got to stay fit to keep these souls in line."

"Ah, then, you must still be rock climbing? Up there at Risky Peak?"

"Oh yeah, I do, some. When I can."

I shook my head. "We did some crazy climbs back in the day. And those were some beautiful days at Pinnacle. Do you remember? With my brother? We were just starting out, then. You guys went on to do a lot more of those pitch climbs, though. Impressive!"

"Yeah. Your brother was the best climber I've ever seen. Those were some magical times. But I don't do that much anymore. And you know, I haven't seen your brother since he went into the Navy. What's he doing? He all right?"

"He's been living up north. He got out a while back and sort of…I don't know. He's been living up there."

"I actually had a little climbing…incident, a while back. Kind of shut things down for me." He held up his hands as if to ward off a curse. "Nothing traumatic. But I was leading a little group, you know, me the wise elder, and there's this pretty little girl just wide eyes and innocence and fear and, well, maybe a little lust? And I'm saying, 'Why, here now, you need to use a fist jam, you know, where you just jam your whole fist back into the crack, here,' as I'm attempting this problem, trying also to insert a cam into a crack, and the next thing I know, whoof, I'm dangling three feet below them and upside down, knocked my head against the rock and opened it up, bleeding, a super mess."

"Jesus."

"It was no big deal. A little embarrassing, being the expert and all. I still climb, though. Rock is pure, and when you get up in it, it's pure sky, pure wind, pure… you know, like your life! The closest thing to real freedom." He looked at me as though he might have said something offensive. I didn't mind. Then he grinned and said in mock Irish, "I kicked me heals in heaven."

And that's when Thane showed up. He had spotted me. He materialized out of a black vapor at my side, leering in that cool way, everything about him a kind of mirage, his eyes two deep red stones. "Tom," he said, smiling and moving from side to side like a hypnotizing cobra. "What am I seeing? What am I seeing? Tell me?" He reached his hand out like one of the monkeys in *2001.* "Yep, you're real. Now, how? How? Howya doin?"

"I'm good," I said, and I smiled.

"I bet you are, my man."

"Now, Thane," Jimmy said, "don't you start messing with him. He's fresh in the world."

"Why, I'm not the bad guy!" Thane said, and he looked around like someone was going to agree with him. "Am I the bad guy? I'm not the bad guy!" And he pouted and shuffled his feet and aww-shucked it pretty good so that even Jimmy laughed. Of course, Thane is a careful, intelligent operator. Like all my friends, he was once just a kid, a little wilder than most but with this unusual, almost karmic pattern for being on the wrong side of the law and getting away with it. Thane's story has always run like a secret movie in the background of mine. When we were kids, he liked to skateboard, and he had some favorite spots on the college campus, but of course, there were signs all around saying *No Skateboarding* that he ignored because skateboarding was his meditation, his religion, and nothing as frail as a college regulation was going to keep him from his art, his prayer. He was run off more than once by the campus security. Eventually they knew him by name and by sight, and one campus security guard with the unlikely name of Officer Freeman "arrested" him, even though campus security technically weren't allowed to arrest anyone. But Officer Freeman was sick of this kid ignoring the rules. To him, Thane was trash, not even a student at the university, and he decided to step beyond the bounds of his authority and picked Thane out of a group of skaters on Suicide Hill and zip-tied his hands behind his back and took him off to the security offices and detained him there without allowing him to call anybody, just to make an impression. Well, it did make an impression on Thane. And after that, he became a rebel with a single cause—to antagonize Officer Freeman. He skated all over that campus just hoping Officer Freeman would see him so that he could escape, which he always did, and so send a message to this authority stand-in who in Thane's mind violated a bigger law of the universe and represented no authority he respected or recognized. Thane even began breaking into buildings on weekends and skating down the corridors and leaving definite, even scatological, signs of his trespass wherever he went, a rose for Officer Freeman. Eventually, Officer Freeman moved on from campus security. Indeed, Officer Freeman became a city cop, and he made it his mission to keep an eye out for that young thug Thane. Then it was almost cosmically comic. Thane had a beat-to-shit car with only one windshield wiper, and that wiper was on the passenger side. If it were raining, he had to lean over to see. So, one rainy night, we were out driving around, and Thane was doing that rubberneck thing so he could see through the window. We were laughing and not really going anywhere. Then he pulled into an intersection and barely, just barely, hit a woman who was walking with her boyfriend in the crosswalk. The boyfriend freaked out and started kicking the car, and who should show up at that moment but Officer Freeman. After administering a sobriety test, in the rain, Officer Freeman gave Thane every citation he could think of: entering a crosswalk when pedestrians are present, reckless driving, faulty windshield wipers... Time goes by, and Thane's apartment building has to be bombed for bugs, so he climbed into his car and headed up to the park to sleep the night. Who should come along and find him there but Officer Freeman, who promptly arrested him for vagrancy and trespassing. Officer Freeman was getting his revenge, and to Thane, it was a sign that the universe was no friend. After all, the forces were coming after him. I don't know if that was any kind of a turning point for Thane. I don't know if his life would have turned out any differently or if he would have made any different choices, but from that time on, the only law Thane respected was the law of what he wanted.

"And you're out," he said like a baseball umpire, "all the way out?" He was playing dumb, drunk, like some buffoon, but he was, I knew, deep down clear and calculating all the time. Then he stopped, looked at me, and smiled.

"That's right," I said. "I'm out."

"Do they know?" he asked.

"It's official."

"Well, welcome back to Phet, my little thanage in the wilderness. Hey!" He looked around as though scanning for spies, rubbing his hands together like Nosferatu, then turned back to me, eyes rolling and head lolling, acting hopelessly drunk. He raised one finger and said, "Give your thoughts no tongue! Be familiar but by no means vulgar. And the friends you have..." and here he placed his hand most ceremoniously on his chest, "...by all means loved, and their loyalty tried, grapple to your soul with hoops of steel."

"Why, Thane, I didn't know you swing that way," Jimmy said.

Thane smiled and bowed and then dropped the drunken act. "Do not dull your time with the entertainment of every new-hatched, unfledged comrade. And beware of entrance to a quarrel! But of course being in it, bear yourself so that your opponent shakes in terror!" Now he stared at me, stone cold sober.

And he leaned in close and whispered, like he was telling me a secret, "You're out? You're out. Out? Do you need anything? Would you like to come back into the world?"

"Nope," I said. "Got work."

"Really?" He sat down next to me and nodded to Jimmy, who evaporated from our proximity.

"Not that kind of work," I said.

He batted his eyes mawkishly and said in a falsetto voice, "What kinda work you doin?"

I drank, smiled, said, "Workin work. Real work. Blue collar stuff."

"Workin up there, huh?" He narrowed his gaze. "Among the cloud miners?"

"Yeah..."

"Well, it's probably not so bad, huh?" He leaned back and stretched his arms wide and then dropped his elbows onto the bar and spun out a Southern accent as he said, "Why, you probably got those family men in there with ya, the high school drop-outs doin forty to life, right? Ah... now, don't get me wrong. They's the salt o' the earth like yourself, and I do love each and ev'ry one of them. World wouldn't work without them. You know, I've been bound to labor before, myself. Sure, and you know, it's good for the soul and all, builds character and all that. Say, though, my friend, if you start getting bored or worn down, well there are alternatives—"

"I bet you've got a million plans."

He smiled from ear to ear. "Well, now, you know I'm always thinking."

Then Chuckie appeared, and he was lit up, swaying with a grin he couldn't quit. He was talking, his mouth hanging open, perpetually stone-faced, saying, "Man oh man oh man it's good to see you." Crazy Chuckie, and he reached out and gave me a light, bony finger insect embrace and just sort of drifted back and looked at me and said, "Man oh man oh man." He reached out to me again, but Thane slid off his stool and guided Chuckie into it and stood there with one arm around Chuckie's shoulder sort of holding him up.

"All your friends are here," Thane said as he swept his arm back in a P.T Barnum bit, displaying the fat pool players with their John Deere hats, the old men with toothless grins and red rheumy eyes, the shriveled potato crones crouched down in their corners. "Your people..." And he had the most extravagant smile on his face, I couldn't help but laugh.

"Yes they are," I said.

"Well, hey, my man," Thane said abruptly, changing again, "It's time I've got to go." And he was so clear-eyed that he didn't seem like he had been drinking at all. "But I'm glad I caught you 'cause I'm having a little party tomorrow night, and I want you to come. I think there's someone there you'll want to meet."

"Intrigue," I said. "Where?"

"Here," he said, and he took out a business card, flipped it over, and wrote down the address.

"Business card?" I said. It seemed like a joke. I half expected him to whip out a top hat and a monocle.

He smiled and handed it to me. I read the address he had written on the back, then turned the card over and read the print:

Thane Volpone
Consultant

"You... you have business cards?" I laughed. "This is good. Very good."

"Do you mock me?" he said. "I will not be mocked!"

"All right! Good enough! Genius."

"So, see you tomorrow, then, buddy?" He glanced around at the patrons once more and then said, "It's good to have you back among the dead."

"Well, you're here, aren't you?" I said.

"Don't get smart." And if he had had a cape, it would have swirled and billowed as he turned and disappeared in a cloud of smoke through the double doors.

"Man oh man oh man," Chuckie said, and I turned around as he gripped me by the shoulder with his claw fingers. "Man oh man, I swear that guy is scary."

"Thane?" I pulled back and plucked his wrist and drew his hand away. "Thane's all right." I took a sip of my drink. "He's a good guy. He just likes to play the devil."

"No, no, no. You know, people say, ah Chuckie, he's crazy, he's just a drunk crazy, says crazy stuff like oh I see the sound waves man, see em in the air swirlin and spinnin and rollin and sendin little streamers down to antennas on cars and antennas on houses and the invisible ones on people's heads, a whole ocean of sound, but you believe me because I tell you it's true, that guy is evil."

I was drunk by the time I got out of there weaving and rocking and trying to unlock my car door with both hands while leaning down like a jeweler to get it open and I got in shut the door started the engine and pulled back and stopped with a lurch and looked back again and then pulled out and rolled into the street nice and slow as I shifted up and eased forward and headed through the dark under the gray stanchions of the overpass and the big graffiti scripted walls around the railroad yard with streetlights floating overhead like dandelion seeds and the river on my right glittering black reflections of industry lights in perfect watery forms as I passed the towers of shipping crates in different colors stacked in such a way that I was convinced that the big blueprint was in the arrangement and the lettering of the crates and that it would give me the key to this whole quivering charade if I just stopped and read it all closely enough but instead I continued up the road and above the river the river the river which carried my reflection like a blue torpedo whoa stay on the road there buddy yeah and as I passed the homes I projected myself into them with their copper pots hanging over stoves and blond people going in and out of rooms hey now wow eyes front as I headed around a curve and into a tunnel of arching elms and then out again where I looked out over The Sound and saw the glittering spires of the city with spotlights swirling in geometric webs over some car lot or theater and I thought Chuckie's not so crazy about those waves as I drove into the dark dark dark they all go into the dark whooee think I'll have a cigarette and I punched the lighter and sang bad bad bad whiskey made me lose my happy home pop and I got an electric ember to light my cigarette ahhh wind comin in through the window as I let my arm hang out and drift with bad bad bad whiskey coming from the radio here we go along the dark field of the cemetery and up on the hill the reservoir tower like some alien ship from the fifties and the homes burning like movie sets I'm peeking through the curtains with all the reactions and dramas there there and there that's my little apartment hovel yeah I'll just oooh glide right in and off with the engine off with their heads as I climbed out and oh fell back in again and then tried it again because I'll try my luck again as I pulled myself up and out of the car and slammed the door and headed up the stairs with the heat curled paint crunching underfoot and there's my door and that's my number and here I come lock lock lock open open open sesame with my hand fumbling damn bandage like filth so nasty I ripped it off and threw it down into the street and inside my apartment I took off my jacket and went to the kitchen and turned on the water and drank from the faucet and then I went to the bathroom and fell on my knees and gave it all up and then finally made it to the couch to lie down in the room room room going round round round like a helicopter blade like a whirlpool like a vortex taking me down down down the dark ladder

N ext morning, ooh did I have a hangover. I must have had a gallon of water and coffee trying to get myself steady for work. And it was hot, getting hotter every moment as I drove out onto the freeway and into the howl of traffic, going toward the airport and the little twin tin cans of my job. Dry, dusty white air burned and swirled in the distance, planes lifting off the runways at stark angles. I rode over the railroad tracks and into the gravel alleyway, my car bouncing like a buckboard as I hit the potholes. I rolled into the lot behind the shop with grit dust swirling up around my car as I got out.

Raphael stood just outside the shop, smoking a cigarette. He lifted one hand, palm high. I got out of my car and took out a pack of my own, lit one up and stood there beside him in the warm shade of the building. "Mornin," I said.

"Hola."

"Sleep?"

"No."

We smoked and watched as someone came skulking out of the house across the alleyway and got into his car and pulled away. Almost immediately, someone else drove up. "Early day for them," I said.

"Yes," Raphael said, blowing a huge cloud of smoke that drifted up and over him.

"They're selling something," I said.

Raphael smiled. "You know, they say I was a cop in Mexico, so I was a crook. That I take people's money. That I fuck with the tourist. They say that. But you know, the police, they're just the same here. Worse. Really, much worse. I love my people, you know? Here, now. You think the cops don't know about this place? They know about it. I know they know about it. I seen them out here. Yes, it's true. They come out here. But they never arrest nobody. That's not why they come out here. You don't believe me?"

"I believe you."

"Watch," he said. "I show you." He went back into the shop. I shook my head and looked in after him. What was he up to? Then I saw him go over to the shop phone. He picked it up and dialed.

I turned back to the bleak sky and stood there in the wide doorway and smoked. I imagined that the moment I went into the shop I would disintegrate. My head was a nest of buzzard snakes. My eyes were puffer fish with poison spines. The air wouldn't move, but the trees and the homes jumped and jittered on the surface of some grainy emulsion. Who could breathe?

Raphael came back out. Two more cars approached and parked next to the house.

"What's up?" I asked.

"I called the cops on them," he said, and he folded his arms and waited.

"Really?"

A few moments later, a bunch of guys all came out of the house at the same time and climbed into their cars and drove away. Finally, the guy who lived there came out. At least I think he was the guy who lived there because he got into the last car in the lot, which was the only one that had never moved, as far as I saw. I had never seen him before, though. He was a skinny guy with bony arms and long black hair in a ponytail. He wore a T-shirt with the sides cut open to expose the lizard rack of his ribs. He slipped into a white, rusted-out machine with four bald tires and a thick patina of dust on the windshield and drove away. His dog barked at the gate.

"See what I mean," Raphael said.

"The cops aren't coming?"

"Oh, they'll come," he said, "in a while. But they aren't the ones. They jus do what they're told. It's the one you don see, never see. You know? You can feel him right now." And he put a finger to his temple, "Thinking!" He went back inside, strapped on his goggles, and began spraying a curved sheet of metal, some anonymous piece of a plane.

I took a deep breath, went in, and punched in on the time clock and nodded to Larry who looked right through me. Then I went back through the door between the tin can shop halves. The kilns were on, baking the enamel on a set of parts, sending out waves of delirious heat. Both halves of the shop were like two fish tanks full of hot oil. Tony was already working. I got a drink from the cooler, then another. My tongue was a dry leather flap. I sat down and started plugging plates full of putty. "Hello," I said.

"Hey," he said. He was deeply involved in his work. The radio was on, and I heard the Byrds singing *Eight Miles High*.

"I feel about eight miles low," I said, blinking, sweating, trying to rid myself of the writhing in my skull.

"Little too much afterburn, eh?"

"You know it."

"In the sweat of thy face shalt thou find bliss," he said.

"I don't know about that." The guitar rippled rapid-fire pulses, rising, higher and higher. "Although," I said, "pretty amazing guitar, there."

"Roger McGuinn?" Tony said. "Definitely a genius. His real name was James Joseph McGuinn. For some reason he changed it around the same time that he got into an Indonesian religion called Subud. Subud? Yeah, that's right." Tony didn't even look up from the metal plate he was working on but continued to rattle off facts: "He was heavily influenced by jazz and modeled the guitar solo you're listening to right now on a John Coltrane song. He played, I believe

35

it was, a Rickenbacker 12-string and had it worked up somehow to sound like a saxophone. And the song, this one, was actually banned because it was considered a drug song, but the band members all said that it was really about a plane flight to London, right, and culture shock, or something like that. At first, it was titled *Six Miles High*, but then Gene Clark thought 'eight' sounded better than 'six' and that it would be a good, catchy title since the Beatles had just recently come out with *Eight Days a Week*. They were trying to catch that wave. Smart, eh? Even the artist has an eye for marketing"

"You know a lot about this song, don't you?" I said. "This group, I mean."

"Oh, sure, I love the Byrds. I love all music, but especially rock music."

"Yeah? What else do you know?"

Again, without looking up from his work, and with his fingers working deftly, filling in the little holes with little bits of putty, he recited. "Let's see. This song came out on their album *Fifth Dimension*. And in fact, David Crosby is listed as one of the composers. Many consider the album to be one of their weaker efforts, interestingly enough, even though this is one of their most popular original compositions, probably because, like Dylan, they were moving on from the folk sound. *5D*, as they were called, actually played a mix of folk and jazz from the very beginning. Their subject matter was always unique, even literary. They have this one spooky song called *I Come and Stand At Every Door* about a child burned in the bombing of Hiroshima whose spirit walks the earth in search of peace, based on a poem written by... Nazim Hikmet and..." he looked up, finding the thought, "translated by Pete Seeger. Yep. Pete Seeger."

"Wow!" I said. "How do you know all that?"

"I hear some of it on the radio sometimes. I read a lot of it. Mostly I read it. Johnny Rogan has a book out on the Byrds called *Timeless Flight*. I read that one. I read a lot of things. I read history, too, mostly about the times when these guys were playing. And I just remember a lot of things. My brain is weird that way. I remember things I have no idea why, random stuff. Like, let's see...when *Five D* came out, in 1966, the US and Soviet Union both landed probes on the moon, the same year; Mao's Red Guard started gearing up in China then, too; Johnson started bombing in North Vietnam after a break of about a month; they started selling little disposable flash bulbs, I don't know, do you remember anything about those? Let's see, what else: some guy named Whitman shot a bunch of people down in Texas at the university, and another guy named Speck killed some nurses in Chicago, a lot of violence that year; um, those two Boeing planes crashed, that was a big deal, and those floods hit Italy and everybody was crying about the art that got destroyed, not the people; FM started getting big around that time, and so did *Mission Impossible,* that was the big show; *Valley of the Dolls* and *In Cold Blood* both came out, and they were big, too; Liz Taylor won best actress for *Who's Afraid of Virginia Woolf?*; the Celtics won the NBA championships; the Orioles won the World Series; hey, and Billie Jean King, do you remember her? She won Wimbledon that year. It's all like a list in my head. They published a study that said monkeys deprived of social contact become emotionally impaired, duh—I could go on forever. I love history, as long as it pertains to the music. Some of it sticks, anyway, obviously. But if there's no connection to the music, I'm not interested. But you know, I usually find there is some connection to the music and the songs these guys are writing and events in history and all these seemingly random facts, especially the classic rock period. It's like something was happening, then. Some pattern showed up. That's my favorite time. Although, I've begun to branch out because classical music and jazz influenced the rock and roll guys, and they influenced the music that came after them. So, I'm expanding my horizons."

"Which comes first?" I asked. "The history or the music?"

Tony laughed. "I often wonder."

"You remember everything in pretty good detail, too," I said.

"Yeah. I remember everything I read. All of it. I can't *not* remember it, in fact."

"Why, Tony," I said, "You're a scholar."

He lifted up a metal plate full of putty and waved it at me. "Yeah, right. I never made it past the tenth grade."

Just then, Raphael shouted from the other shop, "Hey, come check this out. They're here."

I went to the back doors on my side of the shop and looked out. Sure enough, the police were there, cruiser radio with its static voice, red lights spinning. The house was empty. I watched them as they knocked on the door and looked through the windows. The dog barked and snapped behind the fence. Then they went back and sat in their cruiser. One of them wrote something on a clipboard, then got out and posted a slip of paper on the door of the house.

"Raphael call the cops on the drug house again?" Tony asked.

"Yeah," I said. "He's done that before?"

Tony laughed. "He likes to bust their balls."

"The guys in the house?"

"No, the cops."

"What's the note on the door say?" I asked.

"That? Just a warning, says that they got a complaint. That's it. And that's all they'll do. That's all they ever do."

"They never bust the guy, huh?"

"Hell no. The guy that lives there? He's rigged something. He's long gone by the time they come around, if they come around."

"He's tipped off, then."

"I'd say so. Raphael seems convinced that's the case."

"Then why do they even bother to come out?"

"Appearances? Maybe they're just warning the guy to keep it low key. Who knows?"

Larry came in, then, and I went back to the table and got busy putting putty pieces into the metal plates. Larry went right past us without saying a word, and Tony grinned and said in a low voice so that Larry couldn't hear him, "Here we go. Keep your eyes open. Show's about to start."

I glanced over at Larry who was arranging a set of black panels for silk screening. He was lining them up in a rack next to the silk screen and arranging canisters of paint and paddles.

"Control panels, custom jobs," Tony whispered. "They come with these special stencils and have to be aligned very precisely, get it? And not only do you have to line them up properly, but they have to have a sharp line so that they're readable, but in this heat, the paint's going to run." Larry took his time, carefully aligning the stencils, fixing the clamps, setting up his paint. "He has no idea that it's way too hot," Tony said. Then, Larry pooled the paint along one edge, wiped it across the stencil with the bat, pulled back the stencil, and looked at it.

"Mother fuck!" he shouted.

Tony shot me a glance, raised one eyebrow, and grinned. "It's just starting. It gets better."

Larry went through the process again with another plate and pulled the stencil back and looked at it and said, "Mother fuck!" only louder, shriller this time. He wiped the two plates down, stripped them with a rag soaked in solvent, and then set them aside to dry and laid down another plate and tried again. When he pulled back the stencil and looked at what he had done, he screamed even louder, "Mother fuck! Cock sucker!" And he held the plate up over his head like he wanted to throw it through someone's skull, his hands shaking with rage. Then he put it down, wiped it clean, and took one of the previously cleaned plates that was now dry. He started again. Only now, he was more careless, throwing down the plate, slapping on the stencil, slopping on the paint hopelessly. And when he failed for the fourth time, he screamed again, "Ahhhh you fucker, fucker, fucker!" swinging his arms and kicking but not actually hitting anything, his fury thrown into the empty air, his rage going nowhere.

"Can you believe that?" Tony whispered.

I didn't say a word.

"Who could write this stuff?" Tony said, shaking his head. "And I've seen it a million times."

I drove up into the neighborhood where Thane lived, a funky part of town with mostly old apartment buildings and family-owned stores and coffee shops, cheap restaurants and bars and a few fringe theaters, and children in costumes and beggars in doorways, people, crowds, characters everywhere. I was ready for a party. And the heart of Saturday night. A beautiful sunset pulsed in the red flowered clouds. I parked on the street and walked up to the apartment, a five-story brick building with a courtyard and Rhododendrons growing tall and twisted in Dr. Seuss shapes around the lower windows and balconies.

Someone was coming out just as I was about to ring the doorbell, so I slipped into the green carpeted lobby of mirrors and worn couches and fake potted plants. And then anxiety swept through me. Could I be with people? Not working with people, but socially be with people? I felt like the stranger I was, standing there in the lobby. The thought of my next move was a daunting prospect. Maybe this was a bad idea. Gut-sinking nausea hit me. But I made myself go on. It's just old fear, I told myself. I'm a person among people. It's simple and human. And if I turn back, I might get stuck and become some kind of a shut-in suffocating under layers of useless self.

I went up the stairs instead of the elevator, climbing in the windowless green stairwell with its black linoleum steps and ancient tenement smells. Then I came out onto Thane's floor, a dark hallway lined with doors. God, I thought, it looks like a prison ward. Would I ever see clear again? I found his apartment number, heard the music, started to knock, then opened the door and went right in.

Light flooded through the windows, bright blinding and illuminating the room so that the people were only dark shapes. The furniture had been moved out to the sides of the room. People were standing in clusters. I waited for a moment in the doorway, getting used to the light, getting a feel for the energy of the room and looking up at a large painting over the fireplace. Odd painting, I thought. It was entirely black, until I saw a faint, redline silhouette of a woman emerging from its darkness. I felt myself sliding into it. I turned again and looked into the light blazing through the windows and saw a friendly form approaching. "Tom," I heard a voice say, and the form became Thane. "You made it. All right." He pulled me forward and said, "Hey! I want you to meet somebody."

I could vaguely see. Then he turned and lifted his hand like a magician, and a young woman appeared. She wore a dark sleeveless dress with pale Zen koan slashes across it. Wind chime music rose from tinkling gold bracelets on her bare arms. "This," Thane said, "is Natalie." And she moved closer, her slender form haloed by the window light.

She put her hand out, and I held it lightly, perhaps too long, stunned by a flash in her green eyes. I said, "Hello," and "Hello" she said back to me with a voice like an answer to a distress signal. I looked long into the dark of her eyes, the light illuminating her long black hair and one cheek, and for a moment I lost myself in gaze.

But this moment wasn't going to hold. There was Thane, standing with one arm clutched around her shoulder like a raven's claw. He was saying something, but I didn't really follow it. I was drawn into Natalie and not because she was lovely or the first woman I'd been close to in many years. It was the way she had designed herself like a work of art. She had three little glittering jewel earrings along one ear and a necklace so fine the chain looked like a single golden thread. Her hair glittered. Her eyelashes glittered. Her skin seemed to glitter. Her face was a mystery of expressions and smiles, and she looked at me as though waiting for me to say something true, but I just stood there then laughed. Thane raised one eyebrow and said, "Well, I think you better have a drink." And he shook a thumb over one shoulder, directing me toward the kitchen and said, "Follow me."

I followed him as he cut through the crowd, people seeming to step aside without even seeing him. "Nice place you've got," I said, but I was looking back at Natalie who was talking to someone else, though she turned at the same moment and smiled when she caught my glance.

"This old thing?" he said. "It's all right…" And we slipped between people, none of whom I knew. They were mostly slick art-types in black with blasted hair and pouting presentations, stitched-up cutouts posing as stand-ins and extras in this act. I don't know why I thought that. In the kitchen, Thane poured us two tall glasses of whiskey on ice and handed one to me. "To freedom," he said, and he tilted his glass towards mine.

"Here, here." I said, and I drank.

"It must feel good."

"It does."

He pulled a flask from his pocket and handed it to me. "Here. Try this."

"What? Is what we're drinking no good?"

"This is different."

I sipped it. It didn't taste like alcohol. "What is it?" I asked, eyeing him narrowly.

"Go on. Take a good shot. It's all right. I've been drinking it."

I took another drink. It was bitter, earthy. It tasted like it had been sweetened with something, honey maybe. I handed it back to him. He drank and opened his eyes wide. "The elighter," he said, and slipped the flask back into his breast pocket.

"What did you call it?"

"Elighter."

"What is it?"

"Real freedom. Give it a few minutes." Then he produced a fat bomber joint and lit it up. He drew in a big hit and held it and then passed the joint to me. I smoked. He exhaled slowly and said in that tight smoky voice, "Natalie's a beauty, isn't she?"

I nodded. "Definitely." Natalie...but what could I say? She was with Thane. We finished our drinks, and Thane poured another one, tall, too much, but I took a big drink anyway.

"I tell you, she's about the closest thing I've ever come to love. Whoo, and is she a wildcat!"

I smiled, shaking my head, and returned the joint.

"I noticed you taking a shine to my little Lorelei, too, old buddy."

I laughed. "Hey, remember where I'm coming from."

He laughed, then stopped short. "Fuck. Sorry, man. Jesus. We should do something about that."

"Don't worry. I can take care of myself."

"Well, I'm sure you can. I just meant maybe something in the flesh."

"Hey!"

"You seem good," he said, and he stared at me hard, squinting, a little tail of smoke curling from his lips that he quickly inhaled. "I mean, you don't look like someone who lost a chunk of his life." He handed the joint back to me. "So what happened to you in there?"

I took another drag, held it, handed it back to him and sipped my drink.

"Time," I said. "A lot of time."

"I mean there must have been some bad motherfuckers in there."

"There were."

"So, what did you do? Did you have to carve a knife out of your toothbrush?"

"Yeah, yeah. I played it pretty cool most of the time. It's hard at first because you have no idea what the rules are. Everybody's watching you, trying to figure out where you fit in the pecking order. It's constant negotiation, projection. You don't exactly make friends even though you're always around people. You're alone, always alone. And bored. Intense boredom. And until you've gotten some kind of reputation established, you're untouchable. But there's always somebody new coming in, and the whole process starts over again."

"So what did you do?"

"I did what everybody does. I went around with eyes in the back of my head. I didn't approach anyone. I went stone dead, and I made myself invisible. And I believed, I truly believed I was ready to kill anyone. I didn't care. I think that helped, having that in my mind. That kind of vibe. Nothing shows faster than a fake. I spent a lot of time in the library." I felt strange, borderless and light-headed. What was I talking about? Then I noticed Natalie there beside us. How much of that had she heard? I was out of place. Thane was grinning like a Cheshire cat, and it occurred to me that he might have coaxed me into talking about this right at that moment, knowing Natalie was there. It was his way. Or I was just drug paranoid.

"What happened?" Natalie asked. Something in her spirit just about made me drop to my knees. I lifted my hand to touch, but I backed away from that impulse. I knew the super-charged current rolling through me was a combination of nefarious chemical ingredients. And I knew from my lofty distant blur that any language I had to respond to her in a simple reasonable way was locked out because I was watching from a hollow deep inside my skull. Thane whispered into her ear and she smiled, sincere, reaching her hand out and touching my cheek as a blue spark arced between us.

And then others appeared, moving, bobbing around in the living room, little groups dancing, girls with reticulated Shiva arms flowing with the music, voices rising and falling like crashing ocean waves. I was smoking a cigarette by the window. The music changed to Frank Sinatra singing, "I got the world on a string, sittin' on a rainbow, got the string around my finger, what a world, what a life..." Then I felt a click-crack like a lock breaking and a door opening and wind rushing through, and I was standing by some people who were talking, but I couldn't decode their speech. They looked at me with bored rolling eyes. Then, out of that strange assembly, Allen appeared, my old buddy Allen, dressed in fatigues and slapping my shoulder and shouting something like "Killer range," I think.

"What?"

"Maneuvers...I've been out on maneuvers."

I focused for a moment enough to say "What?"

He laughed and said, "You're fucked up!"

I nodded. "Yeah, I was smoking with Thane."

He threw his head back so far it looked like it was going to snap off, and then he laughed and shouted back at me, "Whack, man."

"What?" The editor in my head was taking what he said and stirring it up into word soup.

And he yelled, "Whack...he smokes whack..."

I shook my head, which threw me off balance because I felt wrong-weighted and heavy. I couldn't feel my arms. I remembered drinking something, too, and I said, "There was something else..."

I pulled back, drifting up, back and away. My body was an iron anchor leaning by a window. An almost visible thread of smoke kept me tethered as I scanned and saw other familiar and unfamiliar people. Sure, even Big Jim. Seven foot three and three hundred pounds. We called him the genie of drugs. He was goofing, making wide-mouth freak-you faces. And Horowitz slithered over in his rumpled suit. He was smoking a cigarette through a long black holder, spit like loose teeth in the corners of his mouth. He was droning, "Hoover...Hoover loved numbers...nine on Kennedy...ninth on King, you see?" Old Horowitz, I hadn't thought about him in years...

People came into my sphere...insane conversations. I don't even know what I was saying. I was way out here watching it all. Then I saw Natalie, again, and she was smiling at me almost sad and a little seductive. I couldn't be sure. I lifted my hand, and she lifted hers. A star shot off between our fingertips, traveled on and radiated out of everyone in their burning marionette forms. Out the window I flew. "What a world, what a life…" Apartments glowed in scatter light, and the bay was flowing like the watery page all this is written on, and then Thane had an arm around my shoulder, bringing me back to earth.

"Listen…listen carefully…you listening?"

I nodded and nodded… "Yeah, yeah."

He said, "Now I know you're working, and I know you want to steer clear…I understand that…I do." He was looking down at me through the tunnel of my head with those black snake eyes and a finger leveled at me. "If I were in your place, I'd probably do the same thing…but I just want you to know…just want you to think about…don't even answer now…just think about it…a few contingency plans…nothing firm…just ideas…no pressure…just think about it…all right…you listening…all right…"

I nodded again. "Yeah…yeah I'm listening"

"So when you're ready—"

I put my hand out, and it felt like long-dead numb flesh as I tried to push him away.

"No…wait," he said. "Wait…just listen…if…now…if you're ready…all right… now if you—"

I kept pushing him away with my dead hand. "Nah, nah, nah, nah, nah," I said.

He laughed, lowering my hand, saying, "You know you probably won't remember this anyway." We doubled over. "Just listen," he said again. "…can you do that?" We laughed again. "Listen…listen…if you want, I've got a light little project that's easy…safe…clean…" He lifted one hand as though conducting an orchestra. "Three or four guys tops…and I just want you to know it's there…all right….now…I've said it…I've got the details in place…I've already done the mental work…It's a pure walk-through…all right…I mean…really…look at me…am I hurting for money?"

He kept wavering from my field of vision.

"Am I going to take any unnecessary risks…am I going to be like the rest of these soulless ghouls...?"

Sometimes it seemed like he was standing behind me, and then suddenly, he was in front of me.

"I'm not going to take any chances... I've got a beautiful girlfriend... I'm not going to risk losing that... I'm probably going to marry her."

I leaned in. "You're really going to marry..."

He leaned back. "Now don't go telling her I said that...just keep my offer in mind... if you're interested... it's here... I'm here... all right?"

I swayed back out of the way of his incoming ideas. "All right," I said. "All right."

Then Natalie slipped beneath his arm and said, "Don't be so hard on him, Thane. He's a gentle soul..."

"What, am I the bad guy again? She's defending you from me. How do you like that?"

He swept her away, and I tried to follow, but then I felt foolish and lost. I found myself standing in the middle of the room, completely cut loose from any grounding intention or person or purpose, in a whirlpool of faces. I'm sorry, I thought, as I stumbled and righted myself. I felt sweat coming down my face and into my eyes, and then it hit me, rushing and overwhelming, wave after wave of nausea. I couldn't breathe. So close to so many people. I looked for Thane and saw him for a split second, but in a flash he was gone back into the human energy blob out of which people rose like Allen and then Horowitz, and then Natalie beneath the painting of the emerging ghost woman, as I made it at last to the door and out of there—

—down the quiet hallway with green glow of fuzzy bulb lights and double row of identical doors rippling like jellyfish I moved alone and now in terror of seeing anyone knowing at least in a distant life preserver way my condition and how vulnerable I was and that I could even get arrested and break parole and overwhelming had the desire just to get home going down twisting stairs that seemed to telescope away from my feet as the green walls pulsed and seethed like inner organ flesh leaching wet emulsification and bubbling up and bursting and breathing as I prayed not to see another person as I opened into the lobby with the

mirrors reflecting the shifting ash of my serpent slick criminal monster mask and
then I heard the elevator engine churning and cables whining and doors sliding open
like a gorgon mouth so I slipped spirit-quick outside into the protective nightland of
tilting streets black swaying under a wobbly orange moon orbing over the city
towers as cars swept by with warping passengers inside and siren calls issuing from
distorted mouths while other nightmare insects with articulated limbs and prowling
feelers inserted themselves onto the city scrim of the scary movie-reel my friend had
given me and I took long strides in flux motion jumping jittering in and out of time
schemes and down the steep hill under troll arms of oaks and elms and onward
down through alleyways and empty courtyards with my heart rushing because I
didn't know where I was or where I left my car thinking no no no don't drive even
if you do find it and I went under a red swaying Cyclops eye over the Wall Street
sign and laughed at the joke embedded in the scene as horns howled and elongated
cars slid down the street and I arch-stepped in perfect veronicas up to café windows
liquid steaming with circus clown horror people inside and I tumbled down through
the empty farmer's market and through a ripple of papers that wrapped themselves
like Brazilian leaches around the lampposts and around my legs and when I ripped
them away I found nothing not even me underneath and there at the edge of an
empty stall a man in a long black coat was taking note with eyes that watched and
glowed as I lurched further down cement stairs with no railings on a sloping
cockeyed hillside with weeds silver dancing in the air as creatures under the
overpass leered from their hovels made of cardboard boxes and grocery cart
barricades with cookfires and shade sneers and the freeway bridge overhead
howling with its vehicles and I saw some animal movement on the perimeter while
my feet stretched down steps and slithered over railroad tracks and out into
boardwalk pier lights among people on the stroll from whom I backed away like
some swamp thing crawling to an empty pier and down wooden steps to a ladder
going down to a swaying boom dock where I landed and crouched in cloacal dark
beside the pregnant water with green phosphorous serpentine forms rising up and
other deep suburnal leviathans rolling by with flesh gleaming and deeper still past
sound and sight where motion stirs and rocks its will to streaming I dreamless there
reposed with night upon my back because I couldn't sleep with my brain a fright of

nightmares floating up with claws and tendrils and up there in the street sounds of approaching bandits and cops and all kinds of angry visitations I swore off as projections of the mind nothing more just projections of the mind as the water beneath me issued up its dream debris of murdered flesh and the sky's black mouth above swooped down with cavernous hunger and devouring intent as I huddled among the unveiling grainy sand flea hoppings of the mind as hour after hour I sang a little song to comfort myself…

"…oh hey oh hey come on home now come on home…"

I sang it as a prayer to hold it together as the goblin globe spun round and the dawn light came back at last sempiternal overall.

I rose at daybreak and climbed back to the empty street, seeing no one at all and feeling like I was alone on Earth. I walked through the drained world uphill through ashen dead towers of gray buildings and made my way through the closed kiosks and gravel lots and cold railroad yards and the silent makeshift camps of the transients. All around me, the city slept on, papers tumbling like slow dream ghosts through the streets. I made my way back to my car, climbed in and turned on the engine and headed home, singing as I drove through the empty streets, though stopping at every streetlight, singing hey oh hey oh come on home come on home hey oh hey hey oh hey.

I was able to sleep by about midmorning and woke up later that afternoon feeling pretty good. I was wiped out and charged up at the same time. And I jumped into action—showered, made coffee. I pulled out Thane's card, flipped it over and called his number, wanting to explain my Irish exit and say that I was fine with all mental equipment in standard operating order.

"Hello," I heard over the phone, but it was a woman's voice. I recognized it immediately.

"Hello," I said, "Is this Natalie?"

"Yes, it is."

"This is Tom. Remember me? I'm the one who spoke so eloquently last night."

"Oh, yes. I remember. You were quite stimulating."

"Well, just tell Thane that the snake bites its own tail."

"What?"

"It's an old joke of ours."

"Oh, I see. Okay. So how are you feeling?"

"Nothing wrong with me a little communion with the Sound can't cure."

"The Sound?"

"Yes, you know, late night journeys to the interior and all that."

"Are you still high?"

"I think... I'm finally okay."

"You sound a lot better."

"Have you ever felt like you were given a new life?"

"Sweetheart, every day," she said.

"Then you know what it feels like to know, deep down know, that your next move is charmed, all next moves aligned and right just so long as you stay clear and true and keep your energy good."

"And now you're starting to sound religious. But, yes, I do know that feeling."

"Isn't it Sunday?"

"You preachin?"

"The reverend Wellwish now takes the poisonous snake in hand, and by the grace of God lulls the serpent into trance, thus revealing the power of faith in the lord."

"Well, hallelujah, brother."

"And now he will commence with the speaking in tongues allelamnaregettatitooroo..."

She laughed. "Did you grow up Pentecostal or something?"

"Oh no, no, no. Not me. Hey, I wish your boyfriend hadn't slipped me that Mickey last night. I would have loved a chance to talk to you more."

"And what would you have wanted to talk to me about?"

"Oh, you know, you and why you're you, and how you became...you, where you're from and if all the people from there are beautiful, and what you do, the dream you had last night, and why you hang out with that superfreak friend of mine, Thane. You know, the easy stuff."

"Twenty questions, huh?"

"Yeah, well, it's no interrogation."

"I guess you've had a few of those, huh?"

"Hey!" I laughed. "I like that you're not afraid to go straight for the jugular."

"You understand the rule, though, don't you?"

"Ah. Sure. The rule. No. What's that?"

"Whatever questions you ask, you also have to answer."

"Fair enough. I like that rule."

"You really want to know where I'm from?"

"Yeah, sure."

"Well, long ago, I came from the dark forest..."

"I know that place."

"Really? Do you? You've been to Portland, Oregon? Because that's where I'm from. Portland, Oregon, originally."

"The dark forest of Portland, Oregon, huh? Originally?"

"Yes. Now, don't get cute." And I could feel her smile across the phone.

"And you still have family there?"

"Just all of them. And that's the problem. Going home means going into the madhouse and risking that I'll get sucked back in and lost in the circus."

"Lots of brothers and sisters?"

"Oh yeah, and it's always one crisis after another. One time I was there, my brother got drunk and fell off the back of a friend's boat and got his leg cut open by the propeller. He nearly lost his leg. He can't drive his truck anymore, so he lies around the house collecting disability, watching TV, drinking beer and getting fat. My sister dumps her kids off at my mom's and disappears for weeks at a time. My other brother... now, why am I telling you all this? You don't want to hear this stuff, do you?"

"Oh, absolutely."

"Why?"

"It's the real world. It's your world."

"Not anymore, it isn't. At least, not all the time. Oh, wow… I don't mean it to sound that way. I love my family, but I love them in small doses."

"You don't go back there much, I take it."

"Well, you know, I do love them, but there's this sadness. It seems like we're never just happy together. I go back thinking it will be better, and it's not. It just gets worse. And I want to feel good about my life, which is hard when I'm there because they act like I abandoned them, just for moving away. And they treat me like I think I'm better than they are, like I'm some kind of a snob. And they call me 'princess' and 'precious,' and it's this attitude of…like, if you try to change yourself, you know, to them, you're somehow betraying the whole family. To succeed or even try to succeed at anything, trying to rise above your station, is to become something you're not, and it threatens this fragile reality that says the forces of the universe are against you and that the best way to get through this life is just to endure it. Trying to change is like a crime, and you only risk looking foolish and being put down. So, to them, I'm a disappointment and a threat to that sad, comfortable truth. I can't believe I'm telling you this."

"Reverend Wellwish understands."

"He does, huh?"

"Yes, my angel."

"Now you're sounding creepy."

"I'm only interested in your soul."

"Well, then, reverend, what do you think—is it our families and our environment that make us who we are, or is it some supreme being writing out our lives? Or do we make ourselves and create our own destinies?"

"Some of all three, I suppose, but I think we mostly make ourselves."

"I sometimes think I was stolen at birth. I seem to be so different from my family."

"Perhaps you were stolen from the gods."

"Hmmm. I have to tell you, I overheard you talking to Thane last night about prison and all. That sounds pretty scary. You don't seem like someone who would have gone to prison."

"I was stolen at birth," I said.

"But you made yourself," she said.

"Hey! Now who's getting cute? But I can't lie to you. It was scary."

"Did you ever...have to fight?"

I laughed, but only a short laugh. "Fighting is a practical and artful form of communication."

"I don't really know you. I mean, Thane told me a little about you, how you went to high school together. But I sensed when I met you that you're, well...not a bad person." She laughed. "That sounds wrong. What I mean is, when I think about it, for some people a place like that... it's always got to be awful, but for you, I think it must have been... unbearable."

"Hey," I said, "you don't have to feel sorry for me."

"Well, you know, I thought about it."

"You did?"

"Yeah."

"I didn't think I made that much of an impression."

"Well...don't go getting all full of yourself."

"Try to rise above my station?"

"Nobody actually says that anymore."

"They don't, huh?"

"So...you want to talk to Thane?"

I didn't want her to go. I hadn't talked to a woman—flirted—for a long time. It was easy, playful, fun. I loved the sound of her voice, the way her mind worked and wove together with mine. I felt like a kid.

"No," I said, not wanting this feeling to end. "Just tell him standard operating equipment."

"Standard operating equipment?"

"Yeah."

"You and your secret codes."

"I'm glad you answered the phone," I said. "I enjoyed talking to you."

"We'll talk more," she said. "Don't worry."

"All right."

"Bye."

"Bye."

I was so elated, light, fired up, I thought I'd take a drive through the old neighborhood. So I jumped into my car and headed up through town, thinking, at last, a connection. Until now, I had only been physically here, but now I felt I'd made some true human contact.

I drove up Eighty-Eighth, alert, scanning every yard and alley for the chance to see my kids. I was sure I had seen Stephen for that one fragment of a moment, but I hadn't seen my daughter, Melissa. What would she look like? She was only a baby when I last saw her. The world has ways. And then, when I cruised by the house, I saw them—all of them. They were all out in the yard: Stephen, my ex-wife Carol, the man who must have been her new husband, some other people, friends over for a regular Sunday afternoon get together. And I saw her, Melissa, and I knew her, and I couldn't believe what I saw. She looked so much like Carol it was spooky, and I thought, how could they both be so like us, these children, like seeing our lives starting over again.

But I must have been moving too slowly or gawking too hard because Carol looked over, and her husband looked over, and it seemed like everybody stopped what they were doing and looked over. So I turned and looked straight ahead and accelerated, but not too fast. I didn't want to appear suspicious. I hoped they hadn't seen my face. I tried to act like someone searching for an address. I made myself invisible. And I pulled away, feeling strange, as though I had seen a ghost of another life I lived without knowing.

I had nothing to do, so I drove out by the water. I parked and sat on the hood of my car. There were kids in the play field, bathers on the sand. A train swept by, and as I watched the boxcars bend along the tracks, I felt something pulling me away. Things were always pulling me away, some I saw like work or a thought, the past, and some I couldn't see. Sometimes I just felt it, as though I moved in the air behind my body and nobody could touch me, a gem of fire hovering in another world. It's the hangover, I thought. Stray thought, nothing more.

The sun was fading with a long, silver tail of flame across the water. And I got lost in that blaze and the water rolling out and in at the same time in a collision of waves, and my mind just went. I was calm and blissful and simultaneously this observer overseeing it all and the rattling rocks like thousands of castanets and beautiful cloud genies towering over the mountains and one white gull in arc flight over the vast dreamsea. The night extended tendrils into the world, the sky alive with eyes. And I couldn't shake this feeling that a part of me was out there looking in, untouched, as I looked down at the bones of my hands glowing like dark emeralds through the skin.

I lit a cigarette and walked down to the ragged edge of the shore. Waves rolled up, collapsing into the teeth of rocks. I reached down and touched the water and felt the cool electric shock of it and came back to something and touched my forehead like a blessing. Seals barked out on a derelict barge, and music drifted over from a nearby boathouse. The water gleamed with green phosphorous smiles, and fires rose up in pits along the beach. Then I decided. I'll do it. I'll do it. I said it aloud, "I'll do it."

I called the number. I knew it by heart. I listened. I hoped. She answered.

"Hello?"

"Hello, Carol?"

"Yes?" I could tell she knew it was me.

"It's Tom," I said, anyway.

"Tom?"

"Yeah, hi." My voice sounded faint and papery.

"Tom, it's so great to hear your voice. Are you all right?"

"Yeah, I'm fine."

And then she realized it. "Tom, are you in town?"

"Yeah, I am. I just got back."

"Oh my God, that's great!"

"Thank you. It feels good. You know. Free." Now I had no idea what to say. She didn't either. Uncomfortable silence. Then I said, "Look, Carol, I just thought you should know. I don't want to bother you in any way."

"What do you mean, bother me, come on."

"Look, I know you've got your life, well…the way you want it. And—"

"Don't you want to see Melissa and Stephen?"

That caught me a little off guard. I hadn't even thought to ask such a thing. I certainly didn't think she'd bring it up. I hadn't thought about it at all. I just wanted to call. To hear her voice. Maybe get some highlights.

I said, "I think the question is, do they want to see me?"

"They would love to."

"Are you sure? I don't want to interfere."

"They're your children, Tom."

"I know, I know, but it's been so long. They don't even know me. I don't want to come in there and be some kind of unwanted… disruption. I mean, what would they think?"

"They know you. They remember you."

"But Melissa? I mean, it's been nearly her whole life. Her whole life. I'm…what? A story?"

"I know it's been a long time. But it's okay. I know they would love to see you. They *should* see you."

"Really?'

"Yes, absolutely."

"God, Carol, I don't know. Maybe. I would like that."

"When?" she asked. She was always a clear and practical thinker.

"Whenever is best for you. I—"

"As soon as you want," she said. "Why don't you come over for dinner this week?"

"Dinner? Are you sure?"

"Yes. What about Wednesday?"

"That would be…fine." What could I say? Did I want this?

"Wednesday, then," she said. Another silence, then, "It's good to hear your voice, Tom. I'm glad you're home."

"Thanks, Carol. It's good to be home."

She was so good. Always so good. And we had never fought or had big problems in the relationship. And then I disappeared. It was a shock to her to learn I was... I had thought a lot about it, a seemingly normal family life and home. With the work I had, we were doing well enough to live. Our house was in a good neighborhood. We loved each other, loved our kids. Then, I tore it all down. All she knew was a phone call for bail, confusion, and then an unreal revelation that her husband was a criminal. The trial that must have been a nightmare for her as she sat every day in mute, disbelieving horror listening to this story unfolding of a person, as portrayed by a very hostile prosecutor, like someone out of a cop show: a thief, a liar, a monster no one could love. Then I was convicted. She came to see me in prison at first, asking what I had done and why I had put all of us at risk that way. What was she going to do with me gone? I had no answers. How could she trust me after hearing all those details, a whole life she knew nothing about? At least that was the story.

I walked back to my car. Wednesday. I was going to see my kids, Wednesday. The thought rolled through my mind, building as I imagined it in a wave of hope and terror.

Time progressed slowly. It was hot, and Raphael had the enameling ovens on over three hundred degrees every day, trying to fill an order by the end of the week. The ovens drove the temperature up in the shop so that we seemed to move through a thick, liquid heat-dream, slow motion lifting lead-heavy arms. Even my head felt like a swaying, over-inflated balloon filled with cement. Fool Larry tried again to stencil a set of control panels but couldn't get the paint to adhere properly and cursed and screamed like a besotted character from the Bible. I smoked with Raphael who daily became more and more a ghost of himself as he continued to work his two jobs, showing the strain on his soul in a gaunt face with inflamed eyes.

Ａnd so Tony and I worked to an unending soundtrack of *Moondance, Dark Side of the Moon,* and *Do It Again.* I enjoyed the daily lectures Tony gave from his library mind on the facts of and around any song, say, how Lou Reed started off as a songwriter at Pickwick Records after studying poetry with Delmore Schwartz at Syracuse University and how "Street Hassle," which would never be played on the radio, was the first true concept movie-poem in music, and how Stuart Hendrick, the guitar player, had a vision on acid of Lou burning in the form of a Norse prophet—crazy stuff full of facts I couldn't doubt—the Doors and the arrest of Jim Morrison in Dade County, Florida and the withering trial and flight to Paris and the eventual demise and rumors of a faked death—the timetable of a tour by Buffalo Springfield and the Tet Offensive—Nixon's secret bombing of Cambodia—and on and on. The Nineteen Fifties, Sixties, and Seventies seemed to be his area of expertise, mostly because he liked the music from that era. He seemed to possess an infinite knowledge, as though in his mind resided the entire history of the world all traceable on a web of connections back to songs, entirely accessible if you journeyed down those paths, though traveling the intricacies of memory could take as long as the original events themselves.

I would sit or stand long hours prepping parts or cleaning and saying nothing, seeming to disappear as I did in prison time, whole eternities in which the clock was apparently unable to move. Occasionally, I would see the flash of an airplane rising from the airport in the distance, the trees shimmering unreal in the roiling heat. The cars came and went from the dealer's house. A fine and intricate routine of boredom crept on, and I was caught in its fierce and unremarkable grip.

Ｔhe night was hot and still. My little apartment was a sweltering box. Sonny Stitt was playing on the radio. I went out and stood on the deck just outside my door. Blue moths ticked against the porch light. I lit a cigarette. The night air felt feminine, warm and deep. A full moon cut through a cloud and flooded the street with its yellow light and lit up the broken wall of the schoolyard across the street. In the distance, the black mounds of the gravel mill rolled like whale fins and the thin reed of the steel mill smokestack penciled in white smoke over the railroad tracks. Beyond that and the dark river, the city glowed its green and gold cluster of crowded house stars. One of my neighbors came out then, like me, seeking refuge from the heat. He was tall and thin with long dreadlock hair. He lit up a cigarette, too. "Hey," I said.

"What's up," he said. He looked up at the moon, nodded, then looked down into the street. A heavy baseline of music issued from his apartment.

"I'm Tom," I said.

"Ymir," he said, giving a little salute. "You just moved in, huh?"

"Yeah." I twisted my arm so that the thin stream of smoke drifted up from my hand and swirled around the moths at the porchlight. "How long you been here?"

"About three years."

"Yeah? You like it? Seems like a pretty good place."

"It's a dump, but it's cheap."

I laughed. "That's true."

"You know," he said, pointing at my door with his cigarette, "a guy died in that apartment you're living in."

"Oh, really?" I said, and I took a step away from my apartment door.

He smiled and said, "He was an old wino-dude. Hardly ever came out. Sat up in there drinking all the time listening to old-timey music. He might come out every once in a while and spit. Crazy old fucker. You'd hear him screaming and talking to himself in there. Gave me the creeps. But I guess he paid his rent on time. Then one day…didn't hear a peep out of him. Coupla days go by, no sign. I thought he'd left. Then we started smelling something awful, you know, like a rotting smell, so the manager went in and found him up against his heater in a chair, dead."

"How long ago was that?"

"About two years ago."

"Thanks for the news," I said, looking back into my apartment tomb.

He grinned. "Don't take it so bad, though. A nun moved in there afterwards. You gotta figure she pretty much cleaned up the place, spiritually, you know." He stubbed out his cigarette on the metal railing and flicked it neatly into the darkness. "Nice meetin' ya," he said, and he disappeared back inside his apartment.

I closed my door and went down to the street. What a gala the night was throwing among the parking lots and apartment buildings, little huddles and intrigues and curious shadows. But I stayed away from the main street and made my way through the alleyways where cats glared from porch steps and abandoned cars, and little things scurried off under dumpsters and stairways and were gone before I saw them. Overlapping music and voices wove in and out of the air, the conversations of invisible beings behind the rorschach of low flying clouds. To the east roared the freeway and to the north hummed another arterial. To the south lay a quiet cemetery with a little creek coming out of nowhere, and to the west a power plant chugged away on the old highway that was now a kind of butcher's row of taverns, adult motels, pawn shops and fast food restaurants, a zone of sophisticated vice and boredom. I went south.

A tall hedgerow of laurel surrounded the cemetery, and there at the main entrance stood an arched iron gate laced with ivy. The gate was locked, but the hedgerow had sections that had thinned out, so I passed through and wandered among the quiet rows of tombstones, reading names and dates and the lists on the family plots. Were there any fresh ones? Maybe my old wino was in here. Just count two years back to see. And what would I do with that? Meaning, what did I owe an old wino once tenant of the space I was inhabiting? I hadn't seen him in my dreams. I don't think he'd asked me for anything. Here find Jean Toomer, beloved mother and wife, 1894-1967. Edward Thomas, 1878-1917. A child: Henry Howard 1917-1927. Names in clusters, like Williams, Thomas, Carew, then Jimenez, Vallejo, Thenon, and then Shiko, Joso, Hokushi, in a segregated metropolis of the dead. Grandparents, parents, husbands, wives, sons and daughters, some stones upright and some stones flat, weeping angels of mercy and elaborate monolithic monuments of polished granite.

A light breeze rolled through the trees. I made my way down to the little creek and saw it gleaming in the moonlight. I crouched down and put my hand in the stream, lifted the water and touched it to my forehead. The moon threw down its repeated image on the black surface, and the water rolled in slick, glassy ropes, swirling into back eddies and under reeds, motion and motionless current. Then, in my own form leaning there, I swear I saw another face—perhaps the old dead wino gazing up through my quivering image as though inspecting me from below, the new occupant in the world above among crowds of invisible ghosts all looking into the water at their own reflections streaming and dreaming and moving westward with the moonlight on their backs.

I cleaned up after work, shaved, and put on the only sport jacket I owned. When I looked at myself in the mirror, I realized it didn't fit quite right. It hung on me like a loose robe, like I was a kid wearing his dad's hand-me-downs. I had picked it up in a thrift shop, and it was the best I could find, but now I was locked in obsessive thought that the suit might have once belonged to the old wino who died in my apartment, as though he still inhabited the walls and by some gravitational influence was drawing me into his old life-pattern, to the point of going out and finding his old clothes to wear.

I picked up a bottle of white wine and a red one just in case, a little pint for myself for later, and a loaf of fresh French bread. I drove the old, familiar road feeling more like a ghost than ever. The jumping nerves were firing in my stomach. I parked a little way up the street and smoked a cigarette to calm down. I kept flipping through the radio stations, looking for the right song to launch me into the evening and propel me on to a good conclusion, but I couldn't find one, so I shut it off. Then the thought occurred to me, I can go in, or I can leave. It is a simple choice. That's right. And the effect of that choice on all our lives might be infinitesimal, sure, or it might be colossal. Then again, who knows what kind of pathways our small decisions create and how they affect the fabric of other people's lives, the choices not even considered yet made, the butterfly launching whole lifetimes of regret or even, perhaps, some kid of joy? Now and this decision could be one of those moments. Or is every moment that moment? Or the Big Moment occurred long ago, long before this particular life, setting in motion things I could never see or change. And crazy possibilities hovered just ahead, the unseen door waiting to open, weird dreams we inflate and fly into. Maybe we're just leaves blowing down the street thinking, I'll go this way, or I'll go that way. I'll never know. Not really. Enough of this.

I climbed out of the car and walked up to the house and across the yard I had once worked, though it looked better now (not a good sign for my return and with no Telemachus to great me). I knocked on the back door, not even thinking about the front because I had never used it when I lived there.

Carol answered the door, and I couldn't find any words to speak. I was—

"Hey, come in, come in," she said and embraced me, and I felt the tingling of an old life like a phantom limb. There were tears in her eyes, and I felt my own eyes beginning to burn. We looked at each other for a long moment across an unbridgeable gulf of time. She didn't look any older, though her red hair was cut short, just above the shoulders. She wore a light blue dress I had never seen before. She was beautiful, light, in her life and, yes, I think she looked happy. But I was acutely looking for something else, some evidence that I still existed in there somewhere however small because she also seemed like someone I had never seen before, which made me feel like I no longer existed.

"It's all right, it's all right," I said, and I smiled. I went in, and the kitchen was full of the rich smells of a meal that could save a man's life. I looked around at the pictures on the walls, the family, their family, and I straightened out the arms and the front panels of my impossible and uncomfortable jacket. The place was brighter, freshly painted, better again than I remembered. But I felt none of my old presence there.

"Come on," she said, and she took my hand and led me into the living room.

They were all there, the whole family, dressed I could tell the way they would for company. Up close, I could really see them, my two children, and I was overcome by a wave of vertigo. I was shot back into the halls of my old life, and I had a hard time pulling out of a close focus on their faces in order to play my role or find my role and hear them and know how to act. And I was introduced like a lost relative: "Here's your father," standing there like a ragged specter.

"Hello, Stephen," I said, shaking his hand like my own from a past I had yet to live. He was nervous with a terse smile and a narrow gaze, hanging back, trying to figure this stranger into his world. Then I met my daughter and shook her hand, too. I was conscious of a desire to embrace her, a feeling from when I had been a father and a self I thought long dead, but I knew I couldn't do that. I wanted so much I realized, but I was too far away now.

I met Carol's husband, Don, next. He seemed like a nice man, dressed like a grumpy uncle, meaning he wore a golf shirt and belted shorts, white socks and leather sandals. Maybe that's not true. Maybe he wasn't that bad. I don't know. I felt no animosity towards him, feeling so dispossessed of my past that I knew my claim on this life had run out. We all sat down, waded through some awkward silences. Carol brought me a beer.

"So what kind of work are you doing?" Don asked me, trying in his way to head up his family, present himself, and this was the best question he could think to ask.

"Well, Don, I work for a company that does parts manufacturing for planes. We're out by the airport. It's a nice little operation. I help manage the painting division." I looked around the room at the unfamiliar furniture, a seascape painting with rough water, more photographs of the family at summer get-aways and birthday parties.

"Is this for commercial planes?"

"Excuse me?"

"The parts? Are they for commercial planes?"

"Some, but mostly small planes. Private. Some military."

"You're in management, then."

"Sort of," I said. Stephen wouldn't return my glance but kept looking firmly toward the window. I caught Melissa's eye a few times, and a brief little smile passed between us.

Another awkward silence. I drank half my beer quickly, then stopped.

"Would you like to see some pictures?" Melissa asked.

"Sure."

She got up and went out of the room.

"He doesn't want to see those," Stephen shouted after her. "All she draws are fish."

She came back in with a small stack of crayon drawings, all of fish. They were quite good, though, I thought. "These are wonderful," I said. "I love them. You like fish, don't you?"

"That's my guardian spirit," she said.

I looked through the pictures of green and red-sided salmon with white spots, all of them in motion, all of them drawn within flowing blue lines of water.

"You can have one," she said.

"Thank you," I said. "You know, my brother, your uncle, is an artist, too."

"He is?"

"Yes. He would love these."

"You can take one for him, too."

"Okay," I said, and I picked out two pictures, rolled them carefully, and put them into the inside breast pocket of my coat.

"Say," Stephen said, "didn't I see you the other day?"

"What was that?" I said.

"You were walking on the street. I was playing basketball. That was you, wasn't it?"

"Yeah, actually, it was," I said. I knew I couldn't lie, embarrass myself that way. He would know and lose whatever respect, if any, he might have at that moment, and if I started now, who knows where it would lead. So I told the truth.

"So you've been by the house?" Don said.

What an expression of alarm he tried to conceal, then, and I saw him direct a cool look at Carol, which I was sure had formed in the cauldron of conversations they'd had before I came over in which I figured prominently—and not as the hero.

"You should have stopped," Stephen said.

"Yeah?"

"Sure. I would have introduced you to my friends."

Don laughed and so did Carol, a little, but it was a strange, nervous laughter. Then silence.

Then Stephen said, "So what was prison like?"

"Stephen," Carol said, "give him a break."

"No. No, that's all right," I said, and I could tell Don wasn't too happy about the way this conversation was going. "It's a good question." And I looked at Stephen directly. "I'll tell ya. It's a terrible, terrible place. You never want to go there."

"Believe me, I won't," Stephen said. And then, as if he couldn't help himself, as though he'd had this thought a long time and finally found a way to let it out, he said, "I definitely don't want to turn out like you."

"Stephen!" Carol said sharply.

"No, that's okay," I said. "You're right. You don't want to follow my lead. You're a smart kid. I can see that. And you know, Stephen, I made some bad choices. I admit that, and I know it hurt you guys—"

"It didn't hurt me," Stephen said. "Besides, it's a little late to start preaching, don't you think?"

"Whoa," Don broke in, and I heard him say quietly to Carol, so that I wouldn't hear him though I did, "See?"

"Stephen," Carol said, "what's gotten into you? You really need to take a moment to reconsider—"

"He's right. He's right," I said. "He's just being honest. And I respect that."

"Don't fucking try to defend me," Stephen shouted, "saying you respect me!"

Then all hell broke loose. Melissa went to the couch and sat down and started rocking back and forth a little.

"That's it, Stephen," Carol said. "That's enough!"

"Well what the hell is he doing here? He can't come in and pretend to be our father."

"He *is* your father."

"He is not. He's an ex-con who stopped being anybody's father a long time ago."

"Come on, Stephen," Don put in. "He hasn't done anything." But I could tell he thought differently.

"I love the way you make my point for me, Don," Stephen said, shooting a hard glare at him.

Melissa was crying. She didn't make a sound, but I saw tears going down her cheeks as she sat on the couch across from me, her hands held tightly between her knees, her pictures next to her. And behind her, on the wall, was a portrait of the four of them looking every bit the perfect family. There were no signs at all that I ever existed except in the face of my son who now looked at me with the purest expression of hate.

I stood up. "Look, maybe I'd better go."

Don stood up, ready to show me the door.

"No, wait," Carol said, holding her hand up. Then she turned back to Stephen. "I want you in your room, now!"

"What?"

"You heard me."

"No way!"

"Now!"

He stormed off, and Carol turned back to me. "I'll be back in a minute."

Then she left, and Don and I stood there awkward and silent. What was there to say, now? Don tried, though. He said, "You know, it's hard for him, a kid his age. He's becoming very independent. He doesn't even want to listen to me. It's just all the time you've been away, all the emotions he's bottled up over the years. Would you like another beer?"

"Thanks, Don, but I should go. I didn't mean to disrupt—"

"No. No. Wait till Carol comes back."

Melissa was breathing hard, and I looked down at her and said, "I'm sorry, Melissa. I didn't mean to..." and a whole host of wrongs jammed up in my mind, things I didn't mean to...

"It's not your fault," she said. "He's an asshole. You didn't do anything." I knew she wasn't supposed to swear, but who would scold her now? "Please," she said, "don't go."

"What about Stephen?" I asked.

"He doesn't mean it," she said. "I know." She looked at me, and her face held some tender secret.

"You really want me to stay?"

"Yes," she said, and when I looked into her eyes, I almost broke down, seeing there such a depth of sadness that all I had ever suffered or thought I had suffered seemed like fantasy and self-pity.

"All right," I said. "I'll stay."

I sat back down, and Don brought me another beer. I forced myself to drink it. My throat was tight. Then Carol came back in. And I felt bad because she looked so distressed, but Melissa had put a hold on me so deep, even sitting across the room, I couldn't move.

"Well," Carol said, "I think we should eat. The food's about ready."

"What about Stephen?" Don asked.

"He'll come out when he's ready."

And so we sat down to an enormous meal of baked chicken and fresh steamed broccoli and sautéed apples and wild rice. Don opened up one of the bottles of wine I had brought and lit a dining candle, and then I recognized the linen tablecloth and napkins Carol and I had received from her parents for our wedding gift. I looked at her, and she smiled. I wondered if Don knew.

The food was delicious, but I had to force myself to eat. My stomach was a rock-hard knot. Chewing felt like a bad proposition. I drank a sip of wine with every bite, but my mouth remained aggressively dry.

"So," Carol finally said, "how's your family? How's your brother, Joe, doing? You mentioned him, earlier. That got me wondering. I can't remember the last time I saw him. Way before the kids were born…"

"Well," I said, "I haven't seen him for a while. He's living somewhere up north in the valley last I heard, but he doesn't have a phone, and we haven't stayed in contact much."

"Why doesn't he have a phone?" Melissa asked. "Everybody has a phone."

"Well," I said, taking a big drink of wine. My face felt hot. "My brother's kind of a strange character. He doesn't get along with folks too well, and he has a hard time in big cities and crowded places. He's a little…he's a private person. He's always had a strange way of seeing things, but he's got a good heart; he really does. Although, there was one time…do you want to hear? I'll tell you a story about him from when we were kids."

"Yeah, I do," she said.

So I went on. "I was a bit younger than you are now, and… I suppose this is sort of a cautionary tale, too, now that I think about it. Anyway…we were playing up in the attic of our house, and Joe found my father's rifle, and it was loaded… and… I don't think he really knew what he was doing, but he pointed it at me, right? It was a weird moment, and then he pulled the trigger. Click! But it didn't fire. It was in perfect working condition, and it was loaded, but it didn't fire. It was the strangest thing. A miracle, really. And yet, he said he knew it wouldn't fire, that he just wanted to scare me. He said he kept it from firing with his mind because he was magic. And I believed him. What do you think about that?"

"I think that—wow," Melissa said. "Weren't you scared?"

"It didn't seem real to me at the time," I said. "Kind of like a dream."

Don didn't look too pleased with my story. He and Carol looked at each other for a moment, and I saw all those previous conversations passing between them again even though they didn't say a word. Then Carol asked me, "And your father? How's he doing?"

"He's still up north, too, at the homestead," I said. "As far as I know. I don't hear much from him, either. Didn't he ever check in on you guys? I asked him to check in on you."

"No," Carol said, smiling a little. "No, he didn't."

We ate for a while in silence. I drank some more wine and relaxed a bit. I forced myself to eat a little more of their food, but I had no appetite. I heard music coming from Stephen's room, and I found myself wondering what his room looked like since my memory of it was of a little boy's room full of stuffed animals and cars and posters of dinosaurs.

Melissa watched me, smiling at me. I asked her questions about her friends and her drawings. She gave me short, nervous answers. "What grade are you in?" I asked.

"Fifth."

"What's your teacher's name?"

"Mrs. Poston."

"Is she a good teacher?"

"I guess so."

I wanted to gulp down that wine and climb into oblivion.

Then Melissa asked me, "What are the people at your work like?"

"Oh. Well," I said, "there's a guy named Tony who remembers everything."

"Everything?"

"That's right. And there's another fellow named Raphael, and he's seven feet tall and sings arias."

"What're arias?"

Don cut in, "It's a kind of opera music."

"Right," I said. "Opera." I stopped. What could I really tell her about myself, about my life? So I took another drink of wine. I nodded. "Seven feet tall, and he sings opera."

Stephen never came out. I said my goodbyes and got out of there quick. I drove west to the docks and parked and breathed. Then I took out my pint bottle and guzzled it and looked at the dimming sky and shook my head and laughed.

I sat in my car for a while, smoking, thinking. Going back had been a mistake. I took out Melissa's drawings and looked at them for a long moment and then put them in the glove box. I watched the lights of the freighters as they moved in the distant black. Stars twitched overhead. I drank the last of the little pint I had bought and tossed it in the back seat. I couldn't see myself going back to work. I couldn't see myself going back to my apartment. I suddenly remembered that I had missed my check-in with the parole officer, which put the paranoia on me so that I looked around for police cruisers. I got up, collected the bottles from the back seat, and carried them over to the trashcan. They made quite a clatter as I dropped them in. I looked around. A few people were standing over by the food stand, but nobody seemed to see me.

Now it was night. A streetlamp nearby glowed with a little halo of light projected onto the ground beneath it. I went over to it, stepping into that halo. I reached into my pocket and found Thane's card. I turned it over in my hand. Then, I called. He answered.

I said, "Hello, Thane? Yeah, it's me, Tom. Yeah. I'm in."

II
I Hear the Sound of a Whip Cracking

I called in sick to work and stayed home. I wanted more sleep, but sleep wouldn't come. I sat up in my bed and realized that I was rising not because I wanted to or because I was ready to but because I was still on prison time. So I sat there, listening, discerning. My choice was made. But I still had these walls around me, even if they were semipermeable membranes I could slip through at any time. Walls holding you and walls holding you in whisper similar seductive sentences, the womb versus the tomb. Ultimately, though, what is the difference? Walls are walls, and we're constantly cracking them open to get out, then longing to return to something still and quiet (though a prison is never quiet), a bubble, a hideout, a motionless void. So I sat there listening and breathing it all in. A little music rose through the floor, voices coming in from other apartments, water moving through the pipes, a seagull on the roof calling out that universal flesh complaint, trucks rumbling up University Avenue. I could feel the vibrations of the world.

I got out of bed slowly, swinging my feet to the floor. That old carpet felt thick as a mattress and sticky with time-weight and the layers of lives saturated into it. As I took a step, I felt like I was wading through the swampy muck and swirl of life matter left behind by the previous tenants, their feather bones underfoot. And then I heard the voice of my neighbor, Carl, who lived next door in his own cell on the other side of the wall. I'd seen him a few times going in and out of his room. Once I caught a glimpse of the inside of his apartment through the open door and saw a maze of metal racks loaded with electronic equipment, circuitry of all kinds and husks and screens, contraptions he cobbled together and recombined into new machines to create his own ultimate tower by which to commune with the gods. Or something like that. I heard him through the wall late at night, calling out over amplified pirate band across borders into who knows what. I swear I heard him speaking Spanish and Chinese and other tongues, using his technology to penetrate the weird with the coded blip-language of deep space. He was a tall, hunched Ichabod, a shut-in who scuttled like a crab with averted eyes, and he said not a word to the living souls of the apartment building, even if he was most verbose with the blind and mysterious universe.

In fact, in my short time there, passing on the walkway or going up and down the stairway, I had osmotically come to know more about my neighbors. Their doors and windows were frames around their lives because in a place like that we're all exposed. The one person I hadn't seen, though I expected to and dreaded it, was Rob. His girlfriend never came back, and I felt him trembling like a nasty spider down below, picking up my movements on his electric web. I was sure he'd show up again soon. But others made their appearances like reruns out of the television box apartments. On station one in his cornerstone apartment under the stairs, white-hair Todd was busy night and day composing a screenplay version of this circus. On station two, Ymir came and went through an apartment door laced with purple smoke. On station three, Johnathan, newly emerged, scrub young guy fresh in the world was dating another young tenant on station four named Ronnie who lived in a ground floor apartment on the alleyway side and who was in her second year of the army reserve. He said to me in passing, "I like having sex with her, but she's kind of bony." Much like prisoners, these characters on their open stages wanted to tell their stories and be known, especially to a stranger like me, and my life was equally on display and plain to see because nothing is hidden for long.

I called Thane again, and he told me to come by his place that evening.

"Okay, I'll be there," I said. My own voice sounded like an impersonation.

"Glad you're in," he said.

"We'll see."

"I'm serious. Come by later, and all will be revealed."

And simple as that, I thought, the gears turned under the surface, escapements clicking into indelible, slotted moments.

I made coffee, using one of those Turkish boilers that came with the apartment. It made strong, hot coffee, and I liked that, but it didn't seem to wake me up. I was in a fog. I sat down by my front window and gave in to the world. I heard the screams of the children in the Montessori schoolyard across the street. For a moment, I floated down the corridor of those voices to my own kid days and back into the chaos of the playground amid the wild games with fuzzy borders, the sections of yard divided by class and power and tribes and the lost zones where the mute and feral outcast children clustered near the redbrick industrial chimney billowing ghost smoke. Seagulls circled overhead and shat down on us, and John Fitzgerald spot-watched where the droppings hit, zeroing in to inspect the splattered shapes for secret meanings. His ability to scry would turn him into a light-hearted gambler. And one day I was running—why was I running?—and slammed into another kid and got pow-knocked right out of myself and woke up later back in my body in the nurse's office unable to remember anything that had happened to me that day. I felt like that now as I sat there open and listening. The sound of the schoolyard is so much like the sound of the prison yard—play cry and fight cry, anger cry and shout. Articulated complaints and sometimes expressions of joy, yes, even joy in the prison yard, joy that sounded just like that gull cry up above I followed oversouling as it took off and flew over the schoolyard and circled west and headed through the white sky towards the sea.

I listened and breathed it all in, but even as I tasted that hot coffee and felt the structure of the old building tremble in its doubt as another truck went by, then trembled again as someone ran down the stairway at the end of a long conversation, even as I heard moogy cantina music like an underwater mariachi band and trance jazz sounds and rem rhythms floating through the structure, I had to tell myself I was there. At some low-grade lizard level, over and over, I had to convince myself by concentrated and unpunctuated statements that I was where I was. And I was convinced that that strand of thought was the only thing keeping me in the present tense.

What a construction. Then I heard something else, a shouting out of rhythm with the rest of the schoolyard and apartment sounds, then sirens and cars pulling up. I pulled open the blinds and looked out at the sick, swirling cloud-vapor sky. One gray-wing moth was still battering itself against the light outside my door. I heard its soft dusty concussions. And then I saw a man in a poplar tree across the street. He was straddling a high branch and shouting down at the luckless pedestrians on the ground below, including the police who stood beside their cruisers, doors open, hands on hips and gun handles, heads tilted back, trying to negotiate him down. But I could tell he wasn't going to go easy. That was clear. He had the wild-eye look of a man setting up for a siege.

"Go on! Go on! Get out of here!" he shouted. "I'm not doing anything wrong!" And he tore off his shirt and threw it down and then broke off some branches and threw them down, spitting and shouting out "Don't take me alive!"

I let the blinds fall back on the whole scene. Spectacle that it was, I didn't have the energy to witness it to its conclusion, even as I heard doors opening around me as tenants, realizing what was happening, left their rooms to watch the drama unfold. I stayed inside. The thought of being around people made my mind shudder. I felt vague waves of nausea. I drifted in and out of where I was. I had no idea what was happening for real. I tried a couple of times to read, but narrative was hard to follow. I forgot how my day began. Then, I caught myself waking up a little, saying here I am, here I am, followed by the harrowing swirling whirlwind gaps between words on a page where I stared into the void empty, mind empty, stripped, flayed without hope and left for dead. So I stayed right where I was. I went nowhere and did nothing. I was only a thought. And the day dissolved.

I drove over, nerves jumping. I'm going through with this, I thought. And I kept thinking, this is... I am... I'm like a gambler who knows he's going to lose but can't stop picking up the dice. But there was no way out—not like this. I could be philosophical about it, I thought, imminence here and now tending my garden. A two-note tone rang in my left ear. Buildings faced off with the clouds. Tent flaps fluttered in the jungle camps. Light came out of the chrome. People emerged from water fields and windowpanes with razor blade eyes.

I flowed along with the traffic on the freeway, the sun blazing low over the bay and through the gray cement ribs of the arching bridges, big flag fluttering over the human factory. All the jobs of the world out there, and we line up for execution, working hour after hour until we suffocate to hollow under the dust settling like silica sifting through tedious afternoons onto nails and delicate eyebrows, a slow expiration monitoring sheet metal cutters and assembly lines, cubicle death in glittering office buildings, becoming the manila folders and the invoices, the dockets and the spreadsheets, the phone log, the fiber optics, the digital display, the panic button, the treadmill and the workout shower drain-off of infinite information and the endless little plates full of putty. What a God-awful charade.

Traffic moved slowly along the train yard and up into the penrose overpasses, then back into neighborhood streets and alleyways through the stage set buildings and retaining walls. I drove a three-lane section of road that narrowed down to one between a double row of orange cones, a worker standing like purgatory's acolyte, holding a sign that said "SLOW." A drone backhoe straddled a pit with its piston pounding cement into rubble with a ring of iron on stone. Warning bells of backing trucks rang out while people standing on the hillside with blankets draped over their shoulders looked into the abyss with eyes like meteors ablaze.

I finally came around and into the heart of the city, exited and ascended through tree-shaded streets to Thane's neighborhood and eventually to his ivy-covered apartment building. I parked, and as I walked up the street, I heard someone shout, "Stop! Stop!" I turned and saw a man in ragged, slept-in clothes—a vagabond with a motley dog on a rope. He was trying to cross the street, making his way into the flowing traffic. I couldn't tell if he was shouting at the cars that wouldn't stop or the dog pulling on the rope. He seemed caught between forces.

I went up to Thane's apartment. He answered the door and smiled a broad I-got-you smile, and I followed him into the room. The sun burned through the windows, and again, it was a cave of shadows.

Allen was there. "Hey, muchacho," he said. "Were you lit-up the other night or what?" He laughed, and I saw his entire gothic family in the fabric of his face and the cant of his teeth. "Good to have you back," he said, and he shook my hand, revolutionary-style. He was wearing his fatigues, but he still looked like a lanky high school kid with bad skin and straw hair flopping over his wide white forehead.

Thane unveiled another character, a newer stranger who it turned out was not a stranger at all but another one of our friends from way back when. I slowly remembered, emerging from the fog. And I said, "Hey, Edwin!"

"Hey, man." He spoke with a deep voice through a tight smile. It all came back, this tough, compact antagonist with a black belt in karate. I saw him fight once in high school—I don't remember how the conflict began. He didn't start things, being a person of code. Robert Boyer, who went by the name Boy F. Doggie, got drunk and trespassed some fourth wall. He should have known better—he practiced the martial arts, too. I have no idea what words they exchanged or who threw the first punch, though I'm sure it wasn't Edwin. All I know is that it was over in seconds. Two or three strikes from Edwin, this after telling Boy F. Doggie to back down, and Boy F. Doggie was out, all the way out, you know what I mean? So, imagine my surprise when Edwin said, "I don't go by Edwin anymore. I go by Young Hitter."

"You—huh?" And I laughed.

Then I stopped laughing.

"Young Hitter," I said.

"That's right." He was serious, and through his stance and that tight smile, the line was drawn. I wasn't going to cross it. But Edwin was not Young Hitter. Strange. His new identity must have had something to do with hanging out with Boy F. Doggie and Allen. They were into that paramilitary world of war stuff. Maneuvers were a good thing. They liked maneuvers. Maneuvers were fun.

"All right, Young Hitter," I said. I wanted to respect his new chosen identity, though perhaps it wasn't chosen so much as laden, appointed in some weird fraternal ritual involving survival, combat, and some mild torture. But I kept seeing Edwin the young kid. As much as he was now this other character, he was still Edwin. Stay strong, Young Hitter.

They were all drinking beer, and Thane offered one to me. "Thanks," I said.

"Wanna smoke?" Thane asked. I looked at him, his face a tricky, impenetrable mask.

"Not right now," I said. "I don't think I can afford the mental tax."

He smiled. I glanced around the apartment.

"So, Natalie's not here?" I said.

"Nope," he said, sitting down on his long, black couch, the sun behind him intensely bright so his face was hard to see. "Little Nana's a working girl, tonight."

"Oh yeah? Where does she work?"

"The Shadowbox."

"She works at the Shadowbox?"

"Oh, yeah. That little dancer's got some style."

I nodded.

"You didn't know that, did you?" he said. "She didn't confide that little bit of information with you?"

"No," I said. "I didn't know that."

He looked around at his boys and laughed. "Why, she must like you if she didn't mention it. She's usually quite open and proud of her work, as she should be. You must make her shy."

"It just never came up," I said. And I wondered if he had sandbagged me on purpose that night. I thought about it. Of course, he did. Thane laughed again.

"Hey, wait, wait," Allen said, sitting up in his chair, waving his arms to clear a space for his presence. Something was always a little off about that guy. "Tom, you remember that day you came over to my house and I showed you the pot plants I was growing up on my roof?"

The pause that came after his question was almost violent.

"Yeah, I remember."

"You ever heard this story?" he asked Thane.

"Never have," Thane said, his arms stretched out like wings on the back of his couch, king of his cave. "But I'm dying to."

"Oh, you'll love it. You love this kind of shit. We went up to the roof, you know. This was at my old place when I still lived with my family."

"I know the place," Thane said. "I've been to your house, remember? Your sister still crazy?"

Allen just looked at him.

"She was pretty cute," Thane said. "And then she cut up her own face." He looked at me. "Did you know about that?"

"No," I said, "I didn't."

"Now what would make a person do something like that?"

Allen froze, said nothing, and then went on like he hadn't heard anything Thane said. "We were coming down from the roof. We were so stoned! And just as we came through the door onto the landing, Tom, you were in front, we see my brother sitting there on the landing in front of us, and he's got a single barrel shotgun pointed right at us. Tom, man, Tom just stood there like he didn't believe it was happening, or I don't know what, and my brother says, 'Die motherfucker!' And he shoots, and bang! The wadding hits up against Tom's chest and Poof! Man, if that thing had been full of real buckshot, you'd have been blown away right there. You remember that?"

"Yeah," I said. "I actually do remember that. And believe it or not, it's not the only time I've been shot at by an idiot or a crazy person."

"That was fucked up," Allen said, and he laughed a little too hard, a little too long.

"And your brother still drives an ambulance, doesn't he?" Thane said. "Completely blind to the irony? And mother's still in the nuthouse? Father... mysteriously vanished? That's great, Allen. That's just super."

"Yeah," Allen said, trying to figure out what Thane meant by that. "Yeah, my brother still drives the ambulance."

"All right," Thane said. "Tom's a busy man, a working man, so let's get started."

"Yeah," Allen said. "We've been waiting for this. We want the plan, my man. Show us the plan."

Thane held his hands up as though bringing an orchestra to attention and looked us each in the eye for a moment. He lowered his hands and began. "What never ceases to charm us? Entrance us? Amaze us? What holds a secret so ancient and true, something rare in beauty that reveals through its brilliance a thread of life's magic? Such that we hoard them, use them to beguile, to divinate, to conjure powers beyond the human? One of the few physical things in this world we turn to and find therein the fire of creation burning so pure we've never stopped looking into it? The secret?"

He waited a moment, letting the question sink in.

"Jewels, my friends. The timeless wonder. Jewels. Real, rare jewels. Not cheap forgeries concocted in a lab, but the real thing grown slow in time and darkness."

"Jewels?" Allen asked. This seemed way beyond his practical calculation.

"Precious stones, my little Droogies. The diamond. The emerald. The ruby.

The sapphire. Think about it, what they are and what they've meant to human beings over time and how they still hold magic. Let's review. Back in time, the ancient Mayans placed the emerald in the eye of their god. Charlemagne had a ruby in the crux of his sword to draw forth the power of Christ's blood during the Crusades. Caesar lined his crown with diamonds to draw down the power of Zeus. Sculptures of the one-eyed swan maidens of Phorcides were molded by their acolytes with a singular sapphire eye. The King of Mu in the Chou dynasty carried his emerald talisman across the moving sands and the Fields of Feathers to burn his vision of the world into being. The Mongol Batu adorned the shields of his dog-headed warriors with rubies to make them invincible in battle. And in John's vision of the New Jerusalem, he saw twelve gates of burning pearls. Jewels, my friends, jewels, do you see? Nothing can diminish them. No one can truly duplicate them. They're one of the rarest and most holy things on earth."

"Yeah," Allen said. "Yeah. But wait..."

"We're going to steal jewels?" Edwin asked.

"We," Thane began, then looked directly at me, as though I were the only one getting it. "We are going to hit the Exchange."

I didn't say a word.

He reached under the coffee table and pulled out a pad of paper and a pen. And like some old-time gangster, he chuckled and shook his head and began to draw. We all moved in close to see. He drew a diagram of a building and a parking lot and the streets around them and the layout inside the building, and each line he drew rendered his imagined world into the fabric of the universe.

"This," he said, "is it. It's perfect. Four guys, us, no more. It's almost cosmic. The reason that this is the perfect crime is that the place has been hit before, a couple of times. Not so much that they've gone overboard with protection, but enough so that the people working there know it like a routine. They're not going to freak out and do anything crazy. They're insured, and they instruct their employees not to do anything heroic or stupid. Also, it's set up for a fast, easy, in and out operation. It's got two entrances, one here on the West side, the street side, see, and one here on the North side into the parking lot. That's our penetration and exit point, but we've got the street entrance as an option if we need it. The beauty of the parking lot, though, is that we can get out of it either by way of the street, here, or the alleyway on the other side of the building, here, to the East. Get it? The alleyway will be less conspicuous and quicker, I think, so I propose we use that for our entrance and exit. So, the plan is to come in here, through the alleyway and into the parking lot, do the job, then head back out and leave the way we came. Simple. Clean. Fast." He sipped his beer and nodded over the diagram. "We can be in and out before anyone even notices."

"Sounds good to me," Edwin said. Something about the way Edwin, well, Young Hitter, spoke seemed fake. His voice was too low. Who was he trying to be?

"I don't know," Allen said. "What are we going to do with jewels? I don't want jewels."

"Think of it," Thane said. "Two handfuls each. Two handfuls! And you'll never have to work again in your life. You won't have to do a thing. You'll be free. You can pick your destination, find some undestroyed little spot on the earth and sit back on the beach, snap your fingers, and a servant will bring you a cold Seabreeze. For life. Watching the whole shithouse go up in flames. For just two handfuls. And we're going to get heaps, mounds," and he held out his hands as though holding up a great weight, "mountains of them. Think of it!"

And we did.

"So," Thane continued, "the next question is timing. When do we go? They open at ten, close at six. On every other Friday, they receive a delivery at four. If we time it, we can hit them right after the delivery, and boys, that pussy will be wet! But we've got to time it to the second. And we've got to be synchronized like a sweet machine. As soon as that delivery comes, we've got to be ready to go. Now here's the deal. We'll pull into the alley on the east side behind the building and wait there. The delivery comes and goes on the street side, so they won't see us. Right after they make their drop and leave, we'll pull in and back into a spot as close to the door as possible. We don't want to be walking around outside too much, and with the two exit points, we've got a better chance of getting away if we have to run, especially if the police show up, which they won't, because we'll be long gone before they even know we were there."

"How do you know all this?" I asked.

"You don't ask a magician how he does his tricks, do you?" He took a sip of his beer and smiled at me.

"Well, I probably would."

"What's the fun in that? Trust me. Look..."

And he guided our eyes to the tabletop and expanded his map of the area. "See, the nearest police station is here. That's at least two miles away and on the other side of the freeway. So, we've got at least that distance to buy us some time, right? The patrols are, of course, a variable, but they'll be concentrated in these shitty areas here and here, which is just about the same distance away, and since they tend to be on that side of the freeway most of the time, we've got at least fifteen minutes maybe more before any cops can converge. And we'll be in there just after four in the afternoon, so we'll have the traffic congestion on our side to slow things down too and block an interception. Any surveillance they have, well, we'll wear disguises and use an unmarked vehicle. It's that simple. All right? That's the big picture. Inside, I want Allen here by the street door. Edwin will be in the car, ready to roll. I'll be by the parking lot door, here, and Tom, you're going straight back for the kill, here," and he pointed back down at the building in his drawing and to a line of display cases and a vault he had also put into it. "Get what you can, grab everything in sight. I've checked it out a few times. They sometimes have the vault door open during business hours, which saves us time. We can just grab it all and go. If anyone comes in, Allen, you shuffle them in fast and get them on the ground. They've got one guard, I've seen him. He's old, and he's trained not to confront. He's just there for show. I'll go in first, followed by Allen and then Tom. I'll make the announcement, everybody goes down, Tom goes into action, we slip back out, Edwin's waiting for us, and we're gone. Any questions so far?"

"One thing," I said. "What are we going to do with these jewels? How are we going to get rid of them?"

"That's the beauty of it," Thane said. "I know someone who is ready to take them off our hands. I've already set it up. As much as we can bring him. I tell you, he's the essence of greed. He wants whatever he can get his hands on. If we bring them to him, he'll take them, as long as they're real."

"And you trust him?"

"He's too greedy not to trust."

"I've got a question," Allen said.

"What?"

"Is it BYOG—bring your own guns?" He looked around at us and laughed.

"All right, Myrmidon, I want two handguns—two only—big enough to make an impression. One on you Allen, here, and one on me. And Allen, you're in charge of getting hold of them. All right? You know who to see."

"Craig!" Allen said. "Ha, ha, that crazy fucking bastard!"

"I'll have my trusty little derringer, just in case," Thane said, "but that's it. I don't even like talking about weapons because I don't like the idea getting in there. Thoughts are things. We want this plan to go lightning fast. And we've got to be prepared. But we're not planning for a siege. You got that? If it comes down to it, we can shoot our way out. But I don't want a lot of armament around. It's too unpredictable. Seriously, everyone is to concentrate and act with one thought in mind: safety for everyone, for us, for the people in the store! We're good citizens. You got that? Especially you, Allen."

"What the fuck?" Allen said.

"We are not going to be drama for the late news. Tom, I hope you don't mind. I think you should go in clean. But it's up to you."

"I'd prefer it that way," I said.

"That's…" and he leaned forward and put a hand on my shoulder, "…why I wanted you for the job." He drank his beer, then took out a pack of cigarettes and lit one. "You're the coolest person I know," he said. "If anyone can walk back there, get the jewels, and clear us out of there, it's you. You're the charmed one. I know it."

"They'll be happy to give him everything they've got," Allen said.

"Hell," Thane said, "they'll thank him for being so polite." He turned to Edwin. "Now Hitter, you know your job?"

"Yes."

"Edwin, here, is going to steal us a nice little car, but here's the set up." And he pointed at the map. "Tom, you and Allen are going to park down here, a mile east, see? Bring your own cars. Then you'll walk up here to this block where you'll meet Edwin and me and we'll go in the stolen car. After the job is done, we'll drive back and drop you two off. You get lost in the crowds after that, all right? You guys take off, we scatter. Then Edwin and I will ditch the stolen car. We do it this way, it's harder to follow us. If we're followed from the Exchange in any way, we'll just have to make a run for it, but this way, we can separate out quickly, and no one can identify us by the car. Also, wear a coat, a long coat that's light and inconspicuous, but long enough to cover your general form, and get hats and dark glasses. You'll dump them afterwards when you're sure you're not seen. Keep it simple. We don't need to look like clowns. It might be a good idea to wear gloves, too, just to avoid leaving any fingerprints. And after the job, get rid of everything. Don't even keep the clothes you wore during the job. You got that? Any questions?"

"It's clear to me," Edwin said. "A bit old fashioned."

"It's classical art," Thane said. "It's the wild west."

"I got it," I said.

"Yeah," Allen said.

"All right," Thane said. "Now remember, everybody, Allen..."

"What?" Allen said, lifting his hands, affronted. "Why are you talking to me like I'm the fuck-up?"

"Don't *talk* about it. If you keep it to yourselves, the chances are very high that we can pull this thing off. All right? All right? All right."

It did seem old fashioned. Almost impossible. There would be incredible surveillance, I was sure. But maybe it would work. Maybe. Maybe something would change the old story in which all of this goes hopelessly wrong. Maybe everything is possible before it isn't, and even after that, we never know. Every day, there is nothing that cannot happen. Extra credit if you know who said that.

I went in to see my parole officer. His name was Darren, and he was a thick, low-brow bureaucracy guy. He asked me why I had missed my appointment. I told him I was sick. A fly was buzzing around his office. I kept thinking, I'm not even going to swat that fly, and he'll notice that and think, why look, he wouldn't even hurt a fly. His space was spare, although he did have a calendar on one wall, and each little day grid had an image of the moon on it, growing from sliver to crescent to half full whole and back down again to nothing. Nothing is called "new." I couldn't take my eyes off it, and I saw that the moon was currently an emptied-out circle of nothing. New. Darren was bunkered in by several file cabinets and piles of case folders. I suppose he was a poor drone, worn down by the job from generally kind to mildly suspicious. But who could blame him for jaded, head-down survival? He had a couple of pictures of his kids in graduation gowns. The walls and chairs and desk and even his skin had a yellow tinge, the sickness of fluorescent lights and bad air. He was scanning an open folder, a folder on me, and he was trying to appear friendly and not look like all he wanted to do was get through the checklist of questions.

"The job working out okay?" he asked.

"Dandy."

"And you're still living in your place of—"

"I haven't moved."

"No contact with any known felons or criminal activities?"

"Not that I know of."

He raised an eyebrow. He wrote in my folder.

"I work," I said. "By the time I get home, there's nothing left."

"You don't like the job?"

"No. It's fine. The hours are long. It's fine. I can make it work. Larry, the manager, seems to like me. At least he doesn't hassle me like some of the others."

"And financially you're able to make ends meet?"

"I get by. I'm not going to get rich."

"Well, neither am I," he said, laughing and scribbling in the folder.

I smiled, and my gaze drifted back to the calendar and the picture of the month. Darren must be an art fan. What would you call it? Modern? Surreal? I'm not up on my theory. A man was stepping through a backlit door into a field, and from the top of his head, a second ghostly image of himself swam up into the night sky. It was titled, "4 A.M."

I waited. He seemed like he wanted to ask me something else, something philosophical. I don't know why I thought that because what else was there to ask? This wasn't about support. And then I found myself wanting to ask him something philosophical, like why he had this job. Who chooses a job like this? Did he dream of this job when he was a kid, right after grade school principal and dogcatcher? Of course not, who would? So, what series of moments did he stumble through blindly, unconsciously to end up here? I was curious if there was a moment when he thought, what? Fuck no! Because, isn't that the moment that unites us all? The moment when the line between law and order and criminality becomes most thin? Was he aware of that moment? But I kept my mouth shut. I certainly wasn't here to instruct him, and his message to me was loud and clear. Better to make as little impression as possible. Be invisible, I thought, and I watched my hands evaporate. I'm sure he would forget about me five minutes after I left. So, I waited.

Then, he looked up, biting a fingernail, looked around for a second and then said, "You can go."

I saw him when I arrived home. Rob sat there on the steps, one leg jittering. I couldn't get to my apartment without going past him. My fear brain wondered if he'd been waiting for me. He held a leash with a Pit bull on the other end of it, one of those white snappers with black, ball-bearing eyes and a pink alligator mouth. Then Rob looked up with that bald head and sneer face, and his eyes were dull shark eyes. He wore black jackboots. He was thoroughly tattooed with snake scales, a crucifix on the neck, skulls and swastikas on the arms. Evil markings. I could tell he'd done time. And all I could think was that I had to pass him somehow to get to my apartment.

He was watching me as I approached. My intention was to slip by, if I could. The muscles of my stomach tightened.

"Hey," he said.

I brought my right arm back a little, gathering force in the shoulder. I had no other options, now, I thought. I stopped. The dog sat panting, head-heavy. This was it.

"I just wanted to say thank you," he said.

I kept my weight centered and listened. He took in a long breath. I counted that in my favor.

"You didn't have to come out up there the other night, you know? I don't know if I would have done that. I was out of control, man. I admit it." He seemed deflated, empty, a dull, whispery husk. "Anyway...thanks."

"It's okay," I said. But I didn't let my guard down. He was an explosive waiting for a fuse. His dog shuffled over and sniffed at me. I tentatively reached a hand down and let him smell it.

"I'm Rob Cogland, by the way, case you were wondering. The big guy here is Buddy."

"Buddy," I said, and I pet the dog a little, though I was still wary. Never trust a friendly criminal.

"Yeah, he's my pal," he said. And he jerked the dog back a little and knuckle-rubbed him on the neck. "Something's wrong with him, though. For a couple of days, now, he won't eat, and he's been shitting all over the apartment. That's why we were fighting, me and Sharon. She wants me to get rid of him."

I looked past him and saw the open door to his apartment. It was a dark cave, identical in layout to all the rest of the apartments, of course. But it had its own unique stink I caught a whiff of even from where I stood. And it had its own closed-in dungeon darkness. It could have been a trick of the mind, but I thought I saw a poster of Hitler on a wall in there.

"Did she say where she was going?" he asked.

"No," I said. And I thought, hopefully she won't be back at all, for both of their sakes. Then again, their trouble was their mystery, and I didn't know more than I saw. Sometimes people stay together just to torture each other, crazy as that sounds.

"I don't think she's coming back," he said.

The dog licked my hand, and I saw something wrong and rheumy in the eyes.

"Anyway," he said, "thanks. I don't know what might've happened if you hadn't opened your door." Then he seemed to think about what he had just said and started again. "I mean..." But whatever thought he had dropped off there.

"It's okay," I said, "really." All I wanted was to get past him. So I stuck my hand out to him, and we shook hands. He gave a hard, brief grip that tingled with poison. Then I stepped along the edge of the stairs to pass by him. I got a few steps up. He didn't move. I felt bombarded by electric waves.

"What are you doing here, anyway?" he asked.

I stopped. Was this it? Was the moment changing, now?

"What?" I asked.

"Why are you here? You don't belong here."

"What do you mean, I don't belong here?"

"Nope. Not here. Not with us."

I wasn't sure what he meant. It struck me as kind of funny, though, because the place seemed fine for all of us, run down a little, but good enough for people just trying to stay alive. If anyone didn't belong, I would have said it was him. He hadn't even turned around. He sat there, shoulders bowed.

"I guess I just landed here like everyone else," I said.

"Well don't worry. I got the place covered."

The statement felt like a lure. I didn't ask what he meant.

"Okay," I said.

And I went up the stairs to my apartment. Everything about him felt like trouble. I went inside, closed my door, and waited for a moment. I counted breaths. This was something I had learned. Then I looked out the window. He was still sitting there, his back to the apartment. But I thought I heard him talking. I definitely heard a voice down there. Was he talking? That seemed a little crazy. It made me feel like I was starting to go crazy, too. And I thought that somehow he was watching me, looking through the back of his head and watching me. That was crazy. I leaned against the door. What was this going to lead to? I shook my head. I thought, are the gods fucking with me? Why? Aren't all my debts paid? Wasn't I running on a clean slate? Well, relatively clean. Relax, I told myself. Nothing has happened. Not yet. Not to you. But now I had to calculate all my moves with this character in mind. He was a factor of sorts, although I couldn't tell yet if he was a minor one or not. But the truth of the matter was, I was no longer just another anonymous tenant. The world had another hook in me.

I went to work during the intervening days. Of course, I had no choice. But I was already gone in my mind. I didn't want to throw anything off with my parole officer, though, so I didn't break the routine. I stacked boxes and cleaned shelves; I loaded parts onto trucks, unloaded parts off of trucks. At least the burn on my hand was beginning to heal. Raphael would sing, and when Larry walked by, Raphael would change the words he was singing to things like hijo de la chingada, or pinche cabron, staying perfectly in tune, and Larry never noticed. The action continued at the drug house, the same series of arrivals and departures. And I had a vision of myself slogging through a job like this until my body started to burn out, spending years inside this little hell shop until I couldn't work anymore. And then what? I would die in that apartment just like that old wino? I had this feeling that there were a limited number of stories for a life, and the forces around me were moving me more relentlessly in one direction. Then I thought about the job we were going to pull and the money and the freedom it would give me. And that's all I wanted. Freedom. I just wanted freedom. And I dreamed my future in some nameless, warm paradise with empty white sand beaches and palm trees and pelicans standing around on rocks. I would drink Mai Tais and read and work on that perfect tan and have gray perfect moments every day at ten o'clock swimming in the warm waters without a care in the world, my head this blissful node of all-knowing bobbing on the waves. I would disappear, create a new identity, become a new man.

A t home, I waited, and I watched television and drank beers and sat by the window and listened to the world of sounds out there, just like I was still inside my prison cell. Only now I was waiting for a different release. Still, time couldn't move more slowly.

One night, the walls of my little room began to close in and swallow me. I could feel the pressure in my hands and feet, and I knew that if I didn't do something fast, I was going to disappear. So, I got up and went over to my neighbor Ymir's place. I knocked on his door, and he answered. "What's up?"

"The walls are eating me."

"Come on in."

I had no golden key, and I drank no potion marked DRINK ME. Yet, when I passed through that door, I entered a mystery garden of huge green ferns and jade plants and palms in enormous pots. And on the pots were little painted figures with raised arms unfurling into little blue lines like veins that twisted up and off the pots and spread across the walls. Now, his apartment was no bigger than mine, but it felt like there weren't any walls at all. Instead, the room was the floating world. He had painted everything purple with red and yellow spirals of elaborate and pulsing constellations. And dominating it all was one enormous tree with intricate roots spread out below it along the floor in equal proportion to its branches up above. And at the very top of the tree and across the ceiling, he had painted a golden bird with wings outspread. Weird, slow moody music was playing, something new and strange I had never heard before. His furniture was all black, even the tables. It was a tripped-out place.

"Cool digs, Ymir."

He smiled proudly. "I likes to create my own environment."

And, gentleman that he was, he offered me a glass of Johnny Walker Black. A civilized evening cocktail. Over the next few eons, that became our thing, the Johnny Walker Black, as we drank from Odin's cup.

Ymir was a pleasant, smart artist with the gift of gab. His spirit glowed like a fortune teller's neon sign. And little by little in timeless time he gave me the details of his life. His father had been in the army, and Ymir had grown up with his mother and twin brother schlepping from base to base. "The army's no place for a true man, though," he said. "The army talks about giving you an education and job skills, but that's just bullshit. Maybe at one time, but not anymore. Sure, they'll teach you about electronics and stuff, but not if you're...you don't get those jobs if you're a true man. And I went to their base schools. All they teach are lies, especially when it comes to history. I could make it all up and be more true. I could invent a complete mythology..." And he looked around at his painted world and smiled. "Well, I guess I did."

Ymir's brother was now in jail for petty theft. "Jean Valjean was more guilty than my brother," he said. "And as long as he's in prison, I'm in prison, too. I feel it all the time." As kids, they lived in an insulated world. They were each other's only friends as they went from place to place, especially when their father was stationed in Germany. Ymir spoke German, too. He loved reading and gave me a book called *Hunger* by a Norwegian writer named Knut Hamsun. In my time off, I read it. It was about a man unwilling to do any kind of work other than write. He was starving and wandering around the city streets chewing on wooden pencils in a muttering delirium. He knew an editor at the newspaper. Once he wrote his article, he would sell it and buy some food. But any time he tried to lie down on a park bench to sleep, the police would hustle him off. And so, his sleepless brain blazed. One line he wrote that I liked was, "The animals bearing the original terror and fierceness are the ones that will survive." I liked that, and I showed it to Ymir. He agreed there was truth in it. I wrote it down on a piece of paper and tacked it to my door. I felt that it was important to remember those words.

Ymir ran a small print shop. In fact, he had half-ownership of it and was beginning to make some money. "I'm saving to buy the rest of the business," he said. They printed everything from medical pamphlets to chapbooks. I thought about asking him for a job but decided it was too late for that.

We poured shot after shot from the bottomless bottle of Johnny Walker Black. I wasn't going to turn it down. Work and time became a dream. And we drank through the hazy wildfire evening, looking through his doorway to the east and the burning mountain. At one point, I asked him, "Did you hear that fight the other night?"

"What fight?"

"Seriously? You didn't hear the fight? It was right outside your door!"

"No way, a fight? No. I didn't hear any fight."

"There was a fight, right out here. I can't believe you didn't hear it. I heard it, and I opened my door. This guy was there, and he had a hold of a woman and was dragging her by her feet."

"Wha?"

"Seriously. She was holding onto the railing, and he was pulling her by her feet. I've never seen anything quite like it. Real caveman behavior."

"That's fucked up. Out here?" And he pointed out to the walkway.

"Right out there," I said.

"How come I didn't hear that?"

"I don't know. How come you didn't hear that?"

"That's fucked up."

"I know. I didn't know what to do. I mean, at first, I wasn't sure what was happening. I just heard screaming and scuffling, and so I opened the door. And there they were, going at it. I didn't want to get involved, but once I'd opened that door, what else could I do?"

"You opened the door, man. There ya go. You were in it. Once you open that door... So then what did you do?"

"Well... nothing. I mean, I said, 'Hey, what are you doing?' That's what I did."

Ymir laughed. "Really? That's what you did? You said, 'Hey, what are you doing?'"

"I said, 'Hey, what are you doing?' Oh, and this guy...have you seen him around? Rob? Big bald guy, total Nazi skinhead type?"

"No, man, no. I don't know him. Nazi? Really? I don't think I've seen him."

"Or his girlfriend? She said her name was Sharon? Tall skinny chick? They live downstairs."

"Sharon? Nope. I don't think so. Don't think I know her. Maybe. Maybe I've seen her. I don't know. I'm sure I haven't seen him, though. But people come and go from this place all the time, you know? No one stays in this limbo for long, except me, I guess. Feels like I've been here forever. So, what happened after you said, 'Hey, what are you doing?'" He seemed to like that line and laughed again. Then he said, "You don't look dead!"

"Nothing at all. Nothing happened after that. He just looked at me, and that was it. I thought he was going to haul off and hit me, but he didn't do anything. He just stood there, looked at me, then let her go and walked off. That was it."

"That's it?"

"Yep. Well, then I ran into him on the stairs and, get this, he thanked me for stopping him."

"Nice job."

"What do you mean? I didn't do anything."

"Well, nice job mister peace maker."

"I'm no peace maker. I didn't do anything."

"Are you serious? Of course, you did. You stopped shit from happening. You stepped up, my man. You stepped up, and you made something else happen. For all you know, he might have killed her, right there in front of your apartment. And mine, I guess. And for all you know, he might have killed you!

"That's funny. That's what she said!"

"Ah... ha..." He poured us another drink. "Here, drink this, mister hero!"

"I'm no hero. Oh, man, and then she came into my apartment. I mean, what could I do? And the whole time, I was sure he was going to come back with a gun or something. He was on fire. All I could think was, how am I going to get her out of here?"

"She was in your apartment?"

"Yeah."

"Hmmm. That could lead to some consequences."

"Don't tell me that."

"Just being honest."

"She smoked a bunch of cigarettes and called a friend to come and get her then took off. I'd be surprised if she shows up again."

"Don't be too sure about that."

"Yeah. I was kind of thinking the same thing."

"You never know with that kind of shit. People wrap themselves up in each other in all kinds of ways, and their fates get tangled into each other, and they can't get away no matter what they do. They're like binary stars that lock into orbit around each other and can't break free. So, yeah. I wouldn't be too sure."

"I guess so, but, oh, man... now I'm on this guy's radar, and he's a fucking psycho. What the fuck am I going to do?"

"Lie low," Ymir said.

"Lie low," I said. "How am I going to do that? He lives downstairs."

"Just lie low." He said it as though it were a philosophical truth. Then he pulled out a nice little rolled up number, lit it up, took a deep drag, and then handed it to me. And he said again in a tight voice, "Just lay low."

"I want to lie low," I said. I smoked and coughed and held on. "I want things simple and clean. But I guess it's too late for that."

"It's never too late to lie low, my friend. I highly recommend it."

"Highly," I said and laughed.

"That's right. And don't worry about it. It's all in your head."

"It's all in my head?"

"That's right. It's all in your head, so lie low."

"It's all in my head. Just lie low."

"That's right. Just lie low. That's what you gotta do. Just lie low." And the way he said it, I thought he was going to break out into song.

"Just lie low," I said.

We had the television on with the sound turned off, the stereo playing this strange free jazz. I don't know what we were watching, some old-timey cartoon with blob people that were morphing in and out of various shapes, various animals, even buildings and landscapes. It was like some dream vision of a stoned creator, comic and appropriate and somehow rising right out of the music filling the room. And I lost myself in it, now in my first official moment of attempting to lie low, sliding deeper into the big-armed chair as the walls rippled in waves and the painted world tree slid its roots into my feet and plugged me into the great dynamo. The little screen became a window into the whole weird mechanism of the ongoing cosmic show.

"It's just a dream," he said.

"What is?" And I looked at the screen, looked at him, then at the screen, then...what?

And he looked over at me and smiled with a strange kind of benevolence. At least that's how I interpreted it. So we smoked and watched the screen, and the room filled up with thick, blue waves that rolled and flowed and settled into a broad and borderless cloudscape around my head and all this, yes, all this, and maybe that's what he meant by lying low.

O ne night, the phone rang, and when I picked it up and answered it, it was Natalie. "What are you doing?" she asked.

"I'm just checking the news," I said. Actually, I wasn't doing anything at all, but who says that?

"Is that any way to make yourself in the world?"

"Oh, well, you know. A little environment, a little of my own making. Isn't that the way it works?"

"If you say so. Where do you live, anyway?"

"You mean my address?"

"Yeah. Your address. Your coordinates."

"Funny," I said. I told her where I lived. "Why, so, are you thinking of coming over?"

"I just might," she said. "There's a chance I'll be in your neighborhood later. What would you think if I dropped by?"

I looked around at my dismal little apartment, and then I said, "That's fine. Sure. I'd love to see you. Just know, my place isn't much right now."

"Your environment, huh?"

"Yeah, my environment is a little challenged."

"I don't care about that," she said. "Maybe I'll see you in a bit, okay?"

"Okay," I said.

And then I couldn't move. Nothing. I was locked in place. I don't know if it was anticipation, fear, excitement, dread. And I thought, yes, this was another complication I should probably avoid. I was reading things and people around me like they were signs, but signs for what? The drone of work, the city pier, Raphael, Tony, My ex-wife and my kids, Ymir, none of these were what they appeared to be, which meant… what were they? Rob and Sharon and their fight were a sign for something, too. And that dog. Now this, Natalie, this was a sign for something. But I couldn't figure out what I was supposed to be getting. Think. Natalie is Thane's girlfriend. It's not wise to do something here that would antagonize Thane. That could lead to awful consequences. That wasn't even a sign. That just made sense. Then, a sound like a river rushing came at me, and I whipped out of that moment fast and looked around and scanned what I needed to do.

I jumped up to try and clean, then realized I had nothing to clean. I reached out and then recoiled. It was just a dump. I was living in a dump. I checked my fridge and found nothing there to offer her. An unwrapped brick of cheese. One beer bottle. I wondered how much time I had. She could be here at any minute.

I went to Ymir's apartment and knocked on the door. I glanced down the stairs and saw Sharon going into her apartment down below. She looked up, too, and for a moment, our eyes locked. She made no expression at all. Well, I guess she was back. Ymir answered. He was wearing a pair of purple shorts, no shirt. His place was full of incense smoke. "What's up?" he asked.

"Ymir, can I borrow some bread and wine…maybe some fruit if you have any…blueberries? You have blueberries? Grapes…anything?"

"Huh?"

"Some wine, maybe a little bread. Anything? I've got a friend coming over, and I don't have time to go out and buy something. And I don't have anything at my place but beer."

He smiled a big smile. "A lady friend?"

"Well, yeah, sort of."

He frowned, turned his head, and gave me a wry look. "Not a lady? A gentleman?"

I laughed. "All right, yeah, it's a lady friend. And I've got nothin' to give her."

"Oh, honey," he said with a New Orleans flutter. "I'm sure that you do."

"Can you help me out?"

"Well, you know," he said, adopting a professorial tone, "ahm not really into that sort of thing."

"Come on!" I laughed. "I could use some help, here."

"Okay, of course. Come on in."

I went in, dazed by the air. Incense sticks and candles were burning all over the place. It was like a sanctuary, a dream. The paintings on his walls were particularly active this evening. The little people were on the move, and the golden bird turned its head to look at me. I thought, Ymir's apartment must be some kind of gateway or portal. The arboreal juju was intense.

"You performing some kind of ceremony here?" I asked.

"Just creating the world. Every moment."

"And so this is like the dream kitchen?"

"Exactly."

"Can you give me a romantic moon, then, tonight?"

"Sorry," he said, smiling broad and stoned. "I'm still building a new one."

"And I've been meaning to ask, what are those?" I pointed down at the little figures along the bottom edge of the pots and walls. They were trying to hide, but I saw them.

"Those? Those are my Norns," he said. He gave me a bottle of red wine and some apples and some bread. "Don't you eat anything?" he asked me.

"Nope," I said.

"Man, I should never have given you that book."

"Yeah, well, it's too late now."

"It's never too late."

"You sure about that?"

"Well, maybe it is too late on this one."

"Thanks, Ymir."

"Absolutely. My pleasure. Go get it!"

I went back to my apartment and left the door slightly open so that I could listen. Then I heard a car pull up. I looked out the window and saw Natalie in the parking lot below. I turned my radio on. I threw a towel over the television set, shameful old technology. Then I took the towel off because it made it look worse, and I spread the towel over the scarred-up coffee table. The light was bad, too, with my putrid, stained lampshade. I guess I never looked at my place this hard. I lit a candle, I had one, and threw a bandanna over the lampshade. That softened the light, gave the place a mellower, romantic tone. She came to the door and knocked on the doorjamb, even though the door was open. Then she smiled and bit her lip and came in.

"Hey, you," I said. "Come over here."

She came over and put her arms around me, her bracelets tinkling on her wrists. And she kissed me so perfectly, soft and open and warm... I hadn't expected this and was thrown off at first. But I put my arms around her and felt the gentle, slender curve of her back and hips under my hands and met her tenderness with a soft kiss. I was trembling.

"Hey, you," I said, pulling back a bit. "What made you want to come over here?"

"I don't know." And she kissed me again, and I felt her arms tighten around me, and I drew her back with me down to the couch.

We started gently. I was amazed by the texture of her skin. I didn't know I could move so slowly as I drew my fingertips along her cheek. Her hair was another wonder. We were moving in mythic time, just touching each other, looking into each other's eyes, taking off pieces of each other's clothing in slow motion. And what can I say about what I felt? A rich and dazzling current flowed through us. I touched her lips, her hair, and the little row of earrings along the edge of her ear, my fingers gliding so soft and light I could feel her energy sparking through her skin. And we kissed slow, exploring, eternal kisses. She tasted sweet. Her tongue was a butterfly on my lips. She tasted like new life. She pressed her hand to my chest and nestled her cheek against my neck.

"I thought about doing this the first time I saw you," she said. "I wasn't sure if I would get a chance."

"Really?" I said. "I didn't think I even existed."

She pulled back and looked around my room. "Don't you have a bed?"

I pulled the shutter doors open and lowered the Murphy bed, its huge springs twanging with flophouse age. She pushed me back on the bed, climbed up onto me, and took off the last stitch of her clothing and the last of mine. And when I saw her there in the low light, her honey skin glowing, this woman who came to me like a miracle, I wanted to begin at her feet and kiss my way to her heart with gratitude and awe. The bracelets on her wrists made a light musical sound like wind chimes as I stroked her arms with my fingers. Her soft skin. She was so thin. I ran my fingers along the scape of her ribs, her smooth shoulders, the peaks of her breasts. I kissed her, and she grabbed me and rolled and pulled me to her and into her.

We made love on that Murphy bed, and it squeaked horribly and bounced. I know my neighbors, Carl especially, heard us. I didn't care. I thought I even heard Ymir laughing. Although, maybe he didn't. He hadn't heard the fighting. Why would he hear the love? Natalie and I tried everything we could imagine, beginning by gently facing each other, moving with slow, excruciating intensity, holding close and still, only flexing internal force that pulsed and registered in the widening of her eyes. We rolled back, legs crossed, fingers laced like acrobats. She curled over and raised her hips, and I slid over her, feeling her back against my stomach. We laughed and pulled apart and breathed deep and dove at each other like cats, nails and teeth sinking in, fierce and wild. We exploded. We created a new star. We gasped and laughed and held close. We lingered then in a long, slow moment, glued to each other, mouths linked, one breath between us. Maybe we were trying to impress each other, or maybe we were trying for some final ultimate expression to knock us free of this place. Or maybe, we were together able to reach a pitch that individually we could never have imagined. The inspiration of two, as in what union brings into being so that we can only wonder. That's what I seemed to see in her eyes. Is a feeling outwardly true? It had been so long since I'd touched a wanting hand. And at last, we collapsed, both of us, shining with sweat, the candle half gone, and the bandanna smoking on the bulb.

I leaped up and pulled the smoldering bandanna off the lamp and threw it into the kitchen sink and turned on the water. It hissed, and smoke rolled up, flooding the room. Natalie laughed, lying there naked and beautiful on my ratty old bed. I opened the bottle of wine and brought it to her. We drank the wine straight out of the bottle and ate the apples and bread.

"This is quite a place you have, here," she said.

"Chez roach trap?"

"It's not so bad," she said. "I've lived in worse."

"You have?"

"Oh yeah." She sipped the wine, then handed it to me. I leaned up against the wall, lying beside her on the bed. I took a drink and rested the bottle on my chest.

"So Thane told me you have children," she said, curled beside me, her hand resting on my stomach.

"That's true."

"What are they like?"

"My kids? Kids. Normal kids."

"Are you married, then?"

"Well, no, not anymore. I'm here. I was married, though. Mortgage. The whole bit."

"And what about your wife? What happened?" Then she lifted up onto one arm and looked at me and slid her fingers along my brow. I couldn't remember the last time I had been touched this way. I don't think I even expected tenderness anymore. "You don't mind my asking you these things, do you?" she asked.

"No. The rules of the game, right?"

She smiled. "Right, the rules of the game. But you don't have to tell me if you don't want to."

"I don't mind. My wife divorced me after I went to prison. I guess that's not so surprising."

Natalie shook her head. "I think that's cold. I would never leave my husband."

I looked at her, and I had a thought but kept it to myself. "You know, I put her in a tough position. I don't blame her. I mean, it was a real shock to her. She wasn't expecting anything like that. And I broke her trust in me. It was my fault."

"I think you're way too hard on yourself. But I don't know the entire story. You've got a forgiving soul, though, don't you? I don't think I could be that forgiving."

"In a way, well, in truth, I was dishonest with her."

"And I know that must have hurt. I get that, but if everything else was good... And if you're married, you work through that, right?"

"You just said you don't think you could be that forgiving." I touched the curve of her cheek.

She smiled at me. "That's true. I guess I'm just on your side right now."

"There are no sides anymore."

She looked at me, thinking, concentrating, like she was trying to read me. "You're a good man, aren't you? You're a kind person. I can tell. I just can't imagine you going to prison. It must have been...I mean, why? What did you do, if you don't mind my asking?"

I looked at her. "Well. Hmmm. We're going to do that now, are we?"

"You don't have to tell me anything you don't want to," she said. "I mean that."

"It's just that it sounds like such a cliché. Because, the truth is...the truth is...I was actually innocent." It sounded strange, sketchy even to me. "Right? It's one of those stories. I'm an innocent man! The wrong man! You've got the wrong guy!" I felt nervous telling her this, and I couldn't figure out why. And I wondered if there were some core thing in there that I couldn't see, that I hadn't faced, and if I were to face it, I would see my true crime, my true guilt. "I was convicted of fraud and theft. That's what I went to prison for." That was the simple answer. "I mean, I didn't actually lie or steal anything, in reality. I know it sounds absurd to say that. But the way the law looks at it, my actions..."

"Theft of what?

"Information. I was guilty of stealing information. I was an information thief! Does that make sense?"

"Information?"

"Information. It can be very valuable, you know."

"What kind of information?"

"The wrong kind of information." I laughed a little. "Well, I was working with my brother-in-law...and the real lesson here is never to trust your brother-in- law. Anyway, he had a little company that his father had started, installing security systems. All kinds, from alarm systems to surveillance systems to subtle air information security that made these phony bubble realities so that thieves would get lost in a maze of fake information. It was intricate stuff. Very interesting. And it was good work. Steady. Not a lot of hours. I didn't have the technical know-how for the data work, but I had enough understanding to work with...you'd be surprised by some of the contracts we had. But as it turned out, my brother-in-law had a side job going, too. The catch here is that if you install the security systems, you also know how to get around them. We knew how to get around them. He knew more, of course. Some of it was beyond my pay-scale. And he got involved with some guys who gave him a lot of money to circumvent those systems. I didn't know anything about it, of course. I'm the wrong man! He got in way over his head with these people, though. His argument to me, later, when it was too late, was that most of the places they robbed were insured, so no one was hurt. But insurance companies are smart. Or at least they hire smart people. The insurance company figured it out. The investigators arrived, arrested us, shut everything down, and that was it. And when he went down, I went down with him. I know prisoners are always claiming to be innocent, but no one was going to believe I wasn't involved, not with the kind of friends I had. And how do you prove you're innocent in a situation like that? Hey, but I passed the lie detector test! Well, it showed that I lied but in places where I actually didn't, and it didn't show that I'd lied about things I did lie about, but that's another story. So..."

"That's not fair."

"That's what is."

"It's just so unfair."

"I think what shocked me the most, though, the bad thing about it is that the perception of me changed so quickly. My wife's perception of me, especially, and friends. I was suddenly cast in a new light. And I realized that it's easy to become a criminal. That can happen with the dash of a pen, but it's almost impossible to go back to being an innocent person."

"That is so unfair. I can't believe it."

"Yeah?"

"Yeah!"

I smiled at her. "Now, the real brain twister, the question for you is, how do you know I'm telling you the truth? How do you know I'm not just making it all up?"

"I can tell," she said.

"I used to think I could, too. But something in the mind changes when you're bombarded with a perception. Guilt is like a program, and my mind had to work hard to keep from seeing myself as guilty because there's this process, this force acting on it from all the information around: judgment, people's eyes, cell walls... they make you believe you belong there. I had moments when it seemed painfully obvious that I belonged there. I was very much guilty. In some specific way, I was guilty and just couldn't see it. Or, I was guilty in a broader sense, some vaguely perceived karmic sense, and the reasons for my punishment were just technicalities."

She kissed me. "I see you," she said.

I stroked her hair back from her eyes. Why, I wondered, why was she with Thane? Then again, why was she with me? And was this energy coming from her real? Was this compassion real? And then it struck me. Why should that matter? Why should I doubt it? Why think this gift away?

I took another drink of wine and handed the bottle to her. She drank. "So, miss twenty questions," I said. "What about you and Thane?"

She handed the bottle back to me. "Oh, there's not much to tell," she said. "What do you want to know?"

I shrugged, casual. "How did you meet?"

"He used to come to the gallery where I worked." She looked over at me. "He liked my art. We ended up talking about it. He's very intelligent. And I liked his vibe. He bought one of my pieces. And he knows a lot about art. That was a turn on."

"You're an artist?"

"Well." She blinked, shy and humble.

"That painting at Thane's place..." I said.

She nodded, smiling. "That's the one he bought," she said. "He loves that painting. And... He asked me out after that, and we started going out. He was nice to me. Always respectful. Always a gentleman. And he was funny. Very smart. Everything he said seemed to have a double meaning, very symbolic and mysterious and layered."

"Symbolic?"

"Yeah. Symbolic, doubled. I don't know how to explain it. Never bad. Just more beneath the surface, I thought. You know, the way you can say one thing, and sure it makes sense, but it can also mean something else. He's subtle that way, and it was fun to be around him. And it was sexy, the way he spoke. It's still sexy. His mystery is sexy."

"What about now?"

"What do you mean, now?"

"You two are solid?"

"Well, the problem with relationships is that they're unlikely to last, right? What lasts? And not just because, you know, we're not naturally monogamous. I mean, monogamy isn't natural, right? But monogamy isn't the problem. The problem is that we start out so high, when it's good, when it's all still new. It's like a drug. And we're always acting a little, playing a role because we can, right? And it's fun to be in character. This other person doesn't know it's a role, or doesn't care. We like the character. But he doesn't really know me. And I get to be whatever version of myself I want to be. I can be the best me I can imagine. I even think I'm inspired to be better because it's a performance, and I like it, and this other person is so amazing to bring this out of me or make me feel safe so I can express this stuff of myself, play this role, or however you want to put it, but then we raise the other person up in a kind of conspiracy of passion and illusion, creating these versions of the perfect person in ourselves and the other in this impossible way—who wouldn't fail? Or fall? See, the problem with relationships has a lot to do with other problems of perception, but at the center of it is a core problem, and the core problem is that we're drug people. We seek everything like a drug. For pleasure. And we get addicted. Food. Books. Music. Movies. Drugs, themselves. People. We operate on a principle of addiction. And then, eventually, we develop a tolerance. The drug doesn't work anymore. And the high just isn't as high anymore. And the forces inside us that maybe got checked or buried because we were playing a role for this person start to assert themselves again, and the walls close in, and we're back inside ourselves, that room no one can take us out of. But instead of realizing this, we end up blaming the other person, that poor idiot, who's going through the same disappointment at the same time."

"Wow, so, this whole getting to know you thing..."

"This is the best. This is the drug at its most potent." She drew her fingertip along my chest and down my belly. "And this is as good as it gets."

I kissed her and slid my hands over her shoulders and down her back. Her skin was warm. Her hand traveled down. "So, this," I said, "is as good as I get."

She smiled and kissed my neck, kissed my chest, kissed my stomach. "Yeah," she said. "I guess so."

Then I slipped into another stream of delirium as she stroked and licked and blew the walls out on that little apartment, the seams exploding, the roof coming off, and we were sky gods, if only for a moment. Then she rose up, took the bottle of wine, tilted it back, took a big swig, and swallowed with a smile, as a little wine slid down her chin.

"Well," I said. "You just got a little better."

She laughed, and I pulled her in close to me and kissed her. I looked into her eyes and tried to see inside that paper doll construction that she said she was. And what did I see? I guess every person is a bottomless well.

"And Thane?" I said.

"What about Thane?"

"You two are committed?"

"I have no reason to leave him. At least that's how I feel right now, but who knows? The contract will come up for renewal, and we'll see. I'd say I know him better than just about anyone." She reached up and pushed her fingers through her hair, then turned back and looked into my eyes. She seemed to be examining me, now. "For instance, I know he's got something going on right now and that he wants to get you into it. I can feel it. The way he calculates things, manipulates things. I don't know what it is, and I don't want to know. I let it be because it's his business, and that's fine. I have my own affairs, too." And she smiled. Then her expression changed. "But I think you should be careful. Okay? Understand, I'm not trying to interfere. It isn't my business, but you seem to me like—and I'm not trying to say anything bad—but you seem to me like someone who, well, someone who's trying to change. I mean, I don't know. What do I know, right? But I just think you should be careful."

"Do you love him?"

She lifted one hand, and the bracelets slid chiming back down her arm. She turned her delicate wrist in the air. "We're more alike than anyone I know. I don't know if it's love. Maybe it is. It's a kind of order, like yin and yang. I can't explain it any better than that."

"What's this I heard about you working at the Shadowbox?"

"Did he tell you that?"

"He did."

"That fucker! He...I don't know why he told you that. He really told you that?"

"Yeah."

"Well, it's not true."

"Really? Why'd he say it, then?"

"Oh, he... he... I don't know. He likes to mess with people's heads. Yours and mine, maybe? Yeah. That makes sense. He might have picked up that I was attracted to you and threw that in there to tweak the energies."

"You think he knows about this?"

"Probably. I don't know. He doesn't care, or at least he would never show me that it mattered to him. He's the king of detachment. Although, who knows? Maybe he's just a little jealous. Hmmm." And she smiled, like she liked that thought.

"Well, then," I said, "tell me. Why are you here with me?"

"I like you." She seemed surprised that I asked and smiled. "I like you... because you don't seem to fit. You're different. It's like you're somewhere else and only partially here. I guess I'm curious where that other place is." And she looked intently into my eyes again as though she might catch a glimpse of the other place.

I smiled and turned my face away.

"I guess I just like mysteries," she said.

"I have nightmares," I said, "that some clerical error sends me back to prison. That I get lost inside forever. Sometimes I dream that they have me on a list—and if they can't find the man who committed some crime, they go to that list and they find me on it and they come after me. Total wrong man paranoia. Constantly. I'm getting arrested in my sleep constantly. And it lingers throughout the day, everywhere I go, this dread, this low-grade fear. I try to shut it off, but I can't. And I try to make myself invisible. I try to disappear from everyone's memory the moment I leave their sight, or I try to mind-burn myself into their brains in case I need an alibi. The trick is knowing when to do one or the other." I laughed and said, "The core of my character isn't defined by drug hunger. It's defined by the terror of incarceration."

"God, that sounds awful."

"I tell myself that time is a liberator. In time, a new routine will set in, new memories, and they'll overwrite the old ones. And most of what I am now will be gone."

"That's the beauty of oblivion..."

"How does that children's poem go," I said. "Have you heard it? Something like, I can see your eyes through the back of your head."

She put her hand on my arm and slid it down, her fingers wrapping around my wrist like a vine. "What?" she said. "That doesn't sound like any children's poem I ever heard."

"Sure," I said. "Didn't you ever hear it? The one about the magic woods? The black woods? The woods are full of shining eyes, or something like that, and the woods are full of creeping feet. The woods are full of tiny cries: you must not go to the woods at night! You never heard that one? And there's a man with eyes of glass and fingers curled like wriggling worms and hair all red with rotting leaves and a stick that hisses like a summer snake. And he sings a song with backwards words and draws a dragon in the air and makes a penny out of a stone and shows me the way to catch a lark. And he asks me my name and where I live, and I tell him a name from my book of tales. And I follow him deep into the woods to dance with the kings beneath the hills. And his eyes turn to fire and his nails grow long, so I say my prayers in a rush of words and make my way to my father's house."

"What kind of scary stuff did your parents read you?"

I shook my head. "It was a poem."

Time writes and erases as we go. This is something I realized when I drove down the alleyway on my way back to work and saw that the drug house had burned to the ground. It was a charred husk with a few black beams sticking out and yellow caution tape strung around it. I went into the shop, and before I clocked in, I went over to the painting bay and signaled to Raphael to come have a smoke. He pulled back his goggles, glanced in the direction of the manager's office, and then came over. We went out into the yard and stood there looking at the black burned husk of the house.

"Can you believe that?" I said.

"I do believe it," he said.

"What do you think? They do it themselves?"

"Coo be. Or the police did it, if they din't pay the rent."

"The rent? Ohh… I get it."

He nodded, smoking, squinting at it like he'd seen stuff like that a thousand times before. "That business can be brutal," he said.

"Must have been fairly recent," I said, because faint streams of smoke were still rising up from the burnt wood and swirling in the sick morning mist, and that smoky air coiled around us as though we were inside the lungs of a giant smoker baking out. Planes flew up from the nearby airport, shimmering like escape artists. I wouldn't miss any of this. And for a moment I had a big ego thought that my intention to leave was destabilizing the whole area. It was disappearing behind me as I went.

I drove around the neighborhood. I don't know what I was hoping for. To rewrite the disaster? I'd learned the hard lesson long ago that you can't redo your past. So, I drove around, circling my old house like a trout nosing upriver, some mechanism going off in my brain I couldn't resist or shut off. I knew I had no home. How much had I ever really known of home? I only remember an empty house and a living room cave when I was a kid alone and paralyzed before a television absorbing alternate realities I willed myself into, as outside the eternal rain fell dissolving the world. Is that possible? Is that even true, that memory? How could I know? Or had I simply imagined it? I lived in a watery dream back then—a kind of fluid and boundless fantasy of a child who's like a flower, head just floating in the breeze, wandering around in the empty field, pulling open the tilting door of a farmer's shack with its iron snap-jaw traps and ropes and chains and tinctures of poisonous fluids in murky brown unlabeled bottles, a little hut out of the long ago frontier past with a hidden entryway through which the spirits came and went. Which house is ever home? It's the mystery of Odysseus' ship, replaced board by board over time. The past is rolling away faster than we can remember it, then it's right there in a whiff of detergent or the earth scent of fall or an uncle's drifting pipe smoke—we are travelling through morphic fields of home then and home to come in the ocean of time and the never-ending now only now—

And out of the layers of the evening shade settling deep in the trees, I saw him there, alone this time, stepping back from a mid-range shot.

I pulled up and stopped. And I thought, how would this go? Unannounced as I was? I sat there a moment, watching him. He had a graceful shooting style, an economy of motion. Arms up, ball light on the fingertips, throw, release, the hands flicking forward at the wrist giving the ball a smooth backspin as it arced up and fell back and swept net-clean through the hoop. It was a beautiful thing to watch, shot after shot.

I got out and walked up the driveway, careful, quiet in my energy as though I were approaching a wild animal that was alert and ready to bolt. I didn't want to scare him off. And then he saw me. I stopped there and stood for a moment. I brought a hand up to shade the low sunlight from my eyes so that I could see him more clearly.

"Nice shooting," I said.

"Yeah? Thanks," he said, and he dribbled the ball a few more times, looking over at the house, then looking back at me, then looking out at the street, like he was trying to decide something. Oh, his mind was working hard. Or maybe it was just mine.

"What are you?" I said. "A forward? Guard?"

"I play forward mostly," he said.

"You any good?" I said.

"I'm okay," he said, smiling.

"I bet you're fast. Looks like you handle the ball well. You good at driving to the hoop?"

"There're guys better than me. I like shooting from the post and the top of the key. I'm good at rebounding. Not so much long shots from the outside."

"Sounds like you're good getting in there, though. Top of the key's a good distance, too."

"Yeah, pretty good."

"I've played some, too, you know," I said. Where I'd been, I played a lot.

"Yeah?" he said. "You any good?"

"Hey—" I laughed. "I'm okay. There're guys better."

And he passed the ball to me. I dribbled and took a few steps forward. He had invited me into his space. I slid into that time of timeless being on the court when the light is fading, and I dribbled a few more times, stopped, pulled the ball back, and shot a solid brick dead against the front of the rim.

"You good at driving to the hoop?" he said, smiling. And he picked up the ball and dribbled back to the top of the key and stopped and looked straight at me as he threw the ball up and sent it, swish, no contact but the net, a perfect shot.

"Ah, ha!" I said and got the ball and dribbled back to the top of the key. "Clear it after a point?"

"Sure."

"And change of possession?"

"Whatever you want."

And I moved forward. His arms twitched slightly. He didn't come any closer.

He was giving me some space, daring me to shoot. So, I did, and the shot went in.

"Not bad," he said.

I stepped forward and turned as he went past me to the top of the key to clear for the next play.

"But it's kind of like what they say about stopped clocks," he said, and he did some fancy footwork and dribbled the ball between his legs and crouched down and put his chin out.

"And what's that?" I said.

He lunged forward, and I jumped back a step. He stopped and shot—the ball went right in. He stood there with his hands on his hips and said, "It's right twice a day." And he smiled that beautiful, confident, taunting kid-smile, strolling past me toward the hoop and getting the ball and quick-passing it to me. His eyebrows went up, and he stood there, mid-key, arms at his sides, half-smile on his face, shifting from foot to foot.

"I'm not sure that means what you think it means," I said.

I put the ball in motion.

"Think about it," he said.

And I drove forward on the right because I can really only dribble with my right hand. My left feels about as coordinated as a chicken wing. He moved in, arms up to block me, and I stopped and was stuck. He had his hands in my face, and I jumped back and shot at the same time, and the ball went nowhere, didn't even hit the rim. He went for it and got it and back stepped to the top of the key again as I came forward. And then he ducked down and ran right past me and threw up an easy, graceful layup.

"Very nice, very nice," I said.

He passed the ball to me, and I went out and cleared it and came back in, keeping my left side to him and the ball at a distance, protecting the ball and working arc-like back and forth inside the key and head-faked and drove quick under his arm and made my own half-way decent layup.

"Nice," he said. He took the ball, and now we were down to business.

He drove forward, faked to the right, switched hands, jumped fading back on the left, shot, and made it. I cleared, lunged left, stopped, stepped back, and shot—it was good. He took the ball back and again rolled right, and I stayed in close to him this time and reached in and knocked the ball loose. We both chased it down, and he got it and stood there. I was in front of him and hand-swatted as he lifted the ball. I knocked it clear and got it this time and cleared it at the top of the key. I turned, smiled, and shuffled back and sent up a nice floating bomb shot from two steps off the top of the key. I sank it clean.

"What are we playing to?" I said.

A slight shift occurred, and I saw the shadow of the evening fall as something in his stance changed. Not many people would be able to notice such a thing, but I saw it and knew what it was. And so, time began again.

"It's getting dark," he said. "I think I'm gonna go in."

I stood there, nodded. "Okay," I said. "Okay. Thanks for shooting with me."

"Yeah," he said, and he turned to go up the steps. Then he stopped. He turned back, not quite facing me. "I was disrespectful," he said. A beat. I don't know if his mother had told him he had to apologize or if this was his own idea. Did it matter? "It was wrong," he said.

"It's okay," I said. "I probably would have said the same thing."

He nodded a couple three more times and then went up the stairs and into the house. I went down the slope of the driveway. Then I stopped, and I looked back for a moment at that house, my one-time home. And the time between my living there and the moment I now stood in rushed by in a quick wind that rose and set the tree limbs swaying. I had just played basketball with my son.

W hen I got back to my apartment, Rob was out on the deck not far from my door snapping a bullwhip over the street below. "Ha!" he said when it made that sharp cracking sound. And he pulled his arm back and snapped it again like a circus trainer in a nightmare. The soft mad children in the schoolyard across the street looked up at him like he was the devil himself. Parents arriving for pick up glared at him. I'm sure complaints were made. As I went up the stairs, he stopped, looked over at me and laughed and said, "I'm just getting the hang of it. I got it in Tijuana!"

"Nice," I said, and I stood for a moment watching him. He wanted an audience. Don't we all? This was the place for it. What a bizarre scene. And then I went into my apartment, nerves jumping every time I heard that cracking sound. He stayed out there for a long time with his fury, terrorizing the evening with that whip.

W e met back at Thane's place once more to review the plan and to clarify all the details. That was when it hit me, the unreal reality of what we were doing. Allen was oiling handguns and slapping in clips like he thought he was a movie gangster preparing for a turf war. Edwin didn't say much. He had brought some cocaine and was carving up lines for everyone. "Have a bump," he said in that deep, odd voice. I did a few lines and felt an immediate speedy edge. I looked at Thane. Did he know about Natalie coming over? I felt the unease of the betrayer and a low-level gut-fear that my actions might foul up the course of things. The oldest lesson of all served me well. I kept my mouth shut.

The plan was clear. But the actual robbery was a terrifying idea. I'd never done anything like this before, and I still wasn't sure why Thane wanted me to be a part of it. I tried to imagine it from the first step. That was simple. We would park near the market and meet there. Nothing strange about that, just meeting. I had to imagine it in that way, an actor preparing for a role. I was simply going to the store to shop and nothing else. I would just walk through the rest of it like a performance. A daydream. All reality is a daydream. Thinking about it that way made it seem simple, like Thane said. Easy. But my stomach was a fierce knot of nerves, and my neck burned with apprehension. Mistake, mistake...I was making a big mistake. I wanted to tell Allen to quit jerking those guns around, but I kept quiet. Thane picked up on my vibe and said, "Don't worry, brother. It's already done."

"I don't know..." I said. His concern eased my mind in a way because it seemed that he didn't know or care about Natalie coming to see me, but it also tweaked my guilt. The way things were going, and with the forces at play, I didn't feel there was room for any errors on my part.

"I tell you, it's all right," Thane said. "You're experiencing fear. That's all. It's natural. It's good, really. I'm not worried about you. It's these clowns like

Allen that need to snap into it. But what you're experiencing is just fear; that's all it is. Now, remember, some fear is a good thing because it keeps you on your toes, too much and you freeze up. But like I said, I'm not worried about you. You're smart. You know it's all inside your head, that it isn't real."

"Tell me more about this guy who wants the jewels," I said.

Thane smiled and put an arm around my shoulder. "You don't want to know anything more about him. Trust me." He swirled the ice in his drink, looking down into it, then he swept his hand and drink out as though addressing the world. "He's just desire. That's all. He's hunger that has no limits. We're feeding it and taking a little piece for ourselves. We're part of a natural order, here." He smiled and drank the last of his drink and swallowed the ice.

T he night before the job, I lay on my bed smoking in the darkness. Headlights from the passing cars floated across my ceiling. Engines rumbled and shifted down as traffic crested the hill, and I felt the walls shaking from all that movement. I watched the orange tip of my cigarette burn and glow more intensely as I drew in the smoke. I heard the paper hiss. I felt the smoke in my lungs, in my blood. But I was in another place. I kept thinking of what Natalie had said, that I was only partially here, and it made me reach behind myself to see where I really was because somehow I felt that she was right, as though behind every movement, every thought, every cursory beat of my heart, I walked in another world.

Then I heard something outside my door. At this point, I was getting a little paranoid. It was a strange sound, like someone rubbing sandpaper on the door. I listened hard. What was that? And I waited. Then I heard nothing. I waited a little longer. I didn't hear anything. Then I felt something. And I thought, just lie low. Right? Like Ymir said. Just lie low. But I got up anyway and opened the door. I saw Rob outside on the deck. He had dragged a mattress out there and was lying on it with his dog, Buddy. The dog was motionless next to him.

Rob saw me. "Oh, hey," he said. "Sorry, I know this looks strange."

And it was a little strange, but I was getting used to strange.

And then he said, "I think Buddy's dying, man. The vet told me he's got

Parvo."

"Parvo?"

"Yeah. They gave me these pills for him, antibiotics I think, but he keeps throwing them up."

I looked at him for a long time. "I'm sorry," I said.

"Yeah. Thanks, man."

I waited for a moment, standing there, and then I went inside and sat by the back window looking down into the alleyway. I opened a beer and listened to the sounds of the night and the hubbub of the building, the television sounds, the music, the voices of the world, and Carl on his machine calling out to the aliens. And I thought, you know, maybe it would work. Maybe, just maybe this simple, stupid scheme would help me get an edge on things for a change because the way I was going, I was never going to rise through the ranks. I mean, what ranks? There were no ranks where I was now. In the machine shop? There was no rising from that dead end. Not with my record. That was for sure. I was going to be stuck in the same low-level life of a half-prison—permanently. And there was no way I could ever bring my kids into my so-called world. Even if I could get a relationship going with them, I couldn't bring them back to this shooting-gallery apartment building of mine. Carol would never allow it. But maybe, just maybe, there was a chance for me, and this was it. A chance enough at least to live decently and to be free because the truth was, I was far from free. I was a wage-slave worker bogman, and I was going nowhere, ever. I pictured it in my mind, pictured it step by step, the plan, all the details we had discussed, and I leaned forward as though I could cross an invisible line into the future, imagining my way...

Then I heard weeping. It was a gut-hollowing sob of deep sorrow. I got up, went across the room and opened the door. I saw Rob out there on the mattress, crying over his dog. He saw me come out, and through his pain-crunched face he said, "He's dead."

I went over and sat beside him. The dog lay in his lap, yellow vomit still oozing from its mouth, its eyes closed. And Rob was sobbing hard, unselfconscious, rocking back and forth like a child, looking down, looking up as though he wanted to kill whatever god above had done this to him. And I put a hand on his shoulder. There was nothing to do. There was nothing to say. So I sat there with him as a witness, this sad, violent criminal with his dead dog and broken heart.

I pulled my car over, stopped, got out, and walked up the street to the parking lot of the market. My heart was going fast. My mouth was dry. Every face I saw seemed to express some critical judgment, as though they knew they were looking at a criminal. The air was hot, and I felt conspicuous in the silly coat I had bought, but in the shuffle of shopping carts and the coming and going of cars, I knew people were thinking only of themselves and their own inner furies and perpetual dramas, and that they were paying very little attention to me. I checked my pockets to make sure I had my sunglasses and hat and gloves with me. They were there. Then another car pulled up before me, and the door opened. I saw Thane in the front passenger seat, smiling at me from behind a pair of dark glasses. Edwin was at the wheel and Allen was in the back seat. I had the feeling that everything was both incredibly natural and completely unreal.

I climbed in and shut the door, and we pulled slowly out of the parking lot. My mind drifted in and out of the scene. I was there and not there, and I couldn't fully concentrate on where I was. I knew I had to focus, get into character, get into place.

I looked over at Allen who was sitting beside me. "How long ago did you get here?" I asked.

"What are you talking about?" he said. "I was right in front of you, man. Didn't you see me?"

"No, I didn't see you."

"Well, you better wake up."

"You all right, there, buddy?" Thane called back.

"I'm good," I said. "I'm ready."

"Good! Glad to hear it. Now, let's all stay sharp, all right?"

"Don't start spending your money, yet," Allen said. "They say people spend more money when they think they're going to make more money. That's economics. The invisible hand, or something like that."

"Not now," Thane said. "See, this is just what we don't need. No talk of spending any money. No more talk about anything other than what we need to accomplish, all right? When we're finished, then you can start spending your money. You can do whatever the fuck you want. But we have to get through this part first."

"Got it," Allen said. Edwin kept quiet.

"Oh," Allen spoke softly to me. "Check this out," and he nudged his foot forward against a black duffel bag. "This is for you. Got it? You're in charge of it." I nodded.

We moved with the slow traffic. What a simple, beautiful working day. We stopped at a light. The human world went on about its business as though we weren't even there, the lights and drones and driverless vans and pedestrians with blank, unscripted faces. We were one in the many.

"Okay, Hitter, just stay in this lane," Thane said. "We're doing all right. Just a little way still to go. Just cruise along."

Unreal, unreal, I kept thinking, all of this is unreal. I pushed my palms down on the top of my thighs to keep my legs from shaking. I tried to focus on things around me. Be here, be here, I kept telling myself. I didn't want to make any stupid mistakes. I didn't want to drift. I looked up through the window and saw a man on a rooftop blowtorching a fresh layer of tar. With black gloves and black clothes and black bug-eyed goggles he looked like a man-moth in a wave of heat. The sunlight pierced the clouds like a bright idea, intensifying everything. The very atoms were blazing, and in the shadows of the street, I saw forms moving back and forth like stage hands behind the set and other characters emerging as if on cue, like the one old man pushing his way through a drugstore door to stand at a bus stop, shielding his face with both hands, his mouth fish-gaping as though sunlight were the most painful thing in the world. Well performed, old man. I believe it.

"Say," Allen said, backhanding me on the shoulder. "You ever heard of Urantia?"

"What?" I said, coming back in. "No."

"Urantia. You've never heard of it?"

"No, never heard of it."

"I'd never heard of it either, but this friend of mine was telling me about it the other day. He said it's this place, kind of like a country, only it doesn't have borders. You know, it's like a place where people show up when they're sick of the rat race and slaving away. You go there, and you're free, you know? You just work on what you want to work on, do what you like to do. Let's say you're good at electronics—well, then, you work on refrigerators. You're a carpenter—you help build stuff. You're good at math, you know, you do whatever, design things, whatever. And they grow all their own food there. And everything is voluntary. No one tells you what you have to do. But you're supposed to contribute in some way. So, say some old lady needs her house painted. People just help out. There's no money. You don't do anything for money. You trade stuff."

"Sounds like a commune," Edwin said.

"That's what I thought at first," Allen said. "I don't know, maybe it is. Is that a bad thing? But you know, you get to do whatever you want. You're totally free. That's better than most people's lives, don't you think? And there are a lot of pretty young girls there, too, and they don't have these sexual hang-ups like in regular society, so they're always having lots of sex, and it's no big deal."

"Who told you about this?" I asked.

"You don't have to go to Eurantia for all that," Thane said. "In fact, let me give you a little Thanism. These people out here, these working stiffs you see all around you? They're dead. They're all dead, but they don't know it. They're lost in the grand illusion. And the place you're talking about, Allen, it's in the mind, but these people haven't figured that out yet. Nor have you for that matter. Every moment, every single moment is a chance to be absolutely free, and nobody knows it. They're sheep. Nabobs. Dots, nothing but dots. Yet all these people, they've heard the basic truth I'm talking about in one form or another, somewhere, but they just don't get it, and if they do get it, they don't believe it. They're lazy. You hear what I'm saying? Every moment the cage door is open, but very few people leave."

"I hear that!" Edwin said.

Allen shook his head, his dream brushed aside.

"And who told you about this place?" I asked.

"A friend of mine. He gave me this book on it, explains how the whole thing works. You have to read the book and then you have to know someone who lives there. It's not an easy place to find. Not just anybody can go there, you know. They have to protect themselves because it sort of goes against mainstream society." Allen had a look I'd seen before, the gleam of the fanatic in his eye.

"You think this place really exists," I said. "You believe this guy?"

"It's true," he said. "It's better—"

"All right," Thane said, lifting his hand like a cattle driver. "Let's get into character. The show's about to begin."

Edwin drove up the street and pulled into the alleyway and stopped in the shade behind the building. The parking lot ahead was full of sunlight. A few cars were parked there, but no one was coming or going. Thane got out and walked forward and stood by the corner of the building. He looked around the corner, one hand pressed against the wall, and scanned the parking lot, then came back and got into the car. "We're on," he said. "Everything looks good."

Edwin drove us out of the shadow of the building and into the parking lot. I put on my sunglasses and my hat and my gloves. Edwin moved forward and then backed into a parking space just this side of the entrance. There were three other cars in the lot. One man came out of the store and walked to his car. And we waited for a moment as he got into his car, backed up, then pulled forward and exited the parking lot.

"All right my little Nibelungs," Thane said. "Go straight to your positions. Once inside, I'll give all the instructions. And remember, once we get started, keep your mouths shut. No chatter and no names. Don't use anyone's name. Now, like I said before, we've got maybe ten minutes, and then we're out, no matter what. Ten minutes. And I repeat: don't talk. And don't say any names. Just listen to my voice. I'll call it all out nice and easy, do-si-do. Got it? Ready? Let's go."

I took a deep breath, then grabbed the duffel bag, opened the door, and got out of the car. Outside, we were odd costumed characters that stood out like tarantulas on a birthday cake. A few steps, and we were at the door. Thane went in first, followed by Allen. I went in last.

The place was smaller than I imagined, simple, functional, with two display cases beside each other in the form of an L. Behind the display case on the left was a desk and behind the desk, a partially open door to a room dim lit and, I was hoping, empty. Beside the door was the vault door, closed. And high up in one corner was a small black dome—an all-seeing camera eye viewing the entire space, recording everything. Six people were in the shop: a man and a woman standing before one of the display cases, two other men, a middle-aged clerk behind the display case, and the uniformed guard. But the guard was not old, like Thane had said. He was a young man, and he looked confused, wide-eyed, realizing that something was happening but not sure what it was. Time was starting to speed up.

Everything had a dim, theatrical look through my dark glasses. Then Thane shouted, "Everybody get down on the floor! Everybody get down on the floor! Lie face down, now!" He repeated it several times, as the people looked up, startled at first, in that state of confusion and wonder.

Unreal. I saw it in their faces. It was all unreal, and I felt the same way, too. Allen stepped to the side, opened his coat, and took out a big, silver gun. He straightened his back, stationed himself next to the door to the street, and swept the room with the point of his gun. And he didn't say a word. Thane leveled his gun at the people in the shop, holding it near his waist. And as soon as they understood what was happening, which was both very quickly and in very slow motion, they did just what they were told. They got down on the floor. And none of them said a word.

"Cooperate," Thane said. "Do what I say, and we'll be out of here in five minutes. We like you all, individually and as a group. So just go with the flow, and nobody will be hurt."

Just then, a man came in through the street door, saw what was happening, and tried to turn around and leave. Allen said, "Hey!" And that was it. The man turned back with his head bowed and his hands partially raised and lay down on the floor next to the door. He didn't have to be told what to do.

Thane looked over at me and said, "Go."

I moved forward, carrying the duffel bag. I had to actually step over the guard to get around to the back of the display cases. I leaned down and said quietly to the clerk, "Open up the cases for me. Move very slowly."

He got up and unlocked the cases and opened the sliding back panels, and without being asked, he got back down on the floor and lay there, face down. Unreal. His suit was black, and his hair was oiled and slick, and through my sunglasses, he looked like a seal lying there with one shiny spot of white light reflecting off the top of his head.

I worked fast, going from case to case, each loaded with mounted jewelry on little blue velvet display pads, and I kept hearing a commercial voice in my head as I grabbed the stuff: These are the heirloom pieces, and here we have items for those special occasions. I dropped the rings and bracelets and necklaces into the duffel bag, all kinds of fine gems that glittered under the display lights and then paled out when they fell into the bag. They weighed almost nothing. I emptied the display cases in a matter of moments. And the people all lay there silent, motionless, very careful not to look at us. And in some kind of honor pact of crime between us, I tried not to look at them either. Then I leaned down to the clerk and said, "Vault."

Now he hesitated.

"Vault," I said again. But he wasn't moving.

I stood back and nodded to Thane. He came forward, fast, leaned over the counter and placed the gun against the clerk's head. "Open it up, motherfucker," he said.

The clerk rose, turned, and within seconds opened the vault door. Then he stood there, waiting for more instructions. His face was pale terror.

"Back down on the ground, buddy," Thane said. The clerk slipped back to the floor like a crumpled doll. Thane stepped back.

I went in and began opening the shallow metal drawers in which I found manila envelopes of various sizes. The vault smelled like machinery. I looked inside some of the envelopes as I plucked them out of the drawers, and I saw the loose gems inside. Some of the envelopes held diamonds. Some held sapphires. I recognized those. Some held rubies. Some held stones I'd never seen before, and I had no idea what they were. But each envelope held dozens of gemstones at least. And unreal as it was, I was dazzled by what I saw. I couldn't believe it. There were so many, and the vault was full of drawers that were full of envelopes that were full of jewels. Then I heard that voice again saying, this is it, the motherlode. I sped up, pulling out drawers and envelopes and pouring the jewels into the duffel bag and throwing the empty envelopes onto the floor. My heart was beating so fast that I felt the blood pulsing in my arms. My face burned. I watched my own hands like they were someone else's, emptying out those envelopes. And what a strange dreamy thing to behold as those little star points flowed, clicking as they tumbled into the bag. Unreal, I thought. Unreal.

"Time," Thane shouted. There was so much more in that vault, so much more that I wanted to get, but I listened to Thane's voice. I had in fact grabbed quite a lot. The duffel bag was about half full. Now it had some weight to it.

But things changed fast when I emerged from the vault. The young guard was already three-quarters turned and rising from the ground, his hand pulling out his gun. He looked at me. What are you doing, I thought. I was about to tell him to get back down, but I didn't have time to. I heard an explosion. I saw him roll back as though he had been kicked, his gun dropping from his hand. The right side of his neck near the shoulder was at first a sort of white ruffle of flesh, then a fierce flow of blood.

I stepped forward and knelt beside him. I felt like I was in a trance. I looked up at Thane, who was still standing in a blue coil of smoke with his gun pointed now at me because I was in the space where the guard had been trying to rise. "We ready?" he shouted at me. "Let's go!"

"Get down! Get down," I heard Allen yell. And then I heard one of the customers, I'm not sure which one, maybe a couple of them sort of moaning and pleading not to be killed.

"Get back down!" Thane said. "Everybody, just stay down!"

I looked back down at the guard. A pool of blood was spreading out in a halo around his head. I looked at his face. He was maybe twenty. He had a look of bewildered concern. He struggled to breathe, just taking in short little breaths, and his hands shuddered, poised at his chest like he was trying to push me away. He was saying something, trying to speak. I leaned down to him, but as I did, I saw the fear rise in his eyes.

"Are we ready?" Thane shouted.

I took off my sunglasses and my hat.

"Are we ready? Let's go!"

"Hey," I said to the guard in a quiet voice, "Hey." I felt the warmth of his blood soaking through my pant leg. I took off my gloves. "It's all right…it's all right," I said. I slowly pushed his hands back. Tears were sliding down his temples.

I leaned in close to hear what he was saying. "I'm scared," he said, "…scared," though nothing came through his lips. He was forming words, but he had no breath to give them sound.

"It's all right," I said. "You'll be all right." And I watched him, his mouth opening and closing in little gasps, struggling to catch a breath. His eyes were stark wide, trying to take everything in. "It's all right," I said in a whisper, so that only he could hear, and I brushed the hair back from his forehead with my fingertips. He looked into my eyes then, and I think his fear faded a little. "It's all right," I said again, and I smiled. I felt my own eyes burning. He reached one hand out and took my arm, very lightly, and he pulled me down to him, trying to say something, pulling me so close that I could feel the heat of his face. I didn't resist. I felt the small concussions of his breath against my cheek, and because I didn't pull away, I felt his breath swirl in as I inhaled. His eyes looked into mine, and something from deep inside of him seemed to move forward while at the same time retreating. In a moment, he stopped breathing. Then he was gone.

"Let's go! Let's go! It's time!" Thane shouted.

I rose to my feet, holding tight to the duffle bag. I held my gloves, hat, and sunglasses in my other hand. I started to put them back on then stopped. What was the point now? It was too late, after all. Here I am. I looked around at the people on the floor. I looked directly into the eye of the surveillance camera. Here I am. There you are.

"Let's go," Thane shouted again.

I was the first one out the door, then Allen, then Thane. We got into the car, and Edwin drove fast, but he was careful, looking around for other cars. He was doing it right, I thought, not to draw attention to us or get us into an accident, getting us out of there quickly.

"What the fuck were you doing?" Allen said.

"Just shut up," Thane said. "Everybody just shut up! Don't say a fucking word."

"But they saw him!" Allen said. "Everyone saw him. The camera saw him."

"I said shut up! Let's just finish this, okay?"

And nobody said a word after that.

Edwin took us out into the flow of traffic. And we all kept our mouths shut. We sat rigidly facing forward, but I could feel us all looking around to see if anybody was coming after us. I reached down and felt my leg. It was soaked with the man's blood. Edwin drove down the street where Allen and I had parked our cars and stopped. Allen jumped out. I started to get out, leaving the duffel bag behind in the seat, but Thane turned around to me and said, "Take that with you, Tom. We can't have it in this car." So I reached back in and took it. "Meet me at my place," he said.

I closed the door, and Edwin and Thane drove off. I stood there for a moment and watched Allen get into his car. He pulled out into the street and sped past me, glaring. Then I went to my car, calm and quiet. I looked around. The street was empty. I saw no one. It was just a quiet little neighborhood. It felt like an end of the world movie. The afternoon shadows were moving across the homes and the lawns, but my car was sitting in the intensity of the sunlight. I felt strange. I felt nauseous. I felt like I could lie down on the ground and go to sleep. I felt like I was in a dream. And I knew I had to do something important, but the important thing was not taking the duffel bag back to Thane. It was something else, but I wasn't sure what it was. I got into my car. Light shot through my windshield—bright, painful light. I turned on the engine and started to drive.

I drove calm and controlled in the evening traffic, but my mind raced ahead on its own through the intersections and streets, snaking out and imagining countless paths and every possible way I might get away or might get caught as my eyes tried to take in everything. I was twitching with the fear of pursuit, but I also had a strange floating feeling of detachment. I couldn't shake the idea that it was all unreal. And I couldn't shake the image of that poor kid dying, and all the tension and horror and terror of it hit me in the chest like a black nova as I drove. My eyes burned and blurred, but I kept my face a blank rigid mask of normal, commuting concentration. Cars seemed either to move at terminally slow speeds in front of me, or someone was pulling up beside me and shooting their frustrated, hate-hustle hurry energy at me. Some oversized truck stuck to my tail. But I kept looking straight ahead, though I saw everything happening around me with chameleon eyes of clarity.

As the traffic flow came to a stop, I felt my heartbeat pulsing in my head. When we started moving again, I acutely engaged my hands on the steering wheel, my feet on the pedals. Driving gave me something to focus on. But my mind was a wild scenario generator. I reasoned that I probably had some time before anything happened, time for the police to arrive on the scene, time for them to take statements from people, time for them to retrieve the camera recording, time for them to play back the entire episode, time for them to isolate an image of my face, and time for them to identify who I was. I figured all of that would take at least an hour. An hour, maybe a little more. I had that time.

There would probably be an initial sweep of the area surrounding the store while all the critical information gathering was going on. Then, after the review of the surveillance camera recording, after discerning who I was, they would likely go to my apartment first. When they didn't find me there, they would check my job and question the people there for information. I watched it all happening like a movie in my head. Then they would go down the list of friends, associates, and finally, I concluded, they would go to my family. My family. After the disaster of my visit, I thought, what would this do to them? My mind witnessed the police arriving, the questions, Carol's reaction, my son's definitive anger, my daughter Melissa hearing the news and... what would she think? What would this do to each of them? And now I had done this to them, sent this into their lives. I knew, then, that I would never see them again, no matter what happened to me.

I turned on the radio, trying to find any news about the robbery, hoping I might get some useful information. But I got nothing but techno pop and drive time badgering, commercials, and what is taking so long? Come on, move, keep your wheels turning, keep them turning and don't stop. Strange the way time was warping. I was caught in its sluggish current. People moved like they were underwater, as though I had been calibrated at the wrong speed or moved in a different medium. Sweat poured out of me. A helicopter overhead went back the way I had come. Then I heard sirens as I went up over the viaduct, and the sun blazed its white blind light through my windshield.

I wanted to go back to my apartment, to my little kitchen and the radio, to Fred Astaire on my television set, to the Murphy bed and Natalie lying there with me. I wanted to go back to my tombstone room. I wanted to go back to the shop and work in the infernal heat with Tony and smoke a cigarette with Raphael. In a short time, I had become accustomed to that life, simple and suffocating as it was, and the repetitive patterns of it. So why couldn't I endure it? What was wrong with me that I couldn't endure it? And now what? What was there for me, now? Nothing. That's all I had left. Everything was altered. I can't go back. I can't go anywhere. I have ripped myself from that life. It all began to blur as it formed.

I stopped several blocks from Thane's apartment building and sat there waiting in my car. The radio was still just a bland broadcast of static sound fragments and contests and call-ins. I snapped it off. I lit a cigarette and sloughed off the long coat. Then I saw that my legs were covered with blood. Jesus, what should I do? I looked like a serious monster. People were walking by on the sidewalk. I tried to wipe the blood off my legs, using the coat to soak it out. But that was no use. Most of the blood had already dried in. I tucked the gloves and glasses into one of the coat pockets and put the hat inside the folds and rolled the coat into a ball. I waited a moment for a space in the flow of people. Then I took the duffel bag and coat and at last climbed out of the car, put the coat under my arm and headed down the street towards Thane's apartment.

I saw a dumpster nearby in one of the alleyways behind a building across the street, so I ran over to it and lifted the lid and threw the coat away. Then I headed back towards Thane's place. I looked around, nervous, trying to keep myself turned in such a way that no one would see the blood on my legs. I felt like I was a walking billboard of crime. But people weren't paying any attention to me as they moved along inside their own movie worlds, heads full of dream as they slid along in the cable tracks of their lives. And yet, at that moment, I would have traded places with any one of them.

I didn't see Thane's car anywhere. I didn't even know if he would park on the street. I had no idea what his plan was at this point, and I wasn't supposed to be here.

I was looking for some kind of sign for what to do, and I didn't dare stand around and wait outside. So, I pushed the buzzer for his apartment. Natalie answered, "Hello?"

"It's Tom," I said in the most casual voice I could produce, and she hit the release on the electronic door lock. I went up the stairs, but when I came to Thane's floor, I stopped. I waited for a few moments, looking through the little chicken wire window in the stairwell door. I saw no one. I figured I must have gotten back before Thane. I couldn't face Natalie like this, and unless someone came up the stairs, I wasn't going to move until I saw Thane coming down the hallway. I sat down next to the duffel bag and waited.

My legs trembled. I smoked a cigarette with a shaky hand. Hopefully, no one would use the stairwell while I was there. I wouldn't go unnoticed, that's for sure. Even smoking a cigarette in there was taking a risk. At last I heard the elevator descending, stopping, then a moment of nothing, then ascending, stopping. I waited. I peered through the little window into the hallway, and then I saw Thane get out and approach his door. I pushed the door open, the duffel bag in my hand, and I hissed, "Thane!" He shot a look over at me and then waved me over.

"Come on," he said.

As I went forward, he saw the blood on my pant legs. "Jesus," he said. "Don't let Natalie see you like that."

"What can I do?"

"Just hold the duffel bag in front of you. I'll go in first and then you follow me and go straight back to the bedroom. Get some pants out of my dresser. And make sure you don't leave those here, either. Be sure you take them with you. And get rid of them fast, but not anywhere around here."

He opened the door, and I followed him in, bending forward with the duffel bag in front of my legs. He kept himself between me and Natalie. She was sitting on the couch there in the living room. "What happened to you?" she said, as I waved and slipped by behind Thane without saying a word. "I buzzed you in a while ago."

I closed the bedroom door. There was no lock on it, so I set the duffel bag in front of the door, hoping that would block it for at least a moment if Natalie came back. Then I started pulling dresser drawers open, looking around until I found one with Thane's pants in it. I took my pants off and put on a pair of

Thane's jeans. They were loose, and I pulled my belt tight. I rolled up my bloodstained pants, and I was just trying to figure out what to do with them when Thane came through the door, pushing back the duffel bag.

"Jesus, Tom," he said. "You really put a fucking wrench in it."

"I know. I know. I'm sorry. I blew it."

"Here," he said. He closed the door and handed a paper grocery bag to me. I put the bloodstained pants in the bag. He picked up the duffel bag. And for a moment, we just froze.

"This changes everything," he said.

"I know."

"I'm not sure what we're going to do about it, or what's going to happen."

"Yeah, I don't know, either."

"What happened back there?" he asked, and there was no anger in the question. "Why'd you take off your glasses and your hat?"

I shook my head, but all I could say was, "I don't know."

He looked at me across a great distance.

"What did you tell Natalie?" I asked.

"I told her you had to puke, that you were fucked up."

We froze again, then, listening. Was she coming back?

"What are you going to do with it?" I said, pointing at the duffel bag.

"I'm getting rid of it as soon as possible. I don't have much time, now, I figure. There's a good chance the police will come around eventually. I'll have to coordinate with Edwin and Allen and make sure they have solid stories. I'm not too worried about Edwin, but Allen could be a problem. And I've got to get this stuff out of here, fast. So, I'm sorry to say it, but you'd better get going. They've probably checked the recording by now, and I wouldn't be surprised if they figured out who you are, so it won't be long before they start looking for you. I'm sorry, man. This isn't how it was supposed to happen."

"I know, I know. It's my fault."

"I'll hold onto your share after I sell off the stuff. You can trust me. And eventually..."

"That's fine. I'm not worried about it. I'm just trying to figure out what to do now."

"You're going to get the fuck out of here. That's what you're going to do. And we don't have much time."

"Okay. You're right."

"You have any money?"

"I've got nothing."

"You have enough to get out of town for a while, hide out somewhere?"

"I'll figure it out."

"Well, wait a while. Get lost, and after some time, give me a call, but don't use your name, you know? I'll help you figure out how to get back in."

I tried to slow my mind down and imagine a plan. But there was no plan. There was only this confusion, this chaos I had initiated.

"You better go, brother," Thane said.

"You're right."

I took the bag with the blood-soaked pants in it and went out and down the hall and past the living room. I saw Natalie there on the sofa in the afternoon light, smiling, a wine glass in her hand, and I looked into her eyes one last time, but I never stopped moving. My hand hit the doorknob, pulled the door open, and I saw her face change to an expression of disbelief as I went out and closed the door behind me on everything.

I went back to my car and got in and sat there for a moment trying to think of what to do. Where was I going to go? I certainly couldn't go back to my apartment. Think, think, think. I looked at the flow of the world around me. A mangy dog was low-headed sniffing and pissing its way up the street towards me. I waited. I smoked. Everything was evaporating. I started the engine. A space appeared in the flow of cars, so I pulled forward into the alleyway across the street where I had thrown my coat away earlier. Making sure that no one was around to see me, I took the bag with the pants in it, jumped out, and threw it into the dumpster. Was this far enough away? Who knows? Then I climbed back into my car. As far as I could tell, no one saw me do a thing. I was invisible. I lit another cigarette. I listened for a few moments. Everything was quiet. No sirens. I heard nothing. I pulled out into the street and drove west through the neighborhood and down the hill to the onramp and got onto the freeway headed north.

III
Leaving the Dream

Driving north on the freeway, I sank into the sluggish morass of rush hour traffic. I flipped the radio on again, searching for any news about the robbery. Nothing. All I heard were blasting advertising voices, cheap machine music, and apocalyptic preachers. The end of the world was near, they were saying: scarcity, rations, refugees, chaos rolling as one government after another collapses and hordes flow in, the lost people stacking up in hobo camps throughout the land. And as though their very words were coming into being all around me, I saw them as I drove, packed in under the freeways along mud paths and garbage pits, shelters made out of tarps and blankets hung over ropes tied between the highway stanchions, little blue and orange dome tents, recliners and folding chairs set up around campfires, shopping carts down by the edge of the road. When did all this happen? I was like a space traveler who comes back to the earth after a long voyage. Time had passed but not for me. It was a strange and different world than I remembered. And in the sky above, huge black industrial dragonflies hovered and darted down into little neighborhood valleys and shot out over the big city towers.

The sunlight was hot against my face. I rose with the wave of other vehicles going out over the span of the freeway bridge. And down below, buildings and tenement windows shimmered, black rooftops boiled, and the sunlight shattered itself on the waters of the bay and out to the far mountain peaks. Who could say it wasn't beautiful? Yet I felt exposed in that light, atomizing under gaze. Every chemical of fight or flight was firing in me. This would require impossible concentration. I slipped my sunglasses over my eyes.

I went over the probable narrative of events: the identification of my face on security cameras—had that happened yet? I tried to will a vision of what was happening out there into my mind, to imagine it hard enough and with clarity and reason enough to see it truthfully and not as my fear might believe or my hope might want. I saw the officers drive to the place where I lived, stop, ascend the steps with guns held tight in both hands at the waist, knock on the door, wait, kick in the door, lead with their guns into my empty apartment. I saw them arriving at my job, Raphael pulling his goggles back, Tony listening, nodding, knowing because he'd seen it coming. He'd read it all already. And as my mind went into the vision of the officers arriving at my old home, there, and my ex-wife and kids hearing and taking it in, another layer of what I was fell away.

Every slow moment of driving, every stall in the flow of traffic increased the chances I'd be apprehended as the description of the make and model of my car, as well as images of my face, went out to all patrols who would then be put on alert, looking everywhere and especially on the freeways, knowing that I was trying to escape. That is if some other plotline of disaster and criminal activity hadn't trumped my small part in the big story. Then I looked around at the river of cars, and I realized that in this traffic I was lost in the most anonymous crowd imaginable. Unless a police car was right there beside me, and unless a cop was in fact looking directly at me, I couldn't be more perfectly hidden. It was highly unlikely that this old beat to hell vehicle was trackable. Although being that old and rusted out kind of made me stand out like a bad tooth. But really, I was a needle in a haystack. I had nothing else that might bring them down on me. And so, I relaxed, for a moment at least. But I felt it, felt the close presence of the law like a scanner ray sweeping round, detecting me like a little red blip of wrong on a glowing virtual map of the city. And the thought occurred to me that they might set up roadblocks. Then I thought, no, that would be ridiculous, even as I looked around for them.

Then I glanced down and saw a warning light flashing on the dashboard. The engine temperature was rising. For some reason this made me think that I had been detected. Paranoid, I thought that outside powers were tampering with my vehicle. And in a blind and groping way, I tried to send out my own energy in a vocal blast, like a fool, saying, "Cool down!" I was in a battle of wills with an invisible force.

I turned on the heater, thinking that somehow this might help draw heat from the engine, anything to keep it from breaking down. I wasn't going to resist magical thinking at this point. I even turned off the radio, believing that that too might help the mysterious alchemy of my machine. The sounds on the radio were driving me crazy, anyway. If the police were coming, they were coming. No news flash warning announcement would change that. I was trapped where I was. And what did I think I would hear? Calling all cars. Calling all cars. A dime store version of my story asserting noir television scenes into my script. Besides, I couldn't alter my course now. I kept looking back at that warning light. God, please, I thought, don't fail on me now, not now! But I had no right to pray as heat swirled up from the vents around my feet and heat waves rose up in little flurries over the car. Sunlight burned through the open window, and the air outside was a soupy bog of dragon vapors.

All I could do was think. But thinking wasn't bringing anything good to me. Things like, I was responsible for that man's death. I had stepped onto a path, added my intention to a course of events that brought me to this. It had been my choice to go. None of us would have been there had I not made that decision, at least not this day, not in this way. I set all those acts in motion. And a great weight fell physically upon me, knowing this, feeling this judgment true to the core—and not just legally. And suddenly it didn't matter if I escaped or not because I deserved my fate and whatever it brought me. Hadn't I created it? Wasn't this the world I had dreamed into existence? Crazy thoughts. Desperate thoughts in a desperate hour. And yet something broke. How can I describe it? Right then, I felt free. I would do what I had to do to escape, certainly what any animal would do, but now in another way I was free.

I looked straight ahead, concentrating on the road and my place on it, blending in with the other drivers with my mind. But I kept having this strange feeling that someone was in the car with me, and I kept seeing something at the border of my vision or in the rearview mirror, though when I turned to confront directly whatever I thought it was I saw, nothing was there but the empty back seat and the commuter faces around me.

The traffic moved slowly through the northern suburbs of the city. Exit ramps funneled people to their homes. Neighborhood streets stacked up with a caterpillar congestion of vehicles. And all those thinking souls burned in their cells. Then I passed a shopping mall with parking lots full of cars and flags fluttering on strings and outlying mirror glass buildings blazing like white halls of fire.

Little by little the traffic picked up speed, and with that increase in movement my car engine began to cool. Milagro! What a relief. The warning light went off. That changed everything, as the wind came flowing in and I drove under a bridge with a chain-link fence heavy with thousands of glittering padlocks.

I drove through high cement canyon walls that rose up along the side of the freeway, immense Egyptian barriers with occasional doors into outer nothing. It was all just so much more prison. And slowly, bit by bit, the walls gave way as I passed through the last rings of the city, entering the outer forest groves of pine and fir trees where car lots and schools and homes materialized only briefly. And then, there on the side of the road, a woman appeared standing next to her car, the doors open, bending down and trying to coax a battered coyote into her back seat. The animal must have been hit, though I couldn't see if it was injured. She had no idea what she was in for. And the traffic moved in brief surges of speed, and with it, I moved untouched, unnoticed, until I passed beyond the city limits.

I crossed the first river out beyond the three bridges where it carves through the cattail swamps and into the Sound. From the high point on the bridge I saw in all directions, mountains to the east and out on the peninsula to the west, ocean waters threading through the islands north and south, back and forth. And now I was moving more swiftly, cruising through farmlands and the silver sheen of irrigation sloughs, past a lumber mill with fresh cut raw timber stacked up on one side of the yard, refined clean-line boards on the other. I passed through cornfields and caught that rich sweet smell of ripening corn. A few homes flashed out there in the foothills. Boats flowed by lined up on racks in an empty field. Modular log houses appeared for sale in a lot, then twin lakes with a land bridge between them and water reflecting the last sunlight of day. A hawk soared overhead. My mind was numb. My hands and feet were numb. I kept moving in sync with the traffic in the anonymous center lane. I was the machine I drove.

As I passed through the last outlying town, I crossed the second river, and it felt as though another chain had broken. Another piece of my life had dropped away like burned skin. I thought, I am passing away from my life. And all my memory of it trembled on the verge of oblivion. The bulk of it was the most recent, a life in prison, then a brief dream of freedom. Before that? A childhood dream in an empty home, alone, enormous darkness, then, pulling the door open and entering the backyard and beholding the sun high above, lifting my arms to that opening from which I came, trying for return. I stood in a field of grass burned golden by the sun. Alligators prowled the shadows. I was two years old.

I drove on through a mixture of memory and vigilance. The sun was dissolving into the west mountain range. The islands were lit up like green ghost barges drifting across the cobalt waters of the Sound. The sky swirled mixed light overhead, serpent clouds taking the last golden host on their tongues of fire. Flocks of starlings caught in frenzy rose in a full tight formation and rolled and cut and swept back down along the valley floor, all together, strange and fluid, moving in a way unreal but as real as anything could be, a perfect flight, like a hand painting in the air. And high above them, V after V of geese moving on.

As the land darkened, I wondered, where will I go? If I stayed on this road I would end up over the border, but I knew I would never get across in this car. And as protective night came on, I felt a keening of my senses, a sharpening of clarity as veils pulled back. Small lights glittered pure and bright in the distance. I saw the muted outlines of the hills. Only a few cars were left around me now, hovering at greater distances. They would appear, red taillights far ahead or silver headlights flickering in my rearview mirror, coming and going, and then they gradually disappeared. For a long time I drove alone, the engine a smooth cool hum, warm wind flowing through the open windows, the road nothing more than the quick liquid pulse of blue reflectors and white lane stripes, dash lights glowing beneath my hands.

More of the past swept up from the black sea: I was walking to school in the rain, with the low, gray sky of clouds devouring the hills and the fir trees. I was passing the house on 45th Street with the dog behind the high wooden fence howling and snapping through the slats. I was sliding my finger along the cold metal railing outside the churchyard, water rolling from my hand, gravestones glowing green under thick piles of moss. I was sitting at my desk in the damp schoolroom with its creaky wooden floors and rows of children and coats steaming on the racks, Allen in front of me hunched over his desk and Craig goofing around, throwing wads of paper, rain rolling down over the windows all time warped and trembling, all of us drifting in weird time inside this obscure waterflow world. And outside in the schoolyard on Wednesday at noon all the children stopped in the middle of play in solemn and bizarre communion, cupping their hands over their ears and raising their voices in unison with the air-raid siren.

They arose, the days, the first day I went with Allen to his house and we collected bricks to make a ramp for a bicycle jump. He went through his house and I followed him, black stains from their dogs along the lower half of the walls, the wretched sheets on the couch, the squalor and smell, the insane sister sitting comatose before the television. Allen got a piece of bologna out of the refrigerator and headed into the back yard. I followed him and began collecting more bricks as he stood in the driveway and dangled the bologna over his mouth. Then his brother came out and for no reason threw a wrench at him, hitting him in the hand. A perfect shot. Allen doubled over and pulled his hand in and screamed. The mother came out of nowhere, a big woman in a mu mu dress. I had never seen her until then. But she saw what had happened and decoded it in an instant and dragged Allen's brother inside the house. Allen recovered instantly. He didn't seem hurt at all. Whatever was happening inside was better than his pain. He went to the back door and peered in and began to laugh. So I crept up, too, and looked in over his shoulder and saw the mother there in the kitchen with the brother in her grasp, her fingers gripping his hair as over and over again she slammed his head against the wall. I got on my bike and rode home.

Those long afternoons in our house of darkness, my brother and I in our rooms of darkness connected by a sun porch closed-in by old wire screen windows overlooking the remnants of the forest that hadn't been sold off yet. In the junk that ended up on that porch that was no man's land, we fought our wars with box forts and table bunkers and garden tool weapons. He was on the attack again, and I was defending. He was coming at me, so I ran back into my room, turned, and slammed the door. But our bedroom doors were made with glass windows in them, and the glass exploded and cut my arm. I stood there bleeding, silent. I couldn't feel a thing. And then I was in a hospital. And then I was wearing a cast on one arm. I asked my father, then, what happens when we die, and he said nothing, nothing happens, and there's no use worrying about it. There's a bullet with your name on it out there and no God to help you either.

Much of life is made of brutal memory. And church camp days came with rain even in summer, long, verdant time slow sliding into the evening vespers at the edge of the woods. This was our mother's attempt to give us religion and tend to our migrant souls. A big tire swing hung from the ancient elm there near the alluvial dirt path into the forest. Minister Dale, with his shirtsleeves rolled, threw horseshoes in a pit, and on the porch of the main cabin, people played ping pong and drank ice tea...all of it like something from another age, a frontier past still living in the gray wood floors and double hung windows and door knobs down low on the doors. At night we hiked up through the forest, led by counselor Greg with the light of his miner's cap shining on the trail, up to the settler's cemetery to make butcher paper etchings from tombstones and tell ghost stories and stomp on the graves to hear the hollow ring of decaying caskets underground. And by day we hiked up to Eagle's Roost and the lookout tower and climbed up and looked out over the green feather-brush of the forest top and the hills east and black waters of The Sound. A spooky energy still hovered around the pioneer cabin, fallen and covered with moss. I imagined the cold winters and some family living there deep inside the long dark nights, with a day's horse ride at least just to get to any town (if they even had a horse), playing music on home-made instruments or reading the bible aloud. Our afternoons were cut to silence in the time of listening when no one spoke intentionally and never above a whisper in order to better hear the voice of God in the wind. And no god to help you either.

Driving away, I felt like I was traveling through the murky ruins of my own past. Then I realized I was heading towards my brother. What unconscious choice had sent me this way? I don't know. How much of this was planned at all? How much written from outside? I could almost feel forces at work like the waves Chuckie described. Crazy Chuckie. I didn't feel like I was making any choices. Maybe I never had. But I thought as the road rolled through the foothills towards my brother's place that maybe he could help me.

My brother lived outside of a small town in the valley north, out there back in the woods on a piece of land owned by our uncle. I couldn't call him because he didn't have a phone, and I couldn't call my uncle since the case was altered. I tried to picture my brother. Was he still there? We had been out of contact for a long time, but last I'd heard he'd moved out there just after getting out of the Navy. The cabin had no electricity and no water. It was just a hunter's shack my father and his brother built years ago. There was a post office in town, though. And my brother and I had written each other a few times over the years. But that was about the extent of his connection to this world, other than the odd jobs he did for our uncle and for other people in town and time he spent in the local bars. At least, that was all I'd heard from him and all I knew for now. Things may have changed. He may have changed. All I knew was that when my brother got out of the service, he went straight there. Being in the city, he said, made him crazy. He couldn't live with people.

It was possible, I realized, that the police might anticipate this move, might at least start following leads to my family after they couldn't find me at my apartment or anywhere else in the city. It was possible. But when would they decide that I was gone? When would they suppose or determine that I had left the city instead of burrowing deeper into it and extend their search from there? When would the patrol car waiting at my apartment be called away? Would they have enough resources to keep searching for me? How long would that be? And would they use those resources to try and search for me beyond this state? How important was it to apprehend me? These were the things my flight mind tried to decipher. But I had nothing to go on. They had a robbery; they had a killing in the act of a felony—a first degree charge, as I understood it. So how would they investigate? I was certainly the primary suspect since I was the only one who would have appeared on any surveillance cameras without a mask. I was the face of the crime. Then again, who knows what the hidden eyes are seeing? What penetrating vision discerned through velum, page, skin and muscle right down to the very codes we're made of? How odd to think of myself this way, especially when I had gotten used to thinking of myself as not existing at all.

But I kept going over it in my mind, reaching with my mind to see how it was all happening. There was a lot of ground to cover, I suppose, even for just one man, a lot of human effort following leads. I decided that going to the people and places in the city that were connected to me would be how they'd conduct their first twenty-four or forty-eight-hour investigation. They would exhaust those first, and that would take time. And after that, who knows? Who knows what makes it worth it to hunt down one criminal over another? How the priorities are decided? Not all criminals are caught, either because the victim doesn't matter that much or other, more important cases come along, and then the unsolved ones go cold. So I headed for the cabin. I gave myself one night.

And I drove through blackness absolute. Only a few hints of other things came from out there in the rumpled darkness. My body knew the way. The road behind me was completely absorbed by the void, nothing to see. The road ahead was illuminated only by my high beams, but I saw nothing more than a dark legion of fir limbs unfolding around me like black wings in the filigree night and the occasional flash of eyes in the forest burning bright.

I pulled off the freeway and drove into the small town of long ago. What a relief to be out of the zone of the highway patrol with their scanners out there, at least that's how I imagined them, even though I hadn't seen any. But I felt as though the talons of the law were right behind me all the time. And what a relief to slow down, as I drove over the railroad tracks and under the water tower covered with graffiti from the graduating high school class. But I didn't see another soul. This is the way we used to go on our way to the river and the cabin. That seemed like another lifetime. It was the kind of place you might grow up trying to escape and then romanticize and search for forever after. A diner used to be right over there, but it was gone. I think a laundromat was there. Everything changes.

Three stoplights swayed over Main Street, and though the street was empty, I stopped when the third light turned red. A blue neon arrow twitching over the tavern door said This is The Place, and little sparks of light leaped along the chrome of the motorcycles lined up out front. Specks like cottonwood seeds floated over my windshield and across the brick wall of the hardware store and along the doors of the post office and the shimmering bared teeth of the dead wolf in fierce pose with open jaws behind the window of the taxidermy shop. I felt like I was sitting inside a bizarre snow globe, as fine white ash settled on the street and the hood of my car. And the warm wind blew through the trees making them sway like underwater ghosts. My head was buzzing with engine energy. My thoughts were daggers of perceptions.

I drove through to the other side of town and up into the outskirt dark beyond the bullet-blasted street signs. I passed the trailer park and the junkyard and the Half-Cocked Gun Repair Shop, a mobile home at the side of the road. I drove up through the hills, the road switching back on itself and taking me far back into the magic woods. Then I cut off onto one of the dirt roads, and my car bucked and bounced over the rutted earth. I navigated through the standing people trees that loomed in my headlights. Then I turned down a steep hill and onto a smaller road. Those big cedar limbs hung down low and closed like curtains behind me as I went. I dove deeper into the forest, and another wave of relief hit. I was far away, now. The air was cool and damp. And then the cabin appeared before me.

I saw no sign of my brother as I drove down and around to the back of the cabin. Maybe he was long gone. Who knows, but I still had work to do. I wouldn't be able to relax until I'd hidden my vehicle from sight just in case anyone came looking for me that night. Even if the chances of that were slim, I had to do everything possible, everything I could imagine. I couldn't be careless about even one detail. I turned off the car, and the engine ticked in the darkness. My body shook as a wave of nausea swept through me. I opened the door and leaned out, breathing with my head down. Then I looked up. The cabin was dark. I tried to light a cigarette, but I couldn't hold the match steady. I stared into the darkness of the forest, a vast vibrating nothing. And I felt myself falling through trembling afterimages and howls and shuddering halos of the world I left behind.

I sat for a long time in the car. I simply couldn't move. I opened the glove box and took out Melissa's drawings. I unfolded them and looked down at the green fish forms of her guardian spirits poised in the blue river current and heading somewhere off the page. I rolled the papers up and put them in my pocket and got out of the car. I stumble-stepped across the ground and climbed up the porch stairs and stood before the cabin door. It was shut tight with a padlock on it. I checked around the doorframe and down along the planks of the porch, but I found no key. I sat down, leaning back against the door. I lit a cigarette at last. A cool wind enormous and conscious moved through the darkness. The night hummed. Crickets bivouacked in the tall grass. Up above the stars had set up camp in a sprawling garden of eyes. I listened to the dark waves roll, and I thought that the universe was nothing more than a conversation between giant beings. My actions, the cricket's saw, the star's blink were nothing but pauses and syllables, scattered phrases from that dialogue. What word could it be, of which I was only a syllable? Who speaks the word? To whom is it spoken? Had I read that somewhere? Was that my own thought? I threw my cigarette down, and falling it drew a shining curve like a tiny comet. I could feel the blood sliding through my arms, my heart working away in my chest. I closed my eyes, and after a while I drifted off into a jittery sleep.

I dreamed I was walking along a path on the edge of a cliff above the ocean. It was daylight, but a heavy white fog was around me obscuring everything. And though I couldn't see the ocean below, I heard the sea waves gathering like a great in-take of breath followed by a suspended moment of silence, then the falling of waves on the shore like a long exhale. Then I came upon a tower, or rather a towering sculpture made out of driftwood. It was so high that it disappeared in the mist above. Then I saw a man working on it, fitting more pieces into it. But I only caught the briefest glimpse of him as the mist swept in and out and around him. He was old and thin and bent and was wearing what looked like a priest's cassock. His pale white beard had a greenish tinge. He had flashing eyes and long fingers that were as twisted as the sticks he held. When he saw me, or at least I think he saw me, he moved back around to another side of the tower.

I stopped to admire the intricate work, each piece so intentionally put into place that it rose trembling and solid. Surely this was a work of sacred fellowcraft, something veiled in allegory yet through compass and square at last the kind of thing an astute student of edgework might find embedded in any masonic design. I reached out and touched the smooth wood. I investigated the thick wickerwork of its elaborate structure, so complex that I couldn't see all the way through it. And then I caught a shudder of movement within like the shadows of climbers ascending and descending. My fingers brushed over a small knob, and I looked down and saw that my hand was resting on a skull and that the entire sculpture was in truth made out of bones. My hand recoiled.

"Whose bones are these?" I asked, even though I couldn't see the sculptor. He was on the other side of the tower now and out of sight.

But I heard his voice when he answered, "They come from all over." I moved around the tower, trying to get another glimpse of him.

"And what does it mean?" I asked, as my fingers brushed along the curve of a rib.

"They're the last story we ever tell," he said.

Did I see a smile on that face there in the bones? I put both hands out and gripped the bone rungs and pushed against the sculpture with all my strength and felt it sway, a great fine moveable weight. I said, "But even these will disintegrate one day." And as I let go, the tower settled back into its balanced place.

"Yes," he said, "but there will always be more." I continued moving around the tower, sliding my hand along the hatchings of bonework and its profound heft.

"Besides, the dead don't need their bones," he said.

I laughed. "That's true."

I kept circling, trying for another glimpse of him. I said, "What do the dead need?"

And through the sculpture, as though the bones themselves were speaking, I heard him say, "New eyes."

And I laughed again, trying for one more glimpse, changing my direction around the tower, halting again, reversing course, but it had become a game such that whenever I moved he moved also and ultimately I never saw him.

A black form stood before me. "Hey," I heard it say, "is that you?" I looked up. Was I still dreaming? Or had this dream stopped? It spoke again, "Tom?"

"Yes," I said.

"Tom? What the hell are you doing here?"

"Waiting for you," I said, pulling myself up to embrace my brother.

"Mon semblable," he said, "mon frere!" And he gave me a big bear hug. He smelled of smoke and booze. "How long have you been waiting here?"

"Not long," I said. "Man, I had the strangest dream just now."

"Well, this is the place where the old men dream their dreams."

"God," I said, climbing out of it. "I guess so. I had a doozy!"

"I bet you did. I bet you did," he said, and I could tell he was wavering between stations. "So, uh, hang on a sec," and he fumbled with his keys. "Now, when did you get out?"

"Not too long… a couple of… recently."

He unlocked the door and we went inside. "Uh huh, uh huh, okay..." he said.

He lit a Coleman lantern hanging from a rafter and at last I saw him, the same as I remembered him, though perhaps a little thinner, older in the face. He wore jeans and a jean jacket patched up in different colors and a floppy knitted beret, something one of his drifty dreamy diamond-eyed girlfriends must have made. And on his jacket were pins with strange little feathers and wooden stick figures and flags, and around his neck he wore a black cord with a little leather pouch on the end of it. He had a couple of days of beard growth and the red mark of a scrape or a bruise on his right cheek, but his eyes burned with an intensity I knew well, his child bright energy still shining through.

"Would you like some tea?" he asked, grinning like the kid-catcher, and I laughed. All those codes we shared. One word could summon the dormant past to life.

"Sure," I said.

He went over to the wood stove and opened the blackened door. He had a nice little stack of firewood ready to go. He crumpled up some wads of newspaper and wedged them into the stove and then layered on some kindling and bigger pieces of wood. Then he lit the papers. The fire took fast and began to crackle and glow.

He stood up and looked at me and shook his head and laughed and said, "God, it's good to see you. Alive and kicking!"

"Mostly kicking."

"Man, how long has it been? When was the last time we saw each other?"

"A while ago," I said. "Maybe..." I tried to remember, but the memory wouldn't come. He crouched back down and blew into the stove and raised the flames until the fire was bright. Then he closed the iron doors and adjusted the flues. "I can't remember," I said. "You went into the Navy, then...I don't know. It all blurs as it forms." A big wind swept over the cabin. My ears popped. I watched him pour some water from a plastic jug into a battered tin tea kettle.

He put the kettle on the stove, slapped his hands together and smiled.

"Let me show you around," he said. "All the improvements!"

I laughed because, really, there was nowhere to go, and I could see everything from where I was standing. The cabin was just one room. But he had done some work on it to make it more livable. Before, it had been nothing more than an unfurnished hunting shack.

"Check out the kitchen," he said. And he showed me where he had partially framed in one side of the room for a kitchen space. He had also put in some oak cabinets that were polished and lacquered so bright they seemed out of place. He had installed a counter with a hole cut into it for a sink. It was coming into being, but it was mostly still in his imagination. The floor was a clutter of tools and pipes and plumbing fixtures I'm sure he intended to use if he ever brought in water. He also had boxes with spools of wiring and outlets if he ever got electricity, and then other useful junk.

"It goes kind of slow," he said. "But I've been doing the work myself. I found some drywall, too. I just need to pick it up. Then I can finish off these walls. I'm a total scavenger. And I still need to do some work around the roof, here. I've had some leaking, which is not good. The mice are getting in, which wouldn't bother me, but they keep getting into my food." Then he swept his arm back and said, "And the living room..."

He took a step toward the other side of the cabin where he had a small futon couch set up against the wall by the door. "My bedroom," he said.

He had also built a nice set of shelves on which he had placed a few books. I looked them over: a Bible, an old dictionary, a book on medieval history, a book on chemistry, some Navy texts and navigational manuals, and Nietzsche's *Beyond Good and Evil*.

He grabbed a large fruit jar from the shelf and handed it to me. Inside of it was a set of feathery cat bones and a cat skull with large empty eye sockets and thin-tined nostril slots. He had labeled the jar with a piece of masking tape like a naturalist specimen with the words written on it: FELINUS EXTINCTUS. "My pet cat," he said, laughing his crazy quick-breath laugh.

I scanned the shelves and saw other little objects and totems. He had pinecones carved into faces, stones arranged in patterns and stacked in cairns, an abalone shell with a candle in it, an incense tray, white-tipped feathers in a glazed clay pot with zigzag designs on it, all things charged, I knew, with ritual and significance, nothing merely ornamental. He had a little sculpture of a crouching Buddha, head held in its open hands. I picked it up and balanced it on my palm and closed my fingers around it.

"My Buddha still weeps," he said. I put it back on the shelf. And I saw a ceramic jar that looked familiar.

"This mom?" I asked, touching the jar and turning it with my fingers.

"Yeah," he said. "The holy of holies." And I pulled my hand back.

He had a trunk full of clothes and a small hutch in which he had hung some other clothing and beside this a chest plate from a suit of armor.

"Where'd you get that?" I asked, pointing at the chest plate.

"Found it," he said, grinning fiercely. "I told you, I've become a total scrounge. I'm like one of those Japanese hermits up on the mountain." And as if to prove it, he pointed at a Samurai sword hanging over the doorway. The inside of the cabin was a gallery of self, with pictures he had painted, one of a crow rising from the split skull of a slain warrior, another of himself in a medieval suit of armor, his face gaunt and death-like inside a silver helmet. And in the middle of the room was a large, gray oval stone that glowed in the lamplight.

The kettle began to whistle, and he took it from the stove and lifted the lid. He tapped some tealeaves from a plain brown box into the kettle to steep. I looked around, trying to take it all in and see what it said about my brother and where he had been and what he had become. The Coleman lantern threw a central flame of light into the darkness, and our shadows twitched on the walls and in the grime-bemarked windows. Pitch-blackness hovered at the edges where the light couldn't reach, as though the cabin walls themselves were part of the big darkness outside.

"What time is it?" I asked.

He smiled at me. "It's now."

"No, really..."

"I don't know," he said, eyeing me viciously. "You got somewhere to go?" Then he paused and said in a syrupy, high-pitched voice, "Where you gonna go, Tom? You getting sleepy?"

I laughed at our old joke, and something broke through for the first time.

"Go ahead," he said. "Sit down." He took off his coat. His shirt was spotted with white bleach marks. He looked wasted but strong at the same time. I went to the window and tried to look through, cupping my hands on the glass, but I saw nothing. I turned back. My brother. Myself. That was an old one.

He lived here, far from everything, in a place little more than basic shelter. He craved nothing beyond this, had always regarded the world suspiciously, as though it were a trap. The world, for my brother, was never what it seemed; whereas for me, it was exactly what it seemed, and I had to find a way to live in it. We were of the same blood but different, different but the same. He kicked a few boxes back into the kitchen, trying to create space. Then he picked up the tea kettle and swirled the water and poured us each a cup of tea.

"So," he said, handing me a cup, "What brings you all the way out here to nowhere?"

"Well," I said, sitting down on the futon. "I won't lie to you, brother. I'm running."

"Again?" he said, his face a reflection of all my own disappointment and confusion. "And you just got out?"

"Yes."

"Just got out?" he said again as if he weren't sure what kind of reality I was in. He stared at me a long time and shook his head.

"Well," he said, "we'll figure this thing out."

"We will?" I said. Then I laughed. What could I say? I felt pretty doomed.

He pulled a chair over from the kitchen and sat down across from me. Our knees nearly touched. "First of all, how long can you stay?"

"I'm out of here tomorrow," I said.

"Shit! It's that bad?"

"Yes."

"Then we've got to cover some ground tonight."

He jumped up again and reached into his shelf and brought down a small canvas bag. He opened the bag and took out a smaller, plastic bag and pinched out a few white pieces of dried mushrooms, balancing them on his hand for a moment to better feel the weight and intrinsic power charge, then picked out a few more and said, "Open up."

"Oh, brother, I can't tonight."

"Come on," he said, "especially tonight."

I put out my hand, and he dropped the mushrooms onto my palm. Then he picked out a handful for himself, looked me in the eye, and put them into his mouth. I took a deep breath, looked him in the eye and did the same. The dry, bitter taste of crumbling earth.

I chewed the pieces. I watched his jaw working slowly, chewing. "And I love it," he said, "because it is bitter and because it is my heart."

And we broke out laughing. A world of new creatures and energy streams and flickering lights moved just beneath the surface. Soon there would be no stopping those waves. I looked at him. Here in a land that seemed always night. His face was a mirror of mine. And all too soon we might have been, but I swear I felt the flush of the first wave of it, that jolt of the deep serpent awakening. All too soon.

"There is absolutely no way you are going back in there," he said. "I'll make sure of that!"

"And how are you going to do that?"

"We'll figure it out. Something. Just let the imagination take its course. We'll just see." And he looked around his little shack for a moment, saw the crouching Buddha and picked it up. "I guess your Buddha is still weeping, too," he said. He tossed it to me, and I caught it.

"I guess it is," I said, and I held the Buddha in my hand. The crouching Buddha holding his face in his hands, the top of the head worn smooth and now lighter in color, and I imagined nights my brother sat holding it, worrying his way through some perennial onslaught with this alone to keep him company. And my heart went out to him.

"First of all," he said, "you've got to practice projection, okay? Right through the top of your head. That's what you have to do. They can never catch you. You just have to practice projection."

"Projection, huh?"

"That's right. Projection."

All right," I said. "I'm projecting."

"You do that."

"Through the top of the head?"

"The crown."

He sat silently for a moment, the gears turning. I seriously practiced projecting. I wasn't sure how this was going to come in handy, but I practiced it anyway. And I felt the initial waves come, a gentle breath-suspending upheaval right below the navel. I took in a deep breath. I felt the tingle. I laughed a little.

"What?" he said.

"I'm practicing projection."

He smiled. "Good! Good! You feel it?"

"I do. I do. So, where am I supposed to be projecting to?"

"Nowhere," he said. "You're practicing escape. Pro ba. You have to get out of your head."

"Oh, okay. I get it."

"You feel it, yet?"

"Oh, I feel it…"

And here came the next wave, longer, stronger, a swell rising up and washing through my body and through my head. The shape of the room began to tremble, warp and weft separating and rippling. The elemental breathing of the world was starting to reveal itself.

"Let's go back," he said.

"What do you mean?"

"Let us review, shall we?"

"What are we reviewing?"

"Remember that time with Nicole?" he said.

"What are you talking about?"

"Nicole? Back when we were kids?"

"The little girl from grade school?"

"That's her. Remember when we were walking home, just goofing around, and she hit me in the eye with her umbrella?"

"You're going way back," I said. "Yeah, I remember that. I remember she took off running when she saw all that blood, your blood."

"That's right, and at first all I thought was, why does she look so scared? I didn't know I was bleeding. I just thought my eye was watering until I looked down at my hand and saw the blood."

"You were quite the freak show!"

"I know. I feel sorry for her. What a nightmare."

"I haven't thought about that—"

"You now, that eye's never been the same since."

"Which one was it?"

"The left one."

I looked hard at his left eye. "Can you see with it?" I asked.

"It sees in better than it sees out."

"The vision's impaired, then?"

"Improved!" he said. And he laughed his mad laugh. "You see what I mean? Go back. You just gotta go back. The clues are everywhere. I thought it was…" and he smiled, opening his mouth. "…say it… disaster! At first. But I couldn't see it clearly. You see?"

"Oh, man. Okay. So…projection?" I had a feeling of what he was after, a hint in this case. Free associate and let it slip in, and that provides the direction. The trick is knowing the clue from the ruse.

Then his face changed, and he said, "Okay now, do you remember the Alexanders?"

"Funny, I was just thinking of them." Hadn't I? Which comes first, the idea or the thought? Did I hear it then think it? Or did I think it then he said it?

"You got it, then?"

"Wait, where are you, now?" He was leaping through our common past and scrounging around inside my own recent thoughts.

"You know, the Alexanders? That wreckage of a family?"

"Oh, yes. I remember them," I said. "They ended up down in Guiana. Wait. Right? Do I have that right?" I took out a cigarette and offered one to my brother. My hand moved like a floating jellyfish. How nice that it should decide to help me now.

"Then you remember Paris, the little brother?"

"You guys used to fight all the time." Hands like strange doves.

"He was a little monster then, but you know you have to be careful when you're fighting monsters, lest you become a monster yourself."

"Whatever happened to him?" I took in a drag of smoke and then exhaled, and for a moment the smoke hovered there in the shape of my own image.

"Well, and the reason I bring this up is, you see… I have my ideas about that. It's like, you might not think it's important at the time. Like Paris. I'd see him every day when I walked along the railroad tracks to school, you know. He lived on that run-down street by the west campus, remember? Do you remember?"

"I remember." My voice echoed inside the bathysphere of my skull.

"Bars on the windows and apartment buildings bombed out and junkies in doorways and dogs on chains vicious snapping at you through the fences, you remember that walk? You made that walk, too, when you went to that school. Every day that kid Paris would come out and try to fight me. Every day with, hey, motherfucker! What are you doing here? I know you. Get the fuck out of here! I don't... I wasn't scared, but I wouldn't fight him. I knew his family was fucked up. But he just kept coming at me. As they say, I tried to reason with him, saying, 'Come on, man, I don't want to fight you. I just want to go to school.' That just seemed to make him madder. And he'd taunt me, call me a chicken shit pussy. But still I wouldn't fight him.

"And then one day he came at me, throwing punches. And I never told anyone this... I don't know why... but I just lost it. I picked up a rusty horseshoe I found on the ground there by the side of the tracks, and I jumped on him and beat the shit out of him. And when the smoke cleared and I saw what I had done, I was proud, and at the same time I felt sick about it, you know? I didn't want to do it. But I had done it. I had to do it. I had no choice. You know what I mean? And that's the point. I knew I was capable of it. But in that moment, I had no choice. And the weird thing about it is that I thought that just being in that place, where I was, meant something was wrong with me. Like I was in a terrible place because there was something terrible inside me. You do something terrible like that, you know, or you think it's terrible, and you start thinking there is something terrible about you, like you wouldn't be there in the first place if there weren't something terrible about you. So, I was the monster."

"I don't know. Yes, I see. But also, what happened wasn't because of you. That's like saying if a tornado destroys your home, it's your fault."

"Isn't it? Especially if you're in tornado country."

"Tornado country!"

"You chose to be there. I suppose you have to look hard at what you do, what's in your mind, too, as well as the forces around you. Why are you in the path of that tornado? How do you get out of the path of the tornado? Maybe you want to get up close and personal with that tornado."

Then we both laughed because the tornado was coming.

"Well, how do you know when the tornado is coming?" I asked.

"Because you get the warnings. Hey, motherfucker..."

And we laughed again. The tornado was already here.

"We know a lot more than we think we do," he said with deadly seriousness. "Can't you feel them all around us?" And he waved his hand in the air. "Memories and dreams hovering in the ether?" Then we both laughed again. I blazed. I smoked and exhaled a dream of smoke.

"Wait a minute. If I apply that to my situation, then something is wrong with me... or I wanted..."

"No, you see. That's just the thinking. Pluck it out!"

"Maybe I'm a tornado."

"You *are* a tornado, and there's nothing you can do about it."

My mind circled that for a moment. That's eventually what you have to do, isn't it? Get down to one story of the true thing you are and ride it all the way out?

"And what happened to you?" I asked. "What happened with the Navy? That was your thing, I thought. And then what?"

"That?" He turned and picked up the teapot and poured us each some more tea. The steam rose from my cup and coiled into a brief wave of dreamscape before it disappeared. "I had a good run with it," he said. "Mostly we just partied everywhere we went. We were like a cruise ship for the government derelicts. We'd pick up various dignitaries and their girls and drop them off at coastal resorts. There was very little military about it. We were pimps. It was a party gone way out of all bounds. You'd be surprised. We spent a lot of time cruising around the Pacific, supposedly keeping an eye on the enemy. We made a few trips to The East. Shopping sprees for government contractors."

"Really?"

"The flagging empire. It was pretty disgusting. I mean, it wasn't like that all the time." And he drifted back for a moment. "But I liked the sailing part, being out there, out at sea. I learned the art of navigation, the stars, you know, celestial navigation."

"Beautiful."

"Oh, yeah. The stars are the codes. It's a perfect construction, random as it may be. All you need to know is the location of one star, one star, and you can triangulate your location exactly, wherever you are. You're never lost."

"Any star?"

"Pretty much, if you know what star you're looking at. Especially the North

Star. Just know where Polaris is, if it's visible. That's my star. That's the one fixed star, the North Star. From that, you can establish any location. Simple as that. Once you isolate a constellation you can just do the math. But Polaris, that's my star. Know the North Star and you have the key to the universe!"

"Right on, brother. You found the key to the universe." The geometry of innocent flesh on the bone. This was buckling into some hard truth. I smoked slowly.

"Of course, I was always pretty good at dead reckoning, too." And he laughed a little at that.

Everything was coming in waves and happening at the same time. The not so subtle green architecture of underwater grotto anemones drifted around the room with whiptail poison-dart flagella and glowing grid-flesh that puffed and swelled. Contact was an issue. And they slipped in and out of the layers of darkness that pulsed through the skin of the walls. And then at that moment, the fabric of the futon and my skin began a molecular tango. When I pulled my arms up, material from the futon came up as well, stuck to me like a fine white webbing of ash.

"So what happened?" I asked. "Why'd you quit?" I shook the ash from my arms and watched it float away like dandelion seeds.

"I didn't quit. They kicked me out," and he laughed sardonically. That was an acquired trait. He was a mixture of a No character with root rawness and the brother I had known as a kid showing through the troubled years and other woes. "Fucking captain turned on me. Wouldn't recommend me for a promotion. I called him on it, too. Called him a pig fucker... to his face." He laughed again.

I laughed, too, because I saw that moment. I never could understand why he submitted to that authority. He was always the kid on the verge of trouble or over, wild child full of grace, foster child of silence and slow time. Then again, looking at him now and the way he was living and seeing his spirit like some tough old gnome in the wilderness, I knew his struggle to live both in and out of the structure.

"He wrote me up, said I was insubordinate, started hassling me. I was finally asked to leave, but I've got my discharge on appeal right now. I gave those motherfuckers a piece of my soul. I deserve to have an honorable discharge! The little punk. But I tell you, brother, we did do some wild stuff out there. You would not believe it, but I don't want to scare you."

"Like what?" I asked.

We were in the good groove, now, all ascent and mental theatrics and a part of me going, bring it on. Laughter was a force exploding through us. Trying to explain it is like a turtle doing yoga. Then more laughter spasms attached to nothing at all burst forth, which in some obscure part of the mind I now thought was the cosmic laughter of the huckster at his con, the crooked smile…but every time I tried to look he was gone.

"Oh, man, crazy drinking and bringing girls on board. Shooting off fireworks and scaring the natives. The whole besotted colonial wash."

"Mistah Kurtz, he dead."

"Oh, now—"

We doubled over again, and many selves shook their wings.

"Oh no," he said, snapping into serious. "We chased down a few of those guys. The evil demons are on the loose! We were the good guys, sometimes, I think."

"I bet you were," I said.

"Oh yea verily," he said, grinning.

Laughter dropped another pile-driver, senseless and strange. I held tight to the weeping Buddha.

"And the drugs, man," he said. "Oh… I don't want to scare you." He shook his head, and I looked into the face of my brother and saw the wolf beneath the mask. "I don't want to scare you, but I tell you, I should be dead. I would be dead if I hadn't had divine help."

"Divine help? What divine help?"

"I was gone. Left my body. All the way out."

"You've done that many times, my boy…"

"I'm serious. I got kicked right out of my body. The umpire came in and… let's just say that I was asked to leave. And I wasn't coming back. I was so far gone in fact that I was floating far out in space, or outside of space and time. I was...I don't know where I was. But I saw some strange things out there, man. I saw things like... lives I'd lived before, seriously, and not your noble king sort of lives. We're talking feral, Cro-Magnon animal-in-the-muck lives. And I saw all of our relations, too, saw all their stories in detail like it was written in a book. I could swoop in and examine any moment. It was all laid out and running like some kind of movie that I was inside of, made out of... I don't know... like an endless cosmic strand of narrative DNA. But hey, along the way there were some distinguished representatives, too. You know we're related to Captain Cook, right? I saw his life transpire, all of it, instantaneously. All the places. The sea. I saw his life inside my own, you know, the influence of his life force on mine and everyone in the line, the way... as if everything our relatives did is written in the nervous system. And that's the thing I realize is so amazing. None of it's gone. Everything you've ever heard or thought is still there, somewhere in that vast vault memory. And it's all here now all around. It's true. All of it. And I saw hell, too, man. I saw the people in it, you know, and they were hideous deformed things with faces some of them all covered with pustules and malformations and some just these twisted teeth or ulcers. And they don't see each other as hideous but as normal. It's only when you come in from the outside that you see them the way I did. And I saw Angels, too, seriously. They spoke to me."

"What did the angels tell you?"

"Laugh if you want," he said. "But they saved my life. They told me, that's it. No more. You can't do this anymore, meaning no more drugs, or you will die. You have learned all you can this way. Now you must stop. And so, I did. I stopped. I live like a monk, now."

"Now?" I said, spreading my arms out with tracer shapes appearing like a fanned-out deck of cards in the air, a blazing Shiva, as if to say, see now what are we up to here? Then I said, "What were you doing then?"

"Very bad combinations," he said. "You name it. There wasn't a method I didn't try. I ate it. I smoked it. I shot it up. I was doing heroin, speedballs, crank, crystal, mixed cocktails as we called them..."

I shook my head, hearing my brother's story, seeing it laid it out before me, my brother who couldn't live with people.

"I won't tell you even half of it," he said. "I don't want to scare you. Just..." and he reached out and took the Buddha and held it in his open hand. "My Buddha still weeps!"

"Ah, brother..."

I drank some more of the tea. The room, the walls, the floor pulsed and bubbled, a drifting bursting unreal liquid field. And the underwater grotto squids kept launching themselves green and blue through every breath, out of the membrane of darkness, out of my body, too, now fluttering in the waves of the floating night.

"What are you doing now?" I asked. "How are you keeping it together?"

"Oh, I'm working for a cabinet maker. That's where I got those cabinets."

"You mean you made those?"

"I did."

"Nice." And then I drifted out. Where I went, nobody knows. Then I returned. "So why all the drugs, brother? I thought you liked the Navy and all that and had a good thing going."

"I did. I don't know. We just cruised around like some party barge, and under conditions of peace the warlike man attacks himself."

"You're not a warlike man."

"I've been at war with something. I mean, I don't want to kill anybody. It's just sometimes you have a talent for something, and if it doesn't get expressed somehow, whatever that energy is, it comes out twisted. That's why I'm living like a monk. I get into the world, and I can only be one thing: crazyman. I don't know why. But I'm trying to learn another way. It's a sad road for me. I guess that's what I have to offer you. The story of it. The finger pointing at the moon. You have to write your own story, though, I suppose."

I leaned back and watched the cloud of the bloated ceiling sway in the flickering light of the lantern. A great blue dragon had coiled itself up there and was now spinning in a figure eight and giving a fantastic show of its fire wings, swimming through the walls and sliding along the windows, a playful spirit neither yielding nor supreme. The reality of it wasn't a question or a problem. Shapes in a dream. I was with my brother in our uncle's cabin in the woods, floating in darkness, safe, for the moment, in the golden thread of seems.

The room was growing hot, and I stood up, swaying but clear. It felt good to reclaim my feet again. I was in the zone and relaxed, finally, and able in a way to forget and allow.

My brother got up too and said, "It's getting hot! Isn't it?" That brought on more laughter. He opened the front door with a fierce pull that drew in a gust of wind as though the big vaporous giant who had been leaning against the door trying to listen came tumbling in. We went out onto the porch and felt the cool night air.

I lit another cigarette and stood there between worlds. What was the forest saying, up on its hind legs? Yes, what was it saying?

"Let's take a little walk," I said.

And so we went out into the dark, but now I saw into the depths of the woods with my acute eyes of wide wonder all the seams and little maker's patterns that were solid though sound-made here in the pure land. And it felt good to have my brother's spirit there beside me as we went up the hill. With every step, we passed from one universe to another, and my movement was sure as I went. I had grace I was gradually remembering into being. I felt light, and my mind soared through the tree limbs and the open air and the stars so deep and bright as we walked among them.

"But what about you, brother?" he asked me. "What's going on with you? You just got out of prison and you're already running again?"

"Oh man," I said. "I got sucked into a stupid, stupid scheme. A robbery. Someone was killed. He was shot." I still couldn't believe it or find room for it in my way of seeing my life. "But I don't want to scare you."

"Who was it?"

"A guard."

"Did you do it?"

"You mean shoot him?"

"Yeah."

"No."

"What did you do?"

"What do you mean? During the robbery?"

"I mean when he was shot. What did you do?"

"I didn't do anything."

"Nothing? Think again."

"I didn't do anything."

"You mean you didn't run?"

"No…I didn't run." I stopped on the trail in the trees. I thought back. "I watched him die."

"Then you did do something."

"If watching a person die can be considered doing something, yes, I did something."

"I mean exactly, what were you doing exactly?"

"I just sat there, next to this guy. I watched him die." Why was I getting angry?

"But you didn't leave."

"—"

"Look, you didn't shoot him. You stayed there. I mean, think about it. Your actions. What you actually did. It was a good thing."

"Do you understand the law? In the commission of a felony, if someone is killed during the commission of that felony—"

"Look closer. What were your exact actions? Did you have a gun?"

"No."

"Then look at the act."

"I was not an innocent bystander." The moment flashed back through me.

"You were better than that. Think about it. That's something."

"It was nothing," I said.

We went out onto the main road. I had no concern for the police at this point. I was free of everything, outside the mix. And we went into a clearing overlooking the valley. The lights of the town glittered below like some existential circus, and the stars were pitch perfect notes overhead. The river rolled black through the center of the valley, a reversed mirror of the Milky Way above. The wave of night flowed throughout the land and through our bodies, and I swam untethered in the swells of that dreamtime over bluff and valley and the thin gray ribbon of road.

"There's Polaris," my brother said, pointing to a bright star in the bouquet of constellations to the North. I rose slowly, a deep sea diver ascending as I fixed my gaze on the star he pointed out, and I heard his voice as if from far away saying, "Gaze deep into the abyss, and the abyss will gaze deep into you."

I tried to sleep for a couple of hours, even though I knew it was pointless. My brother kept moving, kept talking. He was on fire, now, caught up in an idea. He was a man who had been living alone for a long time. And I lay on the couch with my mind burning, as he shuffled around like some strange shaman chanting about the sacred five days or seven days, I couldn't tell which, the contracts and the agreements and the unseen forces that guide our lives, and his shadow danced around me and his voice sounded like a non-stop liturgical incantation as he lit incense and mutter-prayed and shook his power sticks and boards and proclaimed that he was sending me out with the magic of projection.

And above me, I saw the great white spider hovering up there in the dark dome sky with its needlepoint lightning legs working together like fine fingers tinkering with the universe.

I drifted on the edge of sleep, tied to my brother's voice that eventually brought me back at last as I heard him say, "You've got to find water."

"What?" I said. I don't know if what he said rang true, but I was definitely summoned back from the hub. I crawled my way back into my body and saw him standing over me with that wild energy. The light was at his back, but his face glowed. "I didn't catch that last bit. Have you been up all night?" I asked.

He turned slightly as though listening to something from far away, and then he smiled and looked back at me and said, "I never sleep."

I pulled myself up, stiff in the limbs, my mouth dry, my mind still vibrating from the great joke-buzzer but slowing down at last. "What do you mean you never sleep? Everybody sleeps. If you don't sleep, you go insane."

"Sleep that knits the raveled sleeve of care..."

"Yes, that sleep. Even troubled sleep. You can't *not* sleep."

"Sleep no more..."

"Really? It's come to that?"

He poured a cup of coffee, handed it to me and said, "Is it so hard to understand? I don't sleep."

I drank some coffee. It was very strong, very hot.

"You know what," I said. "I gotta go."

"I know. I know."

"They might come looking for me, here, so be prepared."

"They won't find you."

"They might hassle you."

He lifted his hands. "You don't exist."

"Hey," I said, "I almost forgot." I reached into my pocket and took out Melissa's pictures. "This is for you. My daughter, Melissa, made it. She told me to give it to you."

I handed one of the pictures to him, and he looked at it for a long moment. "She told you to give this to me?" he said. "She doesn't even know me."

"You could change that," I said.

His eyes began to well up as he looked down at the unrolled picture, holding it like it was a fragile document, his hands shaking.

"A girl after my own heart," he said.

Light now came in through the windows, that pale, deep forest light growing slow and incremental. The cabin smelled of smoke and incense and past lives. The windows were nearly black but for center holes rubbed clean by a need to see. I looked around, but I don't know why. I had nothing, so I had nothing to collect. But I looked around anyway, taking in a last impression of my brother's home, something to carry with me. And if he was right, it would stay with me, even if I thought I forgot it.

Then I looked at my brother and he looked at me. Neither one of us could say what was now obvious. I took a breath and held it for a moment. Then I went out on the porch and lit a cigarette. And I saw in the dawn light a sculpture there that I had missed the night before, a red clay bust of a soldier with hundreds of nails sticking out of it.

"Jesus," I said. "What is that? Did you make that?"

He came out and stood beside me. "Pretty ferocious, isn't it?" And he laughed that quick laugh of his.

"Yeah," I said. "That's exactly what I thought, ferocious. Did you do this?"

"I did."

"It's kind of scary."

"It's a voodoo doll for myself."

"What are you trying to do to yourself?"

"Trying to stay clear."

I looked at him and saw again the red mark on his cheek. It had grown darker. It was not a cut but an abrasion of some kind, and I asked him, "What happened to your face?"

He reached his hand to his cheek, but he didn't touch it. "This?" he said, and he turned to look at his reflection in the cabin window but stopped before he caught sight of himself. He looked back at me and said, "I had a little accident last night."

"When?"

"Just before I came back here."

"You were in an accident last night?" I looked around. "Where's your truck?"

"Well, actually, do you think you could give me a ride down the hill?"

"To your truck?"

"Yeah."

"How bad is it?"

"Well, I'm not sure. But I wasn't able to drive it back here."

"Are you serious?"

"Serious as a heart attack."

"Of course, I'll give you a ride," I said. "You sure you're all right?"

"Right as rain," he said, and he thumped his chest with his fists.

I ran my hands around the back of my neck, stretching into life, sliding back into the world, and gathering mentally to make my next move.

"Do you need anything?" he asked.

I thought a moment, smiled. "Actually, I'm broke."

"Not much of a thief, huh?"

"Not really, it turns out."

"Here," he said. He took out his wallet. He opened it, looked at it, and then closed it. "Take it," he said, and he handed it to me. "There's not much in there, but maybe it will help. You can be me for a while, make it harder for them to find you."

I took the wallet, his wallet. It was old, smooth-worn. I flipped it over in my hand, feeling it, feeling his life in it. "I always wondered what it would be like to be you," I said.

"You did?"

"Yeah, sure. I used to picture you out there. Different places. Having adventures. You were always on some adventure."

"Huh. I always wondered what it would be like to be you, with the wife and kids, the whole shebang. The neighborhood barbecues. Everyone out there mowing their lawns at the same time, drinking iced tea. Normal. Safe. Respectable."

"Huh. I thought you hated that kind of thing."

"Well, I guess you don't know too much about me, do you?"

"I guess not."

I put the wallet into my pocket. "Thanks, brother," I said. "This will help me get down the road a bit, help me get a few supplies."

"You need anything else?"

"No. This'll just about do me."

"All right, then," he said.

He closed the door and padlocked it, and we hiked down around to the back of the cabin and climbed into my car. I started the engine and flipped on the windshield wipers to sweep off the pine needles and pulled back onto the dirt road. Then I gunned the engine and made the leap up the short hill to the main road. Morning light fluttered down in hazy shafts through the trees and over the hood of the car, bright flashes, and we popped and bounced along the road as my brother lit up a smoke and passed it to me. "A little bit of clock," he said.

We headed down the hill, and I asked, "So what happened?"

"What do you mean?"

"The truck."

"Ah, I skidded off the road on a sharp turn. Hit a guard rail."

"You seem like you're okay."

"I am," he said, waving his hand. "I'm fine."

We came out onto the paved road and headed down through the pine trees and the hemlock, the ride smooth and quiet. It was turning out to be a beautiful day, the kind you disappear into. I still had no concerns about the police, not yet at least. But I knew my time was limited. For a moment, right now, I wanted to stay in this dream. For the moment, I felt like we were kids again, just out for a ride.

When I came to a crossroads, I said, "Which way?"

"Right."

I drove to the right, and the road curved around. Then I had a sudden memory of this road and where it went if I followed it far enough. The land out here, I realized, was all completely familiar, and I was moving through the wobbly fields of déjà vu. Maybe my brother was right about the record of the universe or whatever you'd call it, and every detail, every stone, every creek, meadow, road and falling down farmhouse... all of it was logged in somewhere. I knew this land. At least I thought I did. But did I know it because I had seen it and been over it, or was it my imagination reaching across the map of it in the universal mind? My brain was a fuzzy hammer.

"So," I said. "You talk to the old man?"

"Nah. He pretty much keeps to himself. Besides, he doesn't want to have anything to do with me. I'm the fuck-up, remember?"

"He still out at the old place?"

"Ultima Thule? I don't know. I suppose so. Where else would he go, especially at his age?"

"How's his health?"

"That guy? He's strong as an ox! He'll outlive us all!"

We came around a bend and he said, "That's it up there."

And where the road widened out at the bottom of the hill, I saw his little gray truck on the shoulder off to the left. It looked fine from here. Across from the truck on the other side of the road was an abandoned garage with its windows boarded up and out front of it a defunct gas pump and a bunch of old red rusted oil drums. As we approached the truck, I saw the damaged side of it. Up close it looked a little worse. I pulled up and stopped.

We got out and walked over to the truck. Then I was shocked. Coming around to the front of it, I saw that it was completely demolished. The windshield was shattered. The front end was smashed in so bad that the steering wheel was pressed up against the driver's seat, and the battery had flown right through the firewall into the passenger's seat. It was a death trap. I gazed at it in amazement. The fenders were pushed back like accordions, struts exposed, front axle snapped like a wishbone, the frame badly twisted. I looked at the truck, then I looked at him, then I looked at the truck. It just didn't add up. He had come out of it without a scratch.

"You walked away from this?" I said. I couldn't believe what I saw.

He laughed. "I know. It's amazing, isn't it?"

"I mean..." I pointed at the steering wheel embedded in the seat and pictured someone sitting there. There would have been no escape. It would have certainly broken both legs, probably crushed the chest cavity and pelvis. It looked as if someone had been killed inside that truck.

"How could you survive this?"

"I was thrown clear."

"Thrown clear?"

"I told you. The angels are watching over me."

He reached into the bed of the truck and sorted through bags and beer cans and jumper cables all jumbled in a mess. He lifted out a toolbox and opened it and found a rope there and unfurled it and threw one end over the cab and went around to the other side and said, "Help me tie the doors closed. I don't want any kids playing in it and getting hurt." I helped him lace the rope through the windows. The glass had shattered out of both of them. And we wrapped the rope through the handles and around the doors so that no one could get into the truck unless they really tried. Then we stood back, and I just shook my head in disbelief. When I looked over at him, he was grinning.

"I don't get it," I said.

"You know," he said, his voice Pentecostal, "I want you to take this." And he reached up and took hold of the little pouch on the leather cord around his neck, ducked his head down, and slipped it off. He reached out and put it over my head and around my neck.

"What is it?" I asked.

"Medicine pouch. It'll keep you safe."

"I can't take this," I said. Then I pointed again at the truck. "I think you might need it more than I do. Besides, it's sacred to you."

"You can't give it back," he said. "It won't work for me anymore." His eyes narrowed. "And if you give it back it will be worse for you." He was serious about this.

"All right. All right," I said, and I reached up and grasped it and held it in my hand. "Thanks, brother."

"You'll be all right," he said. "Just remember that."

"I will."

I looked over at his destroyed truck, and I wondered, what about him?

"Well," he said. "You best be rolling." His voice sounded like the old man's.

I looked at him for a moment. "What're you going to do?"

"You mean about this?"

"Yeah."

He scratched his head, shrugged and said, "I guess I'm going to hoof it over to the cabinet shop. It's just up the road a piece."

"I'll drive you."

"That's all right. I like to walk."

And we both laughed.

"I guess that's good because you'll have to," I said.

And we embraced. I didn't want to let go. He slapped my back and stood back and picked up his toolbox and threw in onto his shoulder in one slick move.

Then he smiled his mad smile, eyes wide open, turned and started walking up the hill.

"I'll be back, brother," I said.

He stopped and turned. "I'll be here," he said. "Now go get yourself to Arden, get yourself pure." And then he turned again and headed up the road.

I got into my car and started the engine. I had a sick feeling I would never see him again. I wondered. Then I reached up and touched the medicine pouch he had given me. Bless you, brother, I thought. And as I pulled back onto the road, I caught one last glimpse of him in my rearview mirror, dust swirling up around him like creation smoke as he ascended the hill.

I drove north, northeast. All my land memory said that if I kept to this road, I'd end up at my father's house. I don't know why I was going that way. Some homing mechanism had gone off in my script, and I couldn't think of any other direction to go. I suppose I was taking a risk even going near the house. Hopefully, I would be long gone before any police arrived, if they arrived. So I made my way through the foothill forests, traveling through the deep-shaded groves, the sun up above doing a fan dance in the trees.

As I started climbing higher into the mountains, my poor vehicle labored again and slowed to a crawl. It wasn't really built for this kind of escape. But I kept moving through the waves of midmorning heat and the insect buzz and the smell of hot pine needles baking on the ground. The warning light on the dashboard came on again, so I flipped the heater back on and sent my will into the machinery. The inside of the car heated up, and for a while I cruised along in a weird heat dream. Light and shadows flickered across my windshield, rhythmic strobes beating my eyelids. And as I drove through the wickerwork of the forest, I sank into a drowsy no-mind and struggled to stay awake. I lost connection to that tick track of time and knew only that I was moving away from the whirlpool of the city and into another vortex of sunlight and high drifting clouds and granite ridgelines above slopes of gray shale with jagged facades and stone towers and glowing bridges of blue ice. And when I hit the

163

peak, I felt gravity pull back. The sky opened, and I saw the mountain range rolling on white and black at that raw height. Can I say that I pulled the ripcord on a chest full of cargo because at that point I can't deny something lifted and fell away.

Once I crossed the crest of the mountain pass, I felt myself moving more freely, floating downhill with an easy speed. The warning light went off again, and I turned off the heat as I drifted back into the gut of the forest with its maze of service roads that splayed off into backcountry hidden hollows few people ever go down. The trees themselves were a hundred greens and woven so thick I could only see a short distance in any direction. The main highway seemed to dip and climb but never bend, cutting a corridor into the line it finally is far beyond my sight. I encountered very few souls out there. This was what you call a lonely stretch of road. A few semis passed, the occasional camper or pick-up truck coming the other way, but rarely anyone else, and when those other drivers appeared, they were nothing more than simple shaded faces staring forward that swept by and were gone.

When I came down into the eastern valley, I drove for a long time completely alone on that road. Everything was far away. Then I came upon a little roadside station in a field of high grass. It appeared out of nowhere like something from the past, run-down with faded advertising painted on the old slat walls. I could make out the word Durham and what looked like a bull's head. I pulled over into the gravel lot and stopped. An old man came out onto the porch. It was like he knew I was coming. He was wearing overall grease pants and a baseball cap with an emblem worn away to obscurity. He stood there in the shade under the front door awning, squinting at me and wiping his hands with a black rag.

"What can I do you for?" he asked as I got out of my car.

"Hey, good morning" I said, walking towards him. "I was just thinking I might pick up a few supplies." Why did I feel like an intruder? I'm just a lonesome traveler. He certainly wasn't giving me a welcoming vibe. He nodded once, looked me up and down and then took a long hard look at my car. I had the feeling no one ever stopped here.

"Had many customers today?" I asked.

"Nope."

I glanced back at the road and thought that I may have made a mistake stopping there. If asked, he would certainly remember me. It was like he was studying me.

"You got a bathroom?" I asked.

"Round back." And he pointed with his eyes.

I went around the side of the station and found a sloping hillside junkyard surrounded by a wooden fence covered with hubcaps. The lot was filled with old car carcasses rusting in rows. They had shattered bloody windshields and smashed up fenders and side panels. Some were stacked on top of each other. And along the back slope was a clustered tower of oil drums and vehicle parts in barrels and wheels and engine blocks sitting on sawhorses. It was a glorious graveyard of the road.

The bathroom was an outhouse there by the corner of the station, and when I went inside it smelled like the foul depths of perdition. I breathed short, quick breaths through my teeth, taking in as little air as possible while I was inside there. When I came out, I noticed a bumper lying tilted against a smashed car, and on that bumper a license plate dangled by one rusty bolt. I looked around, didn't see the old man, and kicked the license plate off. It was bent, and I stomped it flat and slipped it under my shirt behind my back.

I went up to the shop and pushed through the bell-ring of the door into an ancient mercantile store with stuffed fox and beaver pelts up on the walls and a big jar with amber liquid and a rattle snake floating in it. I half expected to see some old prospector emerge from the gritty layers of hot air. I wandered down the rows of shelves looking at faded magazines and canned foods and dried foods and racks of sunglasses, thinking, what do I need? I grabbed a few snacks from the food aisle, some peanuts and beef jerky and beer, and I put them on the counter. The old guy stood there working that dirty rag around his grease-black fingers, squinting at me like he knew something.

"How much I owe you?" I asked.

"Lemme see here," he said, and he rang it up. Then he looked at me with an odd expression and kind of worked his mouth like he was chewing on something and said, "What you done?"

"What's that?"

"I said what you done, ya takin my license plate like that? You're up to something."

"Nothing," I said. "I just wanted it for a souvenir."

"Ain't worth nothin."

"Then it's no loss."

"Take it. I don't care. Just seems like a strange thing to want for no reason."

"You ever do anything for no reason?"

He smiled a bit, but he didn't give me the impression he was on my side. He was figurin'. Then he said, "S'pose so."

"I'll pay you for it."

"Don't want your money. Like I said. It ain't worth nothin' to me."

"Well, then, thank you, I suppose."

"Don't thank me. It's between you and God." I looked at him for a moment with an urge to explain, but what was I going to tell him? He was reading it just right. Then I wanted to ask him exactly which God he was talking about, but he turned away and went back into the shadows, which was a kind of answer, so I took my things and left.

I went on into the hot day and only stopped for some quick drive-through road food in a no-light town, saying nothing other than to speak my order into the mechanical head at the entrance. Otherwise, I kept on moving. Later, I stopped on an empty stretch of road and pried my license plates off and threw them into the brush and put the plate I took from the junkyard onto the back bumper of my car. That old plate looked like it belonged on a Model T. Then again, my machine was so old the plate didn't look too out of place. All in all, it was a minor diversionary tactic on my part. But once I had that plate on there, I felt like a little cloak had wrapped itself around my vehicle, like a chameleon blending into the leaves.

I drove on, and the blond road cut through the fields, unfurling and hissing, coming out of the distance in a shimmering wave. The white mountain spikes shot up in the distance out there on my left like an ongoing EKG. Theatrical clown clouds drifted into high anvil thunderheads off to the south, flashing with their canny thoughts. The valley floated with swales of heat, and a silver river flowed with its serpent scales flashing in the dream fields and the long grass, gliding parallel as I went. And time rolled slowly in mile-on-mile of road. I felt wiped out, brain blasted. I was a hum, a shining idea. At one point I looked down, and my hands were my father's hands. I felt myself unraveling in the droning driving monotony until I couldn't tell where my limbs ended and the vehicle began. I drove until I was simple motion going forward, road endlessly happening, horizon and wind boiling together until something new appeared: a meadow, a water tower, a town, a man emerging from plowed tracks under an inverted pyramid of smoke. The sun's fierce examining eye looked down on me, and I said, what do you want? What could my mystery mean to you? And the sky answered back, Go moan... go roll your bones and speak your visions well and true. Or something like that. I was a high-speed receiver at that point. I tried to listen to the radio, to see what I could pick up. All I found was preacher talk and static and the deep empty nothing at all.

The sun dragged the day along on an invisible cord, the earth grinding away on its black axis under a cobalt sky. And the evening spread its wings before me, the forest creeping out from itself, my vehicle shadow leaping darkly ahead. I had to stop soon, pull off the road somewhere and sleep.

Just before sundown I went into a sleepy little town with old-time boardwalks and bars and a few weathered shops with local art and furniture and a real estate office with faded photographs in the window of empty land perfect for building a dream home and a few homes from dreams that started but moved on. It was a life almost within reach. But I didn't linger. I didn't speak to anyone. I went into the hardware store and bought a few camping supplies: a little propane cook stove that folded down to the size of a book, a cook set, a knife, a rope, a flashlight, a tarp and a few blankets, and a large, sturdy backpack. Then I went to the market and bought some more food: eggs and bacon and beans and bread and canned hash and soups in both cans and packets and coffee and finally two jugs of water. And I was gone from that town before I could even stun the dust into noise.

I drove with one intention, and that was to find a spot to hide for the night. The last rays of sunlight were dissolving in the upthrust of clouds along the mountain range, and I headed up into the lower hills, the pine trees accumulating again along with aspens and the watching birch trees with a million eyes. The river stayed with me, disappearing and reappearing on both sides of the road, then dipping down again as I crossed a small bridge, its white force surging below. It was the thread, the guideline. I made another turn and drove off onto a forest service road, following the river as it flowed through the hills, going until the road dwindled down to a rut that faded out in a grove of cedar trees. I continued off road and maneuvered my car between four trees with their limbs hanging down like a perfect hide-out. No one would be able to see me, especially in the dark. I was safe.

I worked fast to set up a camp. I laid out my blankets and rigged up a slanting lean-to with some branches and a rope, over which I draped my tarp. If it rained, I at least had some cover. Then I dug out a fire ring and built up a rough kitchen on one side of it with a stack of rocks, angling the flat stones on top towards the center to use as heat shelves. I gathered up some sticks and branches and broke them down and tore up one of the paper bags and wadded it up and stacked the sticks over the paper. I lit it and blew life into the flames and started a nice little fire. I dropped in a few more twigs and leaves and bigger pieces of wood to get it going. Then I sat down on the edge of my blanket, my body still shuddering from all that road time. Everything swirled inside me—my brother, the police, Natalie and Thane, my kids, the guard on the floor bleeding out, the road. My mind was a spider web of anxiety. Be here, be here, I had to tell myself. I reached my hands out and felt the warmth of the fire as the big forest and the granite peaks around me melted into night.

I listened to the ticking of the car engine, the click and skitter of squirrels and a night bird out there singing the dark sky in. I listened and at last heard the voices of the river talking in the big conversation. I need to be near that, I thought, I need to be closer to that source of sound, that dynamo at the heart of the mechanism. Getting close to it would blast away all these ghosts. So I got up and hiked toward the river. Then I stopped. I heard something else: other voices, the voices of people nearby. I went back to my camp and knelt down and listened, and I distinctly heard the voices of people. My heart beat faster. I walked toward the voices, crouching low, sliding up next to trees, stopping, listening, trying not to be seen. Why, you don't exist, my brother said. Didn't he say that? I don't exist. Thoughts are things and bring things into being. That's how hard I was working on my magical thinking. It had gotten me this far. You don't exist, he said. I don't exist. That's even more powerful than being invisible. The thought was a fiery sword cutting away my fear as I went forward through the trees. Then, I stopped again and waited and listened and heard nothing. I looked around and saw nothing. What was it? What was going on out there? I waited for a long time, remaining still, but nothing appeared, and I heard no more sounds, so I went back to my camp.

I sat by my fire trying to penetrate the space around me with my subtle mind: the ground, the trees, the air, the river, listening hard. We are going to determine if this is real or not, now and for good. Then I heard the voices again, and again I crept out wandering in search of them. I was freaking out. I was probably just hearing some other campers. Why did it matter? But I had the irresistible urge to find out if they were out there. Who was talking? But the closer I came to where I thought the voices were, the farther away they sounded, until I heard nothing at all. It was like they were moving away, then coming close, then moving away again. Like some game. Class dismissed. I looked up through the trees. I saw nothing. The forest was utterly dark. I moved slowly with hands out before me. I stopped. I waited. I listened. Nothing again. I went back to my camp.

I stoked up my little fire with some more sticks and sat there listening. Beyond the crackle of the burning wood, I swear I heard the voices again. Like regular conversation, observations, pointed insights and maybe a little mockery. It sounded very close. I took out my flashlight and turned it on and scanned the darkness around me. Then I saw something. It looked like an orange hunting cap out there in the trees. I remained still and held the light on it, waiting to see if it would move. Was someone out there? Was someone watching me? Wasn't it obvious that I saw? That I was looking back at the one looking at me? What are you looking at? What do you want? I stood up and went over that way, keeping the light shining in the direction I was going. But when I got to where I thought the hat was, there was nothing there. No hat. It had vanished. I waited there in the grove, in the open, just outside my camp. Then I backed up to see if what I had seen would appear again. Maybe what I had seen was just a trick of the mind and the way the light hit the bark of a tree. I got back into my camp, but I didn't see the hat anymore.

I sat down beside my fire again and poked at it and corralled the outer pieces of wood into the middle, and it burned clean throughout with a nice set of golden coals collecting in the center. Then I saw movement on the perimeter. I got up to investigate it, going out, moving deeper into the forest. But I found no one, nothing, and I thought, what the hell am I doing? It struck me that I might be going mad. That's right. Whenever I became still, I saw something or heard something. You're going crazy, I thought. There's nothing out there. Just stay put and stop chasing down every phantom you think you see. My heart was racing. My hands were shaking. All of this, I thought, all of it is coming from my mind. I've been here before. These are fears I've carried for lifetimes pouring out, nothing more. So I went back to my camp and stayed there.

I mustn't panic, I thought. I lit a cigarette and sat by the fire and grabbed hold of my brother's medicine pouch. No matter what, I decided, I'm not moving from this spot. I'll just stay put. I'm not the first person to be in this space, and I won't be the last. How I handle this now, though, could make all the difference.

I was assaulted by voices, then, by intense discussions, arguments rising and falling, indictments, monologues, debates, harangues and laughter, insane laughter. And other sounds. But I didn't move. And shadows flowed just beyond the edge of my camp along with flickering, flashes of color and looking eyes, searching, examining eyes, clue-hunting, meaning-making eyes. But I didn't move. It became like some ugly pageant of absurd forest monsters chattering, jumping, taunting me as they strolled in closer and closer, my hands shaking, my heart racing, my guilty fearful mind fighting as I said over and over again, they're not real, I'm not real, they're not real, I'm not real, I'm not real…trying to believe it, trying… and I began to sing a little song to myself, trying to fight it all off, singing, home home heya home, home heya home, the song vibrating in my mind, creating an invisible shield of sound around me so that gradually the voices subsided and the shadows fell back as I rocked and sang and rocked and saw a deer appear there suddenly before me in the firelight, a notch-eared black-tail deer standing at the edge of my camp. I went silent and gazed at it and it at me in an eternal moment during which neither of us moved, and my heart went calm and my mind went still and I just gazed into the black infinity of those eyes in perfect trance communion without words. I mean, if a deer appears, that's a good thing, right? It must mean things are pretty safe, no monsters around. Wouldn't a deer know if monsters were around? Wouldn't a deer stay as far away from monsters as possible? And doesn't that mean I'm not a monster?

Then the deer wandered off. I got up and tried to follow, but I only took a few steps. No, no, I said to myself, stay put. And so I let it go, knowing I had whatever it could offer. I stood there in the darkness with a blanket over my shoulders and listened and heard nothing in the night that was not there and the nothing that was and felt for the first time in… no time that I could remember… peace.

I n the morning, I cooked myself a breakfast of beans and bacon and eggs, and I made a big pot of coffee and stood in the center of my campsite as the sun came up and cast down shafts of light through the mist that drifted up from the river and rolled and flowed and moved through the trees. Blue Jays and camp robber birds worked the edges of my campsite, and I tossed bits of bread to them. They darted in and carried everything I tossed them away, storing their catch in hidden places and coming back for more. And I began to distinguish them and gave them names like Ruffled Jaw for the one with a tuft of brown feathers beneath its beak, Ace for the brave one that shot in first, Spaz for the one so frantic it missed everything because of its furious movement, and Watcher for the one that never came close. Then a flicker flew in overhead and landed on a branch above me. They're holy birds, I've heard, and I gave it a nod of honor and regarded it there with its folded wings of fire.

Then at last I went down to the river, the sound of its braided voices rising as I approached. I pulled back the branches of an ash tree and slipped through and found the rocky bank and the river flowing there and crouched down next to it. And I stared into it, watched as it coursed over rocks with thick, glassy tendons of water, fast and powerful, jade green in its depths toward the middle way, blue and clear along the shallows where the river grass swayed. And in its flowing the river rose and fell and crested in places, circling in eddies that spiraled into themselves. And I caught again that sensation of motionless motion as the quick current riffled the submerged white ash roots that twitched like cilia as they shot out from the black talus riverbed. I reached in and felt the ice-cold power of the water coursing over my skin. I touched the white roots and the rock underneath, and the force of the cold water worked its way up into my bones. Then I raised my hand cupped with a palm full of water and drank.

Up a ways I saw where two rivers came together, joining force and momentum, water flowing into other water. And the sunlight shot straight down through it all, striking the red iridescent side of a salmon that nerved its way upstream. It seemed to regard me, but who knows what it was seeing with its world-absorbing eyes. What I was to that salmon I have no idea, but it didn't move. It just hovered in light as I gazed into that water forever. Then my attention wavered, and the fish shot forward and was gone. I stood up and thought, did I get what I wanted from this, even so? And I could honestly answer, yes I did.

When I walked back into my camp, the birds scattered to the nearby rocks and up into the low tree limbs and chattered away at me. I tossed out another handful of breadcrumbs, and they converged and swept every bit away. But I didn't linger. I packed my gear into the trunk and scanned the camp for any remains and found none. This was important. Leave no trace, not a rack behind for the searching eyes. The air was cool. Glorious day was coming in. I thanked my camp, tossed a few more breadcrumbs to the birds, got in my vehicle and started the engine. And as I pulled out and onto the forest service road, I saw a deer, perhaps the same deer that I had seen the night before. I wanted to believe that. It jumped across the road and stood nearly invisible among the trees, camouflaged as it was, and as I passed by, I felt it watching me.

I drove again the empty road. The river flowed along beside me like a friendly spirit for a while and then slipped away, only to return again jumping in and out of my awareness but always there. I drove in a trance. Visions of past journeys floated up before me, searching out our great grandfather's homestead, a spot near a river in a glen that reminded him of Ireland. It was impossible to find, buried as it was deep in the low-lying hills with misleading signs pointing down roads that seemed to lead finally away as if to trick a stranger. And we only arrived by dead reckoning, laughing, cussing, saying, is this the way? No! You've got it all wrong! Turn back! You're crazy! Keep going! It's just up ahead! His venture to grow crop apples never worked out. It was hardly a get rich quick scheme, and he passed away struggling to reclaim a small fortune he believed he had made and lost. Then our grandfather took it up and kept it as a going concern for a while, but eventually, he moved on when market prices dropped and the apple crops failed to produce enough to live on. The house itself, abandoned for many years, finally burned down in a forest blaze set off by dry lightning, leaving nothing but the wall my great grandfather built by hand using stones he'd pulled up to clear the land, a dry mason's masterpiece. My father and his brother rebuilt the house, hoping one day to return. For years, our father talked of going back, of shedding society and the chains of the city, and when our mother passed on and he was left alone, he did just that. And he never came back. He and my brother were a lot alike that way. They couldn't live with people.

There is a paradise in my mind of a time when we used to go out there to fish and hunt. Open the car door, and my brother and I took off in a wild animal rush running up into the hills. The ghost of the burned house was always there. The new house hovered over it. Everything seemed charged with the potential to burn, the land around us brittle and hot as perfect tinder. And we studied the patterns of the fires of the past, the Ponderosa Pines scorched up their trunks, great patches of forest burned away to nothing but black triggers, green spaces in the middle that were miraculously preserved. A great mystery was always before us. What power picked some areas for destruction and left the others untouched? But that was another life, and I was a thief of those memories now. It was a struggle to think my way back into the present, back into my flight, and it occurred to me that when the police didn't find me in the city they might eventually come looking for me out here. My only hope was that I had made a good start and would be long gone before they arrived.

I flew on up into that wild friable high-altitude land of sky as a light rain rolled in. The same conversations were going on in my head on how to get to the homestead, and the same doubt and final surrender set in. I drove by instinct that wild blue road. A white oblivion mist devoured the treetops and snaked into the depths of the surrounding forest. Wind picked up and more rain. Good, I thought, as I plunged headlong into it. Obscurity, cover me over. I flipped on the windshield wipers, cutting into the watery world, and I dove into that black pupil of distance out of which mile on mile of anaconda road poured without end.

The storm broke and passed on, leaving the land steaming and raw. I relaxed my grip on the wheel and cruised through the lingering mist without thought or fear. The road warped and wriggled and rolled on. I was alone out there as far as I could tell. Then my father's house appeared on its hill above the ragged remains of the apple groves. The windows blazed in the afternoon sunlight. The black river flowed along the north side of the property and out through the dying orchard and then disappeared beneath the road and reappeared further on down the hill where it rose again to join the greater rivers. Clouds fanned out above the house like a mandrake halo. I drove slowly, winding my way up through the orchard. Then I stopped and gazed at the house shining there, gothic and dark, with the windows so bright in the sunlight it looked like it was made of fire.

I lit a cigarette and listened to the crickets. I listened for other things, too, but all I heard were the crickets. White moths fluttered close to the ground. The orchard was an abandoned mess with some trees twisted and overgrown and some nearly lying on the ground. Others were dead from the inside with ashen limbs and gray-black bark and silver green lichen taking over. A few trees remained tall and tough with weighted clusters of apples hanging from their boughs.

I got out and walked up to the house and found the front door open. I didn't bother to call out. I went in. It looked like no one had been there for years. Crowded emptiness. Dust covered the floor and the windowsills. There were animal droppings all around. Some of the windows were broken out. And most of my father's possessions were gone, though a few things remained. It had the look of a place abandoned in haste. There were some cans of food in the cupboards, a heavy brown canvas coat and a rifle in one of the closets, some shot-gun shells in a drawer, and a photograph on the mantle of me and my brother taken when we were little kids standing on a rock with bare chests, snarling like two bear cubs with raised claws. I looked at the picture for a long time, went into the time it was taken, that moment, that long-ago moment...then pulled myself free.

I wasn't that surprised my father had left, but I wondered where he'd gone and if he were even still alive. I hadn't heard anything from him for many years. Nevertheless, as I looked around at what was still in the house, I had the vague, unfounded feeling that he had left these things for me. I wanted to believe that, though of course it would have been unlikely. I hadn't tried to communicate with him, either, in all this time. But magical or not, the thought of him considering me at all gave me power. Wherever you are father, I wish you well. And if you have any say over my fate, please help me to escape! I laughed. Then I went back outside and stood on the front porch from where I could see the road descending through the hills for several miles. I calculated that I had an hour or two of sunlight left, so I unloaded my few supplies from the car and placed them in my backpack: blankets on the bottom and against the back, then canned goods, including the ones from my father's cupboards, the cook set, one water jug and the rest of the food on top, and at last the tarp; then, I put matches and pliers, flashlight and batteries, shot-gun shells and the knife in the outer pouches. It was a nice, lightweight pack, a good set-up. I tried it on, and it felt okay, but after a few hours of hiking I knew it would feel heavier. But for now, it would be all right. It would do. And so, I set it on the porch along with the shotgun and the canvas coat and sat down and smoked and felt the waning light on my face.

I moved my vehicle around to the back of the house and pulled the tarp from the woodpile over it and threw a few pieces of wood on top of it to hold the tarp down. Then I threw some more wood onto it and even gathered up some dry leaves and heaped them up there too. If anyone were truly searching for me, they would easily find it, but my intention was more to hide it from the eyes above.

I stood there beside my hidden vehicle and smoked and looked out to the west where the sun was half dissolving in the talons of a new storm rising up over the far ridge. The light fanned out in beautiful rose hues among the mackerel clouds and punched through in sun bolts that strafed the valleys below. Rogue clouds raced juggernaut in the wind, dragging their shadow forms across the hills. What beauty, I thought, even in the midst of this.

When I came back around to the front of the house, I looked down the hill again, and this time I thought I saw a flash of light. I watched and waited and saw it again, and I felt certain that it was reflected light from a windshield. I stood still and looked and concentrated on the flickering movement and sure enough a car was coming this way. I waited for a moment, thinking that it might be my father. But that was impossible. That wasn't him. I could feel it in my cells. Whoever was coming was coming for me. That road led nowhere but here.

I went up to the porch and tied the coat onto the pack and then pulled the pack up onto my shoulders and cinched the strap tight around my waist. Then I grabbed the rifle and went down the steps and hiked around to the back of the house and jogged across the back clearing and through the orchard and up towards the forest. I went as fast as I could and dove into the cover of trees. And I knew exactly where I was. I knew this landscape by blood. I was code-written from it. And I moved with a natural grace and clarity, my mind a hundred steps ahead and scanning the intricate structures of the forest and calculating possible paths faster than I could know, and as I imagined it, it came into being before me. I felt pumped up with the home field advantage, so to speak, at least for the moment. Then I stopped and listened, checking. I heard nothing and went on.

I hiked up and away from the house, up towards a ridgeline to the north and a little west, as I remembered it. I couldn't see it through the trees, but I knew where it was. There was no trail, so I bushwhacked through the brush, trying not to leave any signs of my passage even though a trained eye would be able to spot every step. I stopped and listened again. Then I heard a humming in the distance. At least I thought that's what I heard. I was deep into the forest and a little way up from the house. I looked back down through the trees and could just see the house below me, but I didn't see anyone there. I listened and listened hard, but I heard nothing. I was certain I had seen that vehicle coming up the road, though, and it seemed likely that whoever it was would be checking the house right about then. They would look around. They would find what I had found, a place abandoned. And at some point they would probably find my car. They would fan out searching, depending on how many there were. I listened again. Then I heard the humming, like a swarm of insects or a storm, a weird sound with a silence of its own. What was that? I turned and hiked on, moving fast. My heart was pounding and sweat was already pouring down my back and my face. I looked up into the metallic sky and wished for quick darkness.

After I had covered what felt like a good distance, I stopped and listened again. And I heard that humming, clearly, definitely now, growing louder like something you might hear drunk or drugged, a kind of droning, a rhythmic pulsing that sounded like one word repeating over and over, whatwhatwhatwhatwhatwhatwhatwhat. It grew louder, and then it hit me. That was the sound of turning blades. I was surprised they had come so soon, but I couldn't believe they had brought out that kind of machinery. I heard it circling up above, whatever it was, buzzing, scoping, scanning through the trees for my outline, the heat of my blood. I looked around to see if anyone was coming my way, but I saw no one. I turned uphill and hiked faster, picking up the pace, thinking and not thinking, using my instinct and the urge to escape.

The sunlight was fading, and now it was dark enough that I couldn't see very far ahead of me through the dense woods, which meant that whoever was after me wouldn't be able to see very well, either. Come, darkness, I thought, come on. Then I saw a beam of light shoot down through the trees about halfway down the hill below me, a spotlight from above. I could feel the burn of those eyes. And it circled, that spotlight, sweeping through the trees, trying to search me out. Then I heard an amplified, mechanical voice coming up from down below, but I couldn't understand what it was saying.

I hit a small plateau, an opening in the trees, and I ran across the clearing. On the other side I re-entered the forest and hiked as fast as I could through the denser woods, climbing over fallen tree trunks and rock outcrops. I hadn't reached the invisible line in my mind that meant I'd gained enough distance to be able to stop, even for a moment. Right then, it was go go go. No road comes this way, of course, and there's no place to land anything in all of these trees, no clearing big enough, so if they were going to follow me, they would have to follow me on foot. And I figured that they didn't know where I was exactly at this point. The forest spread out from my father's house in all directions. And I had the lead and knowledge of the land.

After a while, the buzzing from above seemed to drift off to the west, and I no longer heard the amplified voices. I slowed a bit and tried to get my bearings. I didn't want to go inadvertently in circles. I knew I had to keep ascending and get across the ridge and into the next valley. From there on, it was open wilderness for thousands of miles, essentially borderless. The valleys and canyons went on forever. I would go until I died or found a road or found a town and there reemerge as someone else. The night air was cool, and my breath plumed before me. Stars began to appear overhead through the trees. I heard the river flowing down the hill on my right. I readjusted my pack and tied the rifle on the back to free my hands. I took out the flashlight and turned it on. I listened for a while, pushing my senses out, feeling deep into the woods for any movement or presence of any kind. I heard whispers in my ears like wings in straw, wind, the voices of the water, but nothing of people. I kept moving, my head down, concentrating on my steps, my own little light from the flashlight illuminating the smallest of circles before me. And I kept moving, looking up from time to time but moving, moving. Then I saw a bright star, and I knew what it was right away, my brother's star, Polaris. And that hit me with a wave of bright energy. "Thank you, brother," I said aloud. I kept it before me, hiking on, making sure that I had it in my sight.

I hiked on over the soft loamy branches and ferns and up through a narrow canyon where I had to grab onto the swooping vine-limbs and pull myself up steep slopes and rocky stretches. My ascent went slow, especially in the dark. My hands were getting banged up, and the air temperature was dropping fast. I thought about stopping and burrowing in and hiding, but something told me that I had to keep going. I couldn't stop yet. The ridge was still up ahead, that line I knew I had to cross. After that, I would make my way north. The river was still running off to my right, and I knew I'd have to cross it soon or I'd be forced off into the gorge to the west. And if I went off in that direction, I'd be caught up in all the chaos of bushwhacking my way through much worse terrain, and I was through with all of that for this lifetime. The only conflict left in my mind now was how to get across that river. And I had to do it soon. So, I cut over and picked my way through the sorrel and branch-tangle and black earth muck and on down to the riverbank where I pointed my flashlight into the river's tumbling rush. The current was deep and fast, and only a few big rocks here and there broke the surface of the water, but they were far apart. I couldn't get across there, so I went on up the hill, staying near the river and hoping for a good spot to cross safely and finally get away.

I hiked through most of the night, stopping only briefly to rest and to drink from my water jug. And I listened, listened hard. I heard no voices, no sound of engines or anything. I listened and heard only the sound of an owl hooting somewhere far off. Maybe they had called it off for the night. Maybe they would resume tomorrow. I wondered if they had gone to my brother. From the crown of my will I imagined my way to him, drifting toward him there in his grimy cabin, his face blazing with light. I smiled, thinking of what he had said, and I reached up and touched the medicine pouch he'd given to me. And at least in that moment, I was sure they would never find me.

Now the air was freezing. I had reached that height. I listened and located the sound of the river nearby, and I was sure in my mind where I was. I hung the flashlight back on my pack and hiked on in the pitch-black darkness, my steps purely instinctive but sure and unfaltering. And my vision went out inch by inch as into a stone, disclosing the structures around me, latticework of trees and arc of boulders and dip of canyon like a relief map in my mind, the green burst of the moss, the flaring red eyes of the creatures out there. I kept on going.

Late into the night I felt snow crunching under my feet. I took the canvas jacket out and put it on. It kept me warm and helped cushion the weight of the pack and the rifle. Coyotes howled somewhere far off, and a thin, crescent Cheshire moon rose grinning through the geometry of trees.

Finally, I stopped. I pulled off my pack and sat down on a rock. I sat there for a long time, listening, my shoulders hunched. All I heard at first was my own hard breathing. I saw absolutely nothing. After a while, my heart and my breathing slowed down. Still I heard nothing. I stayed that way for a long time, feeling dispersed and buried in that silence. At the first sign or sound of pursuers, I'd take off on the move again. I knew I couldn't stay there, but at this point, I couldn't imagine anyone following me in this darkness. The woods were dense and hard enough to navigate in the daylight without a trail, so I figured for anyone else it would be impossible now. I was deep in. And I kept thinking of what my brother had said... you don't exist. Well, certainly the marks of my passing had been discovered back at my father's place. But at this point, at this time, I had essentially disappeared.

So now what? It occurred to me that it might be better to set up a dry camp and wait for daylight. No fire. But the thought of that invisible line ahead persisted. That line meant something. It had taken on a mystical charge. It meant safety. It meant freedom. And I felt like it was too risky to get my stuff out and set up a camp where I was. If they were following and should approach, I would have to move quickly, and I might not have time to gather up everything I needed. And I needed everything I had.

I put my pack on and made my way back to the river. I decided that above all else, I couldn't stop until I had crossed the river. Only a fool would try and cross it in the dark, so if I did cross it, then I could relax, if only for a moment. At least from there no one would be able to follow me. I approached the river and listened. The river was all I heard. I turned my light onto it and saw the obsidian current flowing. I saw some rocks, too, but they were too jagged to stand on. I pointed my light up and down the river, looking for a better spot to cross, but I couldn't tell. I could search all night and find nothing better, so I decided this was it.

I took a step out onto one of the rocks and immediately went in, my foot slipping off and going into the water, and I had that quick jolt of hope-fear that my foot would land somewhere not too far beneath the surface of the water and I'd climb my way out of it, but I went down hard and reached out and turning to my left lost all bearing and dropped fast and went underwater. I was lost. My left arm hit rock. My knees hit rock, and I lunged up and caught air and fell back and twisted around and rolled back under and flailed in water darkness, blind and breathless and moving in the current.

My foot hit and stopped, and I came up against another rock. My head seemed poised like an arrow in the current. And I thought, now I can pull myself up. Then my foot slipped, and I was taken up again, free flowing in the black. My movements made little difference. I was more a question or a thought than anything else. And I entered a calm, drifting, thinking, well this is it. I looked through the watery lens at the silver blade of moon above, no notion of the shore. Odd thoughts came to me. This is the way the world ends, this is the way the world ends. What form shall I take from the gallery as I rise and fall in the cool belly of the river? So be it. Then a sound of rushing wind came from somewhere, a sound that I realized was my own throat gasping as I broke the surface and took in air again. And turning, turning I caught hold miraculously to a slick, ropy branch and held myself against the fast force of the current and finally pulled myself back onto earth.

I was soaked through and through. I gasped and got to my feet and coughed and stumbled and felt myself and felt that I wasn't injured, as far as I could tell. I checked my things and found I'd lost my flashlight and my rifle. I was sorry to lose them both. The way would be much harder without them. And I breathed in the night air, harsh and cold, breathed and was relieved. I had made it across the river.

But I was cold, shaking down to the bone cold. My nose and my cheeks felt numb. My hands and feet were numb. I was beginning to shiver in a way that was dangerous. I felt a vague and menacing apprehension. And I knew the air around me was getting colder. I didn't know how high I was in terms of altitude, but I could feel the difference in the atmosphere. The risk of not building a fire was now a critical matter. I was susceptible to the elements. I was going to freeze to death if I didn't do something soon. So, I decided to build a fire.

I found a spot in a clearing and searched around near the base of the trees for dry sticks and twigs and leaves and gathered up enough to get a fire started. My hands shook badly. The ground seemed dry, sheltered as it was by the canopy of the forest. I took off my pack and listened again and heard nothing. Okay, this would do. I opened my pack and took out a few of the cans and ripped off the labels to use for starting the fire. Perhaps they were still dry enough to burn. I couldn't tell. My hands felt lifeless. My fingers were numb. I couldn't feel the things I was touching. I had to concentrate to make my fingers move. I watched my hands working with a strange and distant awareness, as though I were watching another person's hands.

I crumpled up the paper labels and bits of dry leaves and twigs and tried to light a fire. This took real effort, coaxing a little flame to take. The matches were barely sparking. But soon enough I had a fire started, and I found a few seasoned branches and broke them to make smaller pieces and coned them on the flames. Then I had a good campfire burning. And the heat of it began to grow, flowing into me. I collected a few more branches and rigged up some racks near the fire and hung my backpack there and my coat and watched them steaming in the heat. I stood with my back to the fire and felt my own wet clothes heating up and steam rising off my body. I turned and felt the warmth flowing up my chest and my face. Then, for a moment, I panicked, because I thought I might be making a mistake. Anyone nearby, anyone searching from above would be able to see my fire. But again, I fought that feeling back and stayed calm. The forest was thick, so I didn't need to worry about anyone seeing the light of the fire. This is what I told myself. And if they did come, I would douse the fire and run. But those were just thoughts, and I saw them as such. And as it was, I heard nothing. So, I sat there absorbing the warmth and the light, letting my mind settle into the dance of the flames and the pitch-crackle of the wood.

Sensation came back to my hands and feet. And I kept feeding the fire, careful to protect the nucleus but not let it grow beyond a certain circumference. I didn't want a big fire, just a needfire to get me through this. And then I stood there. The cold had left me. But I felt something close. I felt like I was standing outside myself. Had I made it? I felt the surge of a familiar sensation, and my mind opened up, like a child on the first trip away from home. I was light, breathless, floating in space. What a beautiful sense of elation. I didn't want it to end. And it struck me. I was safe. For the moment, nothing was happening, and I was clear. My mind flew back over the roads, the old house, the camp by the river, my brother's place. I was looking for something. Somehow, my flight had taken me over old ground, and a pattern seemed to show itself. A crooked smile.

Then something happened to my vision. Something clicked, and I felt like I was looking down a long tunnel. I felt pulled, like I was physically moving through that tunnel, even though I was only standing there. And something was near. No, someone. I felt it. But I couldn't see it. I knew it, though. I could feel the presence of it. I waited like someone in a haunted house. Ah, was this just fear again? A flash. Wait a minute. A sort of pale blue fire glowed out of everything. Was it close to dawn already? My sense of time was way off. Stay still, I thought. Then two green lights appeared, shining through the trees. Stay still. I fought a growing sense of panic, an urge to make a quick decision and run. But concentrating like that, I kept myself out of it. Then I felt my body again. I made myself feel my body again. And then I saw a pair of eyes.

I was transfixed, staring straight into those eyes in the forest dark. What are you come at last, I thought. It had to be. What I had been running from was materializing before me, now. The mystery had found a form. I gazed at it and it at me in a moment of perfect symmetry. Then it turned, and leaving my pack, leaving the fire, I followed. Quietly into the dark, nothing following nothing, I went. The obstacles of the forest, the interlocking fallen branches, the holes, the uneven ground were nothing. As much as I believed my feet touched anything, I was gliding on my way. And I could feel whatever it was breathing up ahead of me, taking on a panther form. If I made out anything at all beyond the eyes it was the sleek black shape of it in the moonlight. No reason here. I was not following that way. There was nothing reasonable about any of this, its presence or mine. So, I followed. This is the way. I felt the truth of it. But this was not a process of thought. Where it is going, I am going. And I was sure that this was right. It was a piece of the great nothing come to lead me out of the maze. In my life, I had never felt more calm, more comforted. It could lead me off a cliff and I would follow. We could go on past that, and I would follow and keep on following. So, I matched my strides to its strides, my pace to its pace, and in that darkness, I didn't falter but went on. I had no idea where I was going or where I had ever been. I was simply going. And in the going, I became something else. And if I told you I used to know the circular truth of the void and that I have been all over it building this breadth and scope, going for however many lines across this and then this as it rippled its shoulders that were steeped in the power of escape and parting the darkness before me, and that my going was to go up and out of all of it at dead of night, well believe me too when I say that I am speaking to you from where I was shook off, like this, where it turned and shrugged me off, and I stopped there still and silent at the dead of night with my sympathy in the weeds and heard nothing, no further, as clear as if spoken, as if the air itself had said enough.

So, I turned and made my way back to the river. I didn't try to figure out what happened. I just knew. It seemed as if I'd only taken a few steps away from my campsite. And I went back to my fire and crouched there beside it and felt the stars crawl across my back and the forest folding its wings. And I kept my fire going, but I didn't sleep. I listened. No voices came during this time. I had moved past that. I had entered that quiet space where nothing comes. All was stillness. And I stayed there as long as I could, as long as I could make it last.

It was gradual at first, almost indistinguishable, a gray glowing forth of the trees, a gathering of substance in the earth around me. I was coming out of the darkness again, into the world again. So I gathered my things and settled my pack onto my shoulders and cinched it tight and kicked the dirt over the place where I had built my fire. I scattered the heap of twigs I'd gathered. I scuffed up the ground where I had been. I did a good job of erasing any trace of my being there. And I moved on.

In the twilight I made my way. And as I went, I could feel something in the forest change. I noticed it in the light. Not the light of growing day, but something else, the way the light was coming through, the way it was reaching me. The trees were more spread out, now, and I saw farther on through the gaps between them. I was approaching new ground.

And then, I was in an open space, a land between darkness and light where the forest ended and another landscape began. I felt like a creature emerging from hibernation as I moved out of the trees. I saw the world spread out, the white waves of snow glowing out and away. And the sun broke its eastern plane, light flowing over the clouds, clouds rolling deep through the valleys to the west and below me, mountain peaks rising like islands. I was up above it all in a dreamsea sky, seeing in every direction. And I went forward, one black quill tip of a hawk far ahead of me scripting its way on the cool arc of wind. What beauty! What glory! And I thought, I'll try, I'll try my luck again as I made my way into the white field.

Made in the USA
Columbia, SC
20 October 2020

23118625R00117